Good Gone Bad

By

Tony Fisher

Copyright © 2025 Tony Fisher

ISBN: 978-1-918264-42-5

Prologue

Charlie Burrows had made many mistakes in his life.

Nobody's perfect, but in the world of bad decisions, this would come one notch above Kennedy opting for an open-top car.

The sane version of himself wouldn't have contemplated being anywhere near the place he was standing.

A stench of spilt bin juice and dried urine added to his unease. This was a place where desperate people left their DNA, like mad dogs marking territory.

His finger pressed hard on the sticky intercom button by the side of the door; he couldn't hear a buzz but managed to resist giving it a second push. No use antagonising these people before he'd been properly acquainted.

The wait was five seconds, but in Charlie's addled mind, it could have been five hours.

A crackle bled through the tiny speaker, followed by a gruff 'Yeah?'

Sudden panic. He couldn't speak.

'Yeah?' again, this time more forceful.

Autopilot kicked in, and he remembered the phone call the previous night. Maybe it was with the same guy who was barking through the speaker now.

He held up a photograph to the camera, which was set high above the door, and took a step back, half expecting someone to shoot him from an upstairs window or maybe a knife in the ribs from an assailant waiting in the dark recesses of the alleyway stretching behind him.

'I'm here for a quote,' Charlie managed to say through short breaths and a heart rate that would fell a bull moose. A feeling of huge vulnerability fell over him like a concrete blanket.

No reply, just another buzz, and this time the heavy metal door clicked open from the latch.

Charlie hung on a beat, wondering if he should wait for an invite. He stared at the speaker, but the silence was enough, and with one huge breath that burned his chest raw, he grabbed the door and stepped inside.

The room was dark, and it took a while for his eyes to adjust from the harsh sunshine outside into a squalid room lit only by a couple of rusting desk lamps placed strategically on either side of the counter.

The only other illumination came from the screens attached by brackets high up on the walls. One showed fuzzy black-and-white CCTV footage pointing to the spot he'd just stood. A second screen was focussed on a car park, which must have been nestled somewhere around the back of these labyrinthine streets.

Charlie handed the photo over to the guy behind the counter. He was wearing a tight-fitting short-sleeved shirt designed to exaggerate the amount of time he'd invested at the gym. Muscles thick enough to almost tear the sleeves and swirling tattoos that snaked their way down his tanned arms.

He was wearing a mask that was all too common during the pandemic, but now things were at the 'new normal' had reverted to hypochondriacs or surgeons.

His thick head looked Charlie up and down, beady eyes drilling in like tiny lasers.

Charlie wasn't sure where to start or what to say.

He'd been walking round Birmingham's Jewellery Quarter for the past hour, double-checking he'd got the right address and then working up enough courage to press the bell.

'Hang on a sec,' muscle man growled, and then disappeared through a door behind him. As it slammed shut, the pages of a wall calendar depicting a selection of rings flapped in the breeze.

Charlie was nervous, hopping from foot to foot. He badly wanted to sit down, but there didn't appear to be any chairs. Behind him was a blacked-out window with a metal rail running underneath. It was obvious this area wasn't designed for entertaining.

The door opened again, and Charlie straightened himself up like a soldier standing to attention.

The figure at the door was different. This man looked older, and he was wearing an expensive suit, which was no off-the-rail affair, more Ted Baker than Suits Unlimited.

'Come through,' he said. His voice had traces of a Black Country accent with affectations. The sound of the self-made businessman happy to project success while making sure there were still traces of dirt under his fingernails. Hard graft got him where he was.

Charlie stepped behind the counter and followed him through the door.

He was surprised to find himself in a workshop with a scattering of people sat on stools, leaning over high tables absorbed in their work, a halo of light above each employee.

There was a radio playing in the background but way too low to detect anything other than generic lift music.

The man stepped inside a well-appointed office with glass windows all around, giving him a 360-degree view of his kingdom.

There was no denying that the guy offering him a seat opposite his large desk was the boss of this operation.

He looked at Charlie for a moment and then studied the photo he'd handed over to the tattoo man.

The awkward silence was causing Charlie to fidget; his jacket seemed to be swallowing him, and his shirt collar felt to be diminishing in size by the second, squeezing his throat.

'Do you know me?' he asked, just when Charlie was thinking of saying something vacuous about the weather, just to break the unbearable silence.

'No, I heard about what you do from…' Charlie stopped as the man held up a hand.

'I don't need to know who referred you to me, and you don't need to know who I am.'

Charlie didn't know what to say, so just nodded.

To his surprise, the man smiled and leaned forward, causing his chair to creak. 'You have the money?' he asked, sliding the photo into a drawer.

'Yes, it's all here,' Charlie unzipped the bag he had around his shoulders but once again stopped when the man gave a signal. This was turning into something like a musical statues game.

'Give it to the guy who let you in,' he stood up and motioned for Charlie to do the same before opening the office door again.

Walking back through the workshop, he noticed nobody took their eyes from what they were doing. It must be a common occurrence to have nervous strangers wandering in and out. He took comfort in the thought that other people had done what he was about to do. Maybe it wasn't such a crazy idea after all? That had to count as the quickest meeting he'd ever had.

Back at reception, the tattooed man said, 'You got the cash as agreed?'

Charlie nodded and once again unzipped his bag, taking out the bundles of fifty-pound notes. He counted out three thousand pounds in the same mechanical way the girl behind the counter of the bank had that morning.

'It'll be ready by Friday,' he said, scooping up the cash and dispensing it with the ease of a croupier.

'Do I get a receipt?' Charlie asked, foolishly.

The guy gave a smile, 'No, you get to leave here walking without a limp and all your fingers intact.'

Charlie left without another word and didn't look back until the shop was a pinprick in the distance.

'What do you reckon, Mr. C?' Tattoo man asked, pulling off his mask. He was sat where Charlie had been only moments earlier. The leather cushion of the seat was still warm.

'We've got a good one there, I reckon, Andy?' he replied. 'But…'

Andy got closer, the buttons of his shirt at bursting point as he leaned towards his boss.

'I want you to be the guy taking the lead on this. Don't let him out of your sight.'

'So we're going all the way with this?' Andy asked, when he was double sure it was his turn to speak; nobody interrupted Mr. C.

'Oh yeah,' he gave a rare smile that looked wrong on his face, like he'd rented it with an option to buy. 'I reckon we're gonna know a lot about Charlie Burrows.'

Chapter 1

Friday 15th December, 12:08 p.m.

Worcester city centre was busy, and that suited Charlie just fine.

He strolled down the High Street, trying his best to look like everyone else. He was going for anonymity; the last thing he needed was someone recognising him and stopping for a chat. The more people who could swallow him up, the easier what he was about to do would be. Lost among the festive buzz.

He had one hand thrust deep into his pocket, fingers gripping the package.

Pulling the peak of his baseball cap further down, he held his breath, counted to five and stepped closer to the jeweller's. All he could hear was the thudding of his heart and the sound of his boots slapping the polished marble tiles that led to the entrance.

He stopped for the briefest of moments and pushed open the door. A bell tinkled above his head and, although in the real world it was a gentle trill, to him it could have been Big Ben clanking a warning.

His steps softened under lush carpet and, within seconds, a young girl with a sunshine smile and golden hair, exacerbated by the ornate mirrors and overhead lighting, sashayed towards him. She had the name 'MOLLY' printed on a lapel badge, which he thought suited her.

'Can I help you with anything today?' she asked, in a sing-song tone. It gave her an efficient but friendly air, which he guessed was what she was going for.

'Just browsing,' he replied, before flashing her a smile which he hoped would exude trust and ease.

She smiled back. 'No worries, take your time. I'll just be over there if you need anything.'

With that, she left him alone by the counter where he already knew what he wanted. He just hoped it was still there; otherwise, all the planning and sleepless nights would have been for nothing.

He resisted the urge to feel in his pocket again. He had to appear normal, just another guy coming into a jeweller's before Christmas with a few bob to spare and someone special to buy for.

He turned around and made a show of looking at the watches. Thousands of pounds' worth of timepieces glittered and shone. Some had complicated dials performing all kinds of functions, others were so simple it was hard to distinguish which numbers the hands were pointing to.

He gave it a couple of minutes before turning back to the rings. The displays were boxed in groups of half a dozen, all neatly slotted into blue velvet trays, gleaming so hard he had to squint before he found the one he was looking for.

The palpable relief he felt was soon replaced by panic. The ring was still there. This meant he had to go through with it—or did he? Maybe he could give up on this whole insane idea, leave the shop and go home, no harm done.

Then he thought about the kids on Christmas morning expecting presents, the unpaid electricity bill, the mortgage payments rising from January, the next MOT on a car that was already one key-turn from the scrapyard, and finally the face of his wife. She used to be tanned and healthy from regular holidays and a gym membership. Now she was gaunt and frail, as life and circumstances had taken their toll since the first consultation at the doctor's six months ago.

'Have you seen something you fancy?' The girl had appeared behind the counter. He noticed she had a likeness to his own daughter. He wondered if Maisie would be working in this kind of job later in life. This made things even worse.

'Yes, I think so.' The words tumbled out automatically, the way he'd practised them every time he sat planning this moment over the past two weeks.

'I like the look of that one there.' He pointed a finger, which, to his dismay, was shaking slightly.

She followed his direction and slid out the tray with the ease of someone who did this in her sleep. Pulling out a cloth from her pocket, she smoothed it flat on the counter, placing the ring down with ceremony.

'I take it congratulations are in order?' she beamed. At first, he didn't know how to reply; this hadn't been in his mental script.

She looked at his confused face and gave a sympathetic smile and, to his surprise, touched his hand gently. 'Sorry, I meant to say I take it you're getting engaged?'

He tried to laugh at his own stupidity, but it came out louder than he'd intended. If he wasn't careful, his nerves would get the better of him.

She took a step back and looked at him with a mixture of curiosity and sympathy. If he were to take off his leather jacket right now, she would see a soaked shirt; he must have lost a stone in sweat since he'd entered the shop.

'Oh yes, sorry, that's right, I'm getting engaged. I was just a bit shocked by the price.'

She seemed to relax again and switched back into sales mode. 'Yes, it does seem a lot, but you can pay in instalments?'

'How much would that be?' he asked, hoping to sound genuine. This whole conversation was feeling forced, but hopefully she didn't get the same vibe now that a potential buyer was stood before her.

'Hang on, I'll get my iPad.' She turned around and moved towards a desk at the back of the shop.

It was now or never. This was his only chance: do it or don't, but this moment was critical.

Once again, his kids' expectant faces flittered through his mind, the brown envelopes on the welcome mat at home, his wife's degrading illness.

Reaching into his pocket, he pulled out the replica ring and, without wasting a heartbeat, swapped it for the real one, sliding it into his pocket before daring to look up.

She was still squinting at her iPad while a tall man wearing a shiny suit peered over her shoulder. This was obviously the manager, mansplaining unnecessary advice to her.

She looked over and smiled. 'Just be a sec,' she said, and Charlie nodded back, swatting a bead of sweat from his eyebrow.

Every instinct told him to run, but he knew that would alert everyone. He had to stick with the plan.

Before he could flee, she'd arrived back at the counter clutching the iPad and, as she was in full sales glow, didn't seem to notice his face, which he could tell from his reflection in the mirror opposite had turned a very deep crimson.

'I've had a word with my manager,' she said, pointing over to the suit, who gave him a friendly wave with one hand while setting a wall clock with the other. 'The good news is we can let you have it for thirty thousand pounds, which is five hundred off the asking price, and that means it's down to eight hundred a month in instalments.' She gushed this information in a throwaway tone, as if discussing a Netflix subscription.

'Wow, that sounds great,' Charlie said, trying to sound like that kind of cash was passing through his fingers every day. 'I'll just have to go and check my bank before I make my mind up. Is that OK?'

'Of course,' she beamed now, sniffing a sale in an empty shop. 'Would you like me to reserve it for you?'

'That would be great.' His mouth was dry, he could feel nausea creeping in. He needed to get out of the shop before he threw up right there on the floor.

'Could I get a name?' she asked, her Apple Pencil poised above the iPad.

'Er… James,' he said, with a shake in his voice he hoped only he could hear.

'James…?'

'Yeah, James. James Elsworth.' He hadn't prepared for having to give a fake name, so his old PE teacher would have to do.

She smiled, finished the entry and closed the cover on the iPad.

He smiled back and made his steady way to the exit.

'Hang on a second,' she said to his back.

'What is it?' He turned around slowly, imagining police sirens and the cold steel of handcuffs biting into his wrists as he was led out of the shop into a police car.

'There was a price tag on the ring.'

Chapter 2

Charlie wanted to run but his legs wouldn't move. It was like someone had poured quick-drying cement over his shoes.

The girl was looking at him while holding the fake ring. Her face still held the sales smile she'd had when she'd told him the discount, but the missing price tag was causing a slight breakdown of the glow.

Inspiration struck him out of nowhere; the god of quick thinking had sent a thunderbolt at Charlie Burrows and, whatever religion it belonged to, he would be sat in its pew every Sunday from now on.

He felt in his pocket as thirty-one thousand pounds' worth of ring brushed his fingers and, with one mighty tug, managed to pull the price-tag free.

'Here it is,' Charlie said, making a show of bending down and letting the tag fall from his hand onto the plush carpet. 'It must have come loose.'

'Oh, thank you,' she said, taking out another string from an invisible drawer under the counter and reattaching it to the fake. 'As you can see, it would normally be thirty thousand five hundred pounds.'

'I can,' he said with the last of his breath. 'I'll be back in a bit.' He flashed a final forced smile and walked painfully slowly out of the shop, each step feeling like a mile.

The fresh air hit him full on and he hardly noticed anything until he'd walked the length of the high street and reached the Cathedral, his head bowed below his cap, not daring to look back.

The Cathedral Tower looked down its 250 feet on him as if in judgement and he wondered if it were worth going in, taking a walk down into the crypt and saying a couple of prayers for forgiveness. Would the ghost of a 'bad' King John buried in the high altar understand his motivations?

He turned away, hoping that redemption would come once he'd got the money he needed. One thing was for sure: he was never doing anything like this again.

As he paid for his ticket at the over-priced multi-storey he had the feeling of being watched. Was someone following him?

Had the girl in the jewellers spotted the fake and called the cops already? Were they going to grab him the moment he pressed the fob on his car key?

There were plenty of people milling around, looking at the notice boards, loading carrier bags into the backs of cars. His mind was playing tricks—hardly surprising, really.

By the time the barrier to the car-park exit had risen and he pulled into traffic he felt he could breathe for the first time in half an hour.

He switched on the radio hoping for a temporary distraction. BBC Hereford & Worcester were just starting a news bulletin. He half expected to hear about his lunchtime activities.

News just in, a man has walked away with a diamond engagement ring valued at over thirty thousand pounds from a Worcester city-centre jewellers…

But it was all about the wars around the world, a couple of B-list celebrities being cancelled and the successful Worcester Victorian Market. Charlie Burrows had not made the headlines—for now.

Pulling into his drive he turned off the engine. The radio stopped playing an old Wham song and he wondered if this would indeed be his 'Last Christmas'?

He just sat there, hearing nothing but the engine cooling and the distant sound of screaming from the nearby primary-school playground.

No doubt the children would already be excited about the coming days of carol concerts, snowy art projects and dress-down for charity. His own kids were buzzing, even though Maisie was trying to be cool as all sixteen-year-olds are; Dylan still had childish enthusiasm, even though they were prepared for that to vanish next year when he hit the teens.

Charlie reluctantly got out of the car. He didn't want to leave the safety of the driver's seat because he knew once he opened the front door and stepped over the threshold of his home, things would get real again.

Looking up at the fairy lights strewn across the windows he felt another pang of worry. Had he just crushed all the happiness from this house?

Unlocking the front door he had to give it an extra push as the weight of a couple of Amazon deliveries and some ominous-looking final demands had piled up.

'I'm home, Kaz,' he yelled, just in case. He knew she'd be at her sister's but he wanted to make sure she hadn't come back early; he needed some time for himself.

He hated the house being empty. When the kids were playing up and Karen was having a bad day he craved some space from being carer and peace-keeper all rolled into one. But the moment he was alone he felt unstable, like a ship breaking anchor. He loved having the family close and, just for a second, the thought of prison broke into his mind—he would rather die than be separated from all he had.

Swallowing hard, he walked into the kitchen, pulled a glass from the overhead cupboard and filled it with cold water.

He drank it down in one; the dehydration and nausea had built so much.

Slamming down the glass, he slid out a chair and sat at the kitchen table, pulling the ring from his pocket.

He hadn't realised the sheer beauty of the thing that met his eyes. It belonged on the finger of a princess parading the gardens of Windsor rather than a floral tablecloth in a semi-detached in Bromsgrove.

A million thoughts ran through Charlie's mind and he knew he had to get them in some sort of order.

First, he had to hide the ring somewhere safe until he sorted a buyer.

Second, he'd have to go back to work tomorrow and play things normally. He'd phoned in sick this morning, but he could say it had only been a twenty-four-hour thing.

Third, he needed to monitor the news; if nothing happened in the next couple of days he'd probably got away with it.

He thought back to the jewellers. He'd worn a baseball hat and kept his head low; any CCTV would not have captured his face and the girl would only have been able to give a vague description of him at best.

He looked around the kitchen, pulling out drawers and opening cupboards until he found the perfect hiding place.

Over the fridge was a high cupboard where they kept crockery they never used—the kind of gifts from friends who didn't really understand their taste that had accumulated over the years, or those pieces they'd clung on to since they'd first moved in together almost twenty years ago.

He pulled out an ornate butter dish. They never ate butter, even at Christmas. He wrapped the ring in multiple sheets of kitchen roll, put the lid over the top and slid it to the back behind a mountain of egg cups, toast trays and vile ornaments Karen's mother had left them in her will.

He closed the door and took a breath.

Heading upstairs for a much-needed shower, he stopped halfway. He heard something being stuffed through the letterbox.

He stood still, the way he had as a kid when he'd bunked off school and the truancy officer came knocking.

It couldn't be the post or Amazon as they'd already been. He grabbed the bannister hard, holding his breath.

He retraced his steps back down the stairs and pulled out the item caught in the jaws of the letterbox.

He was expecting a plastic carrier for charity clothes donations or yet another pizza delivery menu but, instead, it was an envelope with his name on the front; it had been typed.

CHARLIE BURROWS

With shaking hands he sliced open the envelope. The note was made ominous not just by the message but by the fact it was all in capitals.

**WE SAW WHAT YOU DID
WE KNOW WHERE YOU LIVE
WE COULD CALL THE POLICE
WE CAN RUIN YOUR LIFE
WAIT FOR A CALL**

Chapter 3

Friday 15th December, 1:33pm

Most people are good. In spite of everything you might hear or read, the majority of the population on earth only ever want to do the right thing and help those less fortunate than themselves.

Before you switch off in search of something less 'do-goody', please indulge me for a few more seconds.

The next half an hour may be about the good people I've just mentioned, but sometimes good people can do bad things.

My name is Danny Wade and this is the Good Gone Bad Podcast.

Danny hit the stop button and waited for the wave file to appear. That was the introduction done.

He was all set to record the tenth episode of his podcast series and could hardly believe how quickly it had taken off.

The idea had started in a blog he'd written for himself as part of his amends to those he'd hurt. He began to see a pattern of characters who all had similar stories to him, and the obvious next step was to make a podcast about their experiences.

Quite a few people smiled indulgently when he told them about his idea. After all, wasn't the whole world and his wife doing a podcast these days? Why should his be anything special?

But now, nearly a year later, he had twenty thousand downloads and enough advertising to cover his expenses.

There were nights when he'd get home and have to work hard summoning enough enthusiasm to do the necessary research for the next instalment, but it was only published once a month, which meant he had time for procrastination between episodes.

His latest was the first Christmas edition and he wanted to do something special.

It was at an AA meeting that he'd met Ian, whose story was so gripping that afterwards, when everyone was helping to stack chairs and clear up coffee mugs, he'd done something he'd never done before and invited him onto the podcast.

Obviously, the meetings were anonymous, with many stories and experiences too raw or tragic to bring away from the safe environment of the rooms, but this one was different.

He pressed the cursor on 'record' and began the story.

'On this Christmas edition we meet the man who gave Santa the sack, and how Saint Nick's elfish behaviour caused a mild-mannered charity worker to give him the heave-ho-ho-ho….'

He pressed stop again and dragged in some festive music a friend of his had created on GarageBand. He grimaced a little as he heard himself back. Ironically, he hated the sound of his own voice and squirmed at the cheesy chat. But the feedback he'd got in reviews was pun-positive, so he knew better than to pour hot oil on a winning formula.

Next, he downloaded the interview he'd done in the park a few months ago when the weather was unseasonably warm. They'd sat side by side on a bench under a weeping willow while Danny held the microphone between them and Ian poured out the story as eloquently as he had in the draughty church hall weeks earlier.

He was known as Richard for the sake of identity, and when Danny had asked him why he'd chosen that name in particular, he said the story was about someone who was a bit of a dick.

He looked at the timer on the screen, which had reached 28 minutes. This meant he had sixty seconds for the final link and a couple of minutes for ads. Perfect.

He was about to record when his phone vibrated on the desk. He always kept it on in case a job came in; being a delivery driver on minimum wage meant you couldn't turn an extra shift down, particularly during the busy season.

It was from an unknown number, but the name on the message was familiar.

Hi Danny

Don't know if you remember me but it's Charlie Burrows.

We were mates in sixth form all those years ago and you've friended me on Facebook.

I know it's a bit random but I've heard your podcast and I could really use your help.

I'm a bit desperate TBH.

No worries if not.

Charlie

Danny sat back in his chair and tried to visualise him. It didn't take long.

Back in those days he was drinking with everybody, but Charlie was a proper party animal. They were pub and club friends rather than the real-life variety.

Since Danny had been in recovery, he'd avoided old drinking haunts and the characters he'd been comatose with for all those missing years.

Charlie said he was desperate, and wasn't his podcast all about helping and finding the good, even when it went bad?

He dialled the number and Charlie picked up after one ring. He must have still had the phone in his hand.

'Danny, thanks for calling back, mate.'

He wasn't sure how to respond; it had been such a long time, and the man at the end of the phone sounded much older than he'd been expecting. Maybe it was the stress, or more likely the fact they hadn't spoken since Tony Blair had just resigned as Prime Minister.

'It's alright,' Danny said tentatively.

'No it isn't,' Charlie replied, his voice cracking. 'It really isn't.'

Chapter 4

Friday 15th December, 2:03pm

'I'm just going for a Costa, do you want anything?' Molly asked, shrugging on her big winter coat. If she didn't ask, he sulked for a week.

She didn't dislike her manager, he was just not part of her usual social circle. He was a lot younger for a start, but he treated her like a child, particularly when there was another customer in. She was new to the job, but she had been working sales when he'd have been starting secondary school.

He was what they termed 'management material'. He liked being in charge and spoke fluent jargon. During her induction, he had recited company policy with the same passion as a fan chanting their favourite lyrics at a concert.

She stepped out of the shop and was immediately accosted by a fresh-faced student wearing a tabard and carrying a clipboard. It had a panda on it, so Molly did the old trick of pretending to answer her phone before she could be grilled about her views on wildlife and how the planet was going to end in fifty years.

She was all for the environment, but not when she only had fifteen minutes to grab a mocha and be back behind the counter.

The queue was out of the door, but she reckoned it wouldn't take that long to get served. The one thing about Christmas—everywhere was fully staffed. Everywhere except the jewellery business. For some reason they never seemed to have any extra help, probably because it wasn't that much busier. There were more people browsing, but on the whole it was business as usual.

She thumbed through her phone while she waited, glad she'd decided to wear the bobble hat even though she was a bit self-conscious in it. It kept off the cold, and as she scanned Instagram reels aimlessly, she stamped her feet to keep the circulation going.

'Doing a little dance, are we?'

The voice from behind caused her to spin round so quickly she almost lost her balance.

'Hey, steady, you almost went over then.'

The unmistakable oily tones of her ex, Stewart, were breathing onto her cheek as she regained her footing.

'Sorry, didn't mean to scare you, hun.' There was a smile in his voice, but it didn't reach his eyes.

'No problem,' she lied. 'What are you doing here? I thought you'd moved away to Brum?'

'Hoped' was a better word, but she knew better than to antagonise him.

'Are you sure you're OK?' he said, avoiding the question. He still had hold of her wrist tighter than was necessary. There would be mild bruising in the morning, just when the old ones were starting to fade.

'I'm fine,' she said, her voice ice-cold as she pulled her hands free and plunged them deep into her coat pockets for protection.

'Still working at the ring shop?' he asked. Sarcasm dripped out of his mouth in a virtual puddle.

'The jeweller's, yes,' Molly replied, then turned back to face the café, hoping that would drop a big enough hint that he seriously needed to get the hell away from her.

'Hey babe, there's no need to be like that, I'm just being pleasant.'

He'd raised his voice, and the queue that was lengthening behind her were all listening while trying hard to pretend their attention was elsewhere.

'Are you waiting for a coffee? If not, I'll say goodbye.' She had reached the door now and managed to step inside.

'See ya later then, babe,' he said, and to her horror bent towards her for a kiss.

She reeled forwards and collided with the people in front as she stumbled through the doorway.

'I'm so sorry,' she said to the shocked couple, as Stewart blew her a kiss and disappeared into the crowd like a lizard in a fence crack.

'No worries, mate,' the young girl in front said, holding open the door for her. 'He seemed like a total prick.'

She could have hugged her. To encapsulate Stewart in two words so perfectly. If only she'd been able to do the same before she'd made the mistake of her life and moved in with him.

By the time she'd got served and walked back to work she'd been half an hour in total.

A cold mocha and an even colder encounter. From her expression alone, Graham knew better than to say anything.

She had really thought Stewart was history. After all that had happened between them, she never wanted to see him again.

If he continued to threaten her she'd need help, but she didn't know where from.

Trying to distract herself, she began her daily ritual of polishing the rings.

She pulled out the tray containing the ring that was reserved for the guy called James. She was certain that wasn't his real name, but it wouldn't be the first time. It was a lot of money to spend on one purchase—he might not come back at all, which again was not unusual.

Easing it gently from the cushion, she held it up to the light.

Something looked wrong.

There seemed to be a roughness to the touch. The diamond was not sparking the way it should. Normally, when she took it out for eager customers, there was an audible intake of breath as the stone caught the light.

She gave it a gentle wipe and almost dropped it as the clocks at the back of the shop all struck at the same time, making their pronouncements of the hour in a variety of bells and even a cuckoo joining in.

She placed the ring gently back down on the counter and took a moment. She was a bundle of nerves. The mismatched collection of timepieces on display still held an unmistakable charm for a certain generation, and normally the chiming was just a background noise—no more intrusive than the hum of the air conditioning—but today she noticed everything.

There was no doubt about it. Her nerves were shattered. The encounter with her ex had shaken her badly. She could still feel the imprints of his fingers on her wrists.

'Everything alright?' Graham was by her side, bringing a cloud of Hugo Boss with him. He was looking at her and then at the ring on the counter.

'Yeah, I'm just a bit tired,' Molly sighed, and immediately hated how weak she sounded.

'Tiredness is for bedtimes,' he proudly proclaimed—another pearl of wisdom from the pages of *Management for Dummies*, no doubt.

She gave a weak laugh and tied the reserved tag back on the ring before sliding the tray into the display cabinet.

There was no way she was alerting Graham to her concerns about the ring. It was probably nothing—just her state of mind—and the last thing she needed was her supercilious superior proving her wrong.

Chapter 5

I'd been drinking all afternoon with the guys from work and turned up late for my daughter's Christmas fair at school.

I remember barging into the assembly hall, sweating boozy body odour over everyone as my daughter stood on the stage singing 'Good King Wenceslas' with her classmates. They were all swaying from side to side wearing Santa hats.

I was swaying too—and not in a good way. My wife could barely look at me as I knocked people to one side to get to her. I knew I was in trouble 'cos she had her arms folded and didn't give me eye contact.

I've a vague recollection of singing along, but I must have been way too loud as other parents were staring at me. It didn't occur to me that I was spoiling their precious moments. I thought I was being funny—even charming. Can you believe that?

When my daughter finished, she leapt off the stage and ran towards me.

She flung her hands around my waist—at least she was happy to see me.

I blurted out something about not missing my Princess's performance for one second, and by the roll of my wife's eyes I knew my bed would be the sofa that night.

You know, it's funny, but at that moment I really hated my wife. Looking back, I think it was because she was the one getting in the way of my drinking and spoiling my special moments with our seven-year-old daughter. It wasn't till later I realised those moments were always after I'd been drinking, and my wife had become nothing but someone who tolerated me until some magical cure came along—or I got run over by a bus staggering home one night.

But anyway, things really started to kick off when Santa arrived.

Danny hit pause and rubbed his eyes. The interview sounded great, but he couldn't concentrate on the final edit until he'd considered what to do about Charlie Burrows.

The message had left him reeling. What on earth could an old schoolmate he hadn't seen for years have done that was so bad he'd reached out to someone he barely knew anymore?

Danny had said he'd call him back and they'd arrange a meeting. Charlie seemed reticent to give him details over the phone, and whatever it was he'd done, it was obvious he didn't feel comfortable going to the police.

He pulled off his headphones, double-checked he'd saved where he'd got to, and looked at the calendar on his phone.

He was working all day tomorrow and had to finish the podcast by the end of the week.

Since he'd broken up with his ex a few months ago he thought he'd have all the time in the world, but all the time they'd spent together had just soaked up into his working life. He didn't know how he'd managed to sustain a relationship— but then again, maybe that was the reason they'd split up.

They'd unfriended each other on Facebook, not through bad feelings, just protocol, but he still kept an eye on her account, which he was sure she did with him.

Her last post was taken on holiday somewhere in Italy with a couple of girlfriends he'd never really liked. In one picture she had her arm around a bronzed beach boy, so he guessed she was moving on.

That's what he needed to do—so maybe helping out old Charlie Burrows would be a good next step. Who knew, it might even make a future episode.

He picked up his phone and clicked on the new contact.

This time the phone rang a little longer, and when Charlie picked it up he seemed even more flustered.

'It's all right, Kaz, it's just work,' he yelled into the background. 'One second,' he said to Danny, and by the shuffling he seemed to be taking the phone outside.

'Sorry about that,' he said. 'I'm in the garden now so we can talk.'

'Great,' Danny said, wondering if his tone was a little too upbeat considering the circumstances. 'I wondered if you're free for breakfast tomorrow morning?'

'Breakfast?' Charlie said as if the meal had just been invented.

'Yeah, I'm a delivery driver and I start at nine, but I know a great place by the river in Worcester if you can make it?'

Charlie made a note of the address and thanked him profusely.

Danny hit end and let out a long sigh, wondering what on earth he'd let himself in for.

He'd already looked up Charlie on Facebook and it seemed they were indeed friends. He couldn't remember accepting him, but then again, he wouldn't recognise half the people on his list anyway.

Charlie's profile photo was taken on a family holiday—somewhere hot, by the look of the tanned faces. His wife was squeezed close to him and his two kids pulling faces either side.

They looked happy, but who took photos when they were miserable?

He checked the 'about' info for the third time in case he could glean anything from it to find out why Charlie was in trouble.

He worked at Worcestershire Royal Hospital. He was married to Karen, had two kids, neither of whom were on Facebook.

He clicked Karen's info and saw she hadn't posted in over six months.

Maybe that was when this trouble started.

He put his phone to one side and stood up. It was useless speculating any more—he'd have to wait till the morning when they'd reunite after all those years.

Chapter 6

Friday 15th December, 6:45pm

Molly yanked the coat hangers in her tiny wardrobe one by one, the metal screeching along the rail in protest as she tried to find something decent to wear.

She hadn't seen her soulmate in ages, and although the idea of going into town was about as appealing as root canal work, she had to make an effort.

Budgets were strained and her measly monthly pay hardly covered rent and food, never mind utilities.

The chances of her buying new outfits were low on the priority list, although she'd splurged on a couple of French Connection tops at Oxfam last week.

She opened drawers in random hope and pulled out her trusty jeans. She hoped Gemma wasn't going to be too dressed up.

She'd called her after work just to vent about seeing Stewart again and how she'd felt afterwards.

Gemma didn't waste any time listing her ex's shortcomings before insisting they go out and forget everything.

'I can't get pissed, I've got to open up the shop tomorrow,' she'd insisted.

'We don't have to get drunk to have a good time. We could spend a couple of hours with Chris Hemsworth?' Gemma suggested.

So the cinema it was—the best place really, as the pubs were getting rammed on the Christmas run-up.

After she'd showered and dressed she took a long look at herself in the full-length mirror which was leant precariously against the wall. It was one of the few things she'd insisted on keeping when she and Stewart had split their stuff before moving out of the old flat.

She wondered if people would believe she was thirty next year. Did anyone still think she looked like she was in her twenties—and more importantly, why did she care?

She touched her left cheekbone. The bruise was hardly visible now. She tied back her hair and snapped on a hair-clip. She applied lip gloss and her tongue automatically drifted to the chipped tooth.

She tried a smile and felt better.

Gemma made her laugh. She knew what to say and when to say it.

She heard her phone vibrating on the bedside table and grabbed it, expecting a message from her.

She looked at the screen and covered her mouth in horror. She thought this was all behind her, and here it was again, coming back to taunt her.

Stewart's greasy smile floated unwelcome into her thoughts. She felt his grip on her wrists from this afternoon, swearing she could smell the aftershave she'd bought him for his last birthday before the final time she took his shit.

She threw the iPhone to the floor, not caring if it smashed— rather hoping it would. That way she'd be out of contact. But the moment it hit the carpet she heard it buzz again.

This time it wasn't a message, it was a call.

What did he want? Why couldn't he just leave her alone?

The ringing stopped and she fell onto the bed, staring at the cracks in the ceiling. This was a nightmare, just when she was getting her life back on track.

She'd been steadying her breathing when the phone vibrated again.

This time she grabbed it and hit the answer button with such ferocity she almost pierced the screen with her fingernail.

'Listen to me, you bastard, I don't know what you're playing at but it ends now. We agreed.'

'Molly?' It was Gemma's voice.

'Oh Jesus, Gem, I'm so sorry. I thought you were—'

'Him?' she said.

'Yeah, him.'

'Well I'm not, so let me in. I'm bloody freezing out here.'

Molly ran to the window, pulled back the curtains and spotted Gemma's tiny figure below.

She was stood by the door wearing a ridiculously short dress and visibly shivering.

'Down in a sec.'

She dropped her phone on the bed and took the stairs two at a time before pulling open the door.

They both hugged, and Molly could feel every rib of her quivering body.

She led her into the tiny front room and Gemma slumped onto the ratty sofa, making herself comfortable by flinging off her high heels towards the fireplace, which hadn't seen a lump of coal since the end of the miners' strike.

'So he's called again?' Gemma said, not bothering with preliminaries. They'd been friends long enough to read each other's vibes.

'He's done more than that,' Molly answered, and ran back upstairs to get her phone.

When she returned, Gemma had disappeared into the galley kitchen. She'd managed to find a couple of glasses and was rooting around in the cupboards.

'Please tell me you've got some kind of alcohol in this house?' Gemma's voice was muffled from inside the fridge.

'Just some schnapps my dad brought me back from his work trip, but it's pretty gross.'

'Beggars can't be choosers. Where is it?' Gemma asked eagerly.

Molly reached over her head to the pan cupboard where the sticky bottle was stashed at the back.

Gemma grabbed it off her playfully and began to pour. 'Your dad is so cool, bringing you stuff like this from his world travels. The best I get from mine is an occasional pen he's lifted from the stationery cupboard.'

Molly held back the urge to say something about how lucky Gemma was having her dad at home every night if she needed him. Hers would spend months away while he surveyed a far-flung location for the next block of hotels the company wanted to build.

'So come on,' Gemma said, sinking back into the sofa and spilling a little from the overfull glass. 'Tell me all about it. Remember, there's nothing can touch Gemma and Molly.' She bumped her free fist against Molly's and they both giggled.

Molly felt better already, even though she hadn't begun to process what she'd just seen on her phone.

Rather than say anything else, she just handed it over to Gemma, who stared at the screen.

The glow vanished from her face as she looked up, the reliable smile replaced with creases of worry.

'Man, this is messed up,' she said.

'I know. I should never have let him take those pictures of me. What was I thinking?' Molly grimaced and took a long pull from her glass.

'I remember your dad didn't like him.'

Molly had a flashback to a FaceTime call when her dad was in Hong Kong, his face too close to the screen while he explained all the reasons he thought Stewart was bad news. At the time she'd put it down to him being overprotective, although her mother had been charmed by him when he'd come round for an uncomfortable family dinner and brought flowers.

'Dad was right. He's always right.' She had a sudden ache to hold him, to smell cologne and coffee on his suit jacket while he reassured her that everything was going to be fine.

She couldn't imagine her mother doing anything like that. She was too busy with her book clubs and Slimming World, which she ran every month from a poky room at the community centre. Her insular world only included Molly when she wanted to show her off to a new client. She would insist Molly was in the jewellery trade rather than a shop assistant, as if the idea of her daughter working in retail would crush the family legacy.

She envied Gemma, with her three older brothers and younger sister buzzing around. Being an only child left huge aspirational responsibilities on a girl. It was like her parents were gamblers throwing all their money on one horse.

'So what are you gonna do about him?' Gemma asked, finishing her drink and setting it down on the wooden crate Molly was using as a table.

'I don't know. I'd hate for that photo to get out. He promised me he'd deleted everything.'

'Maybe I should ask my dad?' Gemma suggested, sitting up straight and looking Molly in the eye.

'I don't want to get the police involved.' Molly shuddered. The thought of dragging all this out would mean the kind of bitterness and trouble she just couldn't face.

'How many times do I have to tell you, my dad isn't police. He just works in the call centre. But he does know stuff about the law and I'm sure he'd be happy to give you some advice.'

'I'll have a think about it,' Molly sighed.

'Well don't think about it too long. It sounds to me like a toothache you hope will just get better, and you do nothing till the tooth starts to rot.'

'I wish he'd rot.'

'Amen to that. But now…' Gemma stood up and stumbled slightly. 'Woah, that drink has quite a kick.'

'Let's go to the cinema while we can still see,' Molly laughed and stood up, putting her untouched glass down.

A smash caused them both to let out an involuntary scream.

The sound had come from the window, and a cold wind was already blowing in through the hole.

There was a brick on the carpet and shards of glass all around.

'OK, I think the police idea is great now,' Molly said, picking up her phone and dialling the emergency services.

Gemma slipped her shoes back on and trod carefully through the glass, pulling the curtain to one side and peering out into the street.

Squinting into the darkness, she thought she could see someone in a hoodie running towards the main road.

Chapter 7

Saturday 16th December, 7:17am

The guy playing Santa was pretty good, to be honest.

He'd grown a proper beard and gone to town with the talcum powder.

The kids had finished singing on stage and my wife was still blanking me with just an occasional yes or no reply. The only full sentence I got out of her was when I bought a couple of hot chocolates from an old woman scooping tablespoons of off-brand cocoa into steaming Styrofoam cups.

'There you go,' I'd said, trying to sound festive while not slurring too much.

'This must be the first non-alcoholic drink you've had all day,' she barked back.

Apart from an Alka-Seltzer first thing that morning, she was absolutely right.

My daughter was back by now, hanging onto my arm and asking if I'd wait with her in the queue to see Santa.

My wife rolled her eyes again and said something to her about going to have a look at the class pictures they'd put up on the walls. Loads of snowmen made from cotton wool and lopsided Christmas trees done with glued pieces of green card.

She disappeared, no doubt glad to be away from my exhibition as Dad of the Year, and we made our way to the end of the queue.

A couple of the dads knew me from the pub but only said a quick hello, which I was relieved about. Even in those days I knew my drinking life had no place in my daughter's school, and that was when I got a good look at Santa.

Danny liked to listen to his interviews in the van. He'd done some research recently and discovered the majority of podcasts were heard in the car, on headphones, or on smart speakers round the home.

By listening on the move he'd be experiencing them the way his loyal subscribers did.

He'd stopped the interview just as he pulled into the car park, promising himself he'd finish it off and upload the whole episode by tomorrow.

But first there was the mystery of his old school friend to sort out.

They'd agreed to meet at 7:30, which gave them both enough time to catch up. He had a day of deliveries to pick up from the warehouse at 8:45.

He paid on his phone with a parking app, and when he opened the van door it almost ripped out of his hand.

The crosswind coming up from the river was quite a gust and there was misty rain in the air as he pulled up his hood and walked towards the inviting yellow lights of the café.

He yanked open the door, and a blast of warm air mingled with the smell of frying bacon instantly made his mouth water.

There were only three tables taken. One was a man on his own, dressed in running gear and listening to something on his white earbuds while attacking a sandwich with gusto. He had probably earned every calorie after an early morning jog in the December downpour.

There was an elderly couple sat in silence opposite each other at a table overlooking the river. They both seemed deep in thought, enjoying the companionable quiet only those who've been together for years can achieve.

It was obvious who Charlie was, as he was sitting at a table at the far end of the room just by the disabled toilets, obviously wanting somewhere quiet.

Danny took a second to take in the man he hadn't seen since they'd left sixth form.

He'd put on weight and lost hair; his forehead was higher now, and there was something less eager about his eyes. He was always a hit with the girls in his day but now just looked like every other working Joe in the world.

Seeming to sense him staring, Charlie snapped out of his solo trance and stood up suddenly, making the chair squeak against the floor. The old couple looked across and then turned back to the window.

'Hello, mate,' he said, grabbing hold of Danny's hand as if he'd just presented him with an award. 'How are you, it's been a while?'

Danny smiled, released his hand and took the seat opposite, unzipping his jacket and hanging it on the back of the chair.

'Yeah, it must be what?' Danny frowned, making a show of trying to remember, even though he'd already done his research beforehand, thanks to some old photos and social media stalking. 'Seventeen years?'

'Sounds about right,' Charlie said, seemingly pleased that he'd remembered. 'We both went back to the school for that prize-giving thing.'

Danny didn't remember it that well. He'd arrived late and was a little worse for wear—the beginning of his downward spiral in those days.

'Yeah, and you were getting married,' Danny said, trying a smile.

Charlie didn't return it. 'Yep, to my lovely Karen. She got pregnant and we...' He stopped for a second, the memories coming back and seeming to sting. 'Well, her mum and dad were keen for us and I...'

Danny helped him out. 'How many kids you got now then?'

'Two.' The beam returned as he grabbed his phone, swiped to the photo app and scrolled for a few seconds. 'There they are,' he said proudly. 'Taken at Alton Towers last year. Maisie's sixteen and Dylan's twelve—great kids.' He stuffed his phone back in his pocket as if leaving it out for too long would cause them to escape.

'What about you?' he asked.

'No kids and no one special right now.'

'Plenty of time,' he said sagely. 'Let me get you something to eat, it's on me.' He pushed a two-sided menu in Danny's direction, but he didn't need to look at it. He'd been here a few times before, just never this early.

'I'll do the full English,' Danny said.

'Me too,' Charlie replied, obviously eager to get on with things.

He walked up to the counter, pulling up his jeans over an expanded waistline. He'd put on quite a few pounds since the school cross-country days.

Danny checked his watch and then joined the old couple with their vigil of the river.

It was a beautiful spot in the summer, with boats tied to moorings, bobbing up and down to the beat of the River Severn current.

It was different in the winter months. If the rain continued there would be flooding, as there always was—closing off the main bridge and bringing out the Environment Agency staff in high-vis jackets, manning barriers and laying long pipes across closed roads.

'It'll be about ten minutes,' Charlie said, easing himself back behind the table.

'Shall we get down to business?' Danny said. They could play niceties all morning, but his time was limited and it was becoming obvious Charlie wasn't eager to break the ice.

'I've done something stupid,' Charlie whispered. Danny had to lean forward to hear him.

'OK, start from the beginning,' Danny said. 'Take your time, let's see if we can get you out of whatever this is.'

'I know it sounds a bit daft me contacting you after all these years, but I'm being honest with you, mate—there's nobody else I can turn to. If my wife finds out what I've done it will k…' He stopped suddenly, but Danny resisted the urge to fill the silence. 'She's not been well, you see. Cancer. She's…the kids…the debt…her parents don't…oh Christ.'

His eyes turned glassy, then the tears came. He tried to stifle them but a couple of sobs issued from the wad of napkin he was clutching. Danny noticed his nails were bitten down to the quick.

'Easy, mate.' Danny put a light hand on his heaving shoulder. 'It can't be as bad as all that.'

Charlie looked at him with red eyes. 'It really is, Danny. Very bad.'

'What's happened, Charlie?' Danny was letting his eagerness get the better of him and talking too loud. He moved his chair round so he was sat closer. 'Come on, get it all out—a problem shared and all that?'

'I wouldn't have done it, but I saw something on the telly about forgers and how they work. I thought, hey, there must be someone who could do a good job for me and that way I could clear off a bit of debt, get the kids something decent for Christmas, treat Karen, take her mind off…things.'

'There you are, lads—full English for two. Who didn't want black pudding?' A woman wearing a greasy apron was holding two plates with practised ease and had appeared with ninja stealth.

'That'll be me. When I found out what it was made of I gave it up,' Charlie replied, forcing a smile.

The woman chortled and, after enquiring about any sauces, disappeared as quickly as she'd arrived.

'I can always do banter,' Charlie said, adding salt to his fried egg.

'Comes with the job. I'm a porter at Worcester Royal. You get to see some bad stuff and hear the worst stories. You have to learn to switch off.'

Danny had met people like Charlie before. They had inbuilt coping mechanisms.

Glancing at the clock over the counter, he realised time was running out.

He followed his friend's lead and began to dig in. Charlie continued his story.

'So I found a bloke who did forgeries in Birmingham and made a discreet contact.'

Danny had a million questions about how he'd found the forger and where it was, but whatever he said next would make him an accomplice—or at the very least an accessory after the fact. He'd taken quite a few law courses before embarking on the podcast, and he knew he was now walking on very dodgy ground.

'I found a ring at a jeweller's in Worcester and took a picture of it,' Charlie continued. 'I took the photo to this place in the Jewellery Quarter in Birmingham and they made a copy in a matter of days. It only cost me three grand.'

'Three grand?' Danny interjected, breakfast pretty much forgotten now. 'That's a lot of cash.'

'Not when the real one is worth over thirty thousand.' There was a note of pride in Charlie's voice as he moved food around on his plate.

'So you made a swap?'

'Yep, and I thought I'd got away with it.'

'So what happened?'

Charlie did another double check around the room.

The old couple were settling up their bill, counting out coins onto a plate.

The runner had taken out his earbuds and was reading a magazine, his coffee cooling in front of him.

Charlie slid the note across the table under the palm of his hand. Danny unfolded it and read it a couple of times before folding it up again and handing it back.

'So you're being blackmailed?'

Charlie nodded his head before stuffing the note into his trouser pocket and letting out a sigh, grabbing his cup and gulping down the last of his lukewarm coffee.

'Have they called yet?'

Charlie shook his head. 'I don't know what to do for the best, but I can't have the family finding out.'

'I'm not sure what you want me to do about it?' Danny said, suddenly confused and frustrated. 'Maybe you should go to the police, hand it in and say sorry?'

As the words came out, he knew this was a bad idea. He rightfully wanted to protect his family, and a come-to-Jesus confession would be just as bad as being caught at this stage.

'Please help me,' Charlie said. His demeanour had returned to the trembling man he'd met when he first walked in. 'I've heard all your podcasts and I know you're a good man. You investigate stuff, talk to people—maybe you could find out who these people are and...'

The doors sprang open and the squawk of radios filled the café as three police officers walked up to the counter and ordered drinks.

'Best talk outside,' Charlie said out of the corner of his mouth.

Danny nodded, shrugged on his coat and made his way out while Charlie left a twenty-pound note on the table, not waiting for change.

The door slammed behind them, leaving the police milling around waiting for their order and the runner still sat at his table taking it all in.

The magazine he was pretending to read was discarded and the coffee was cold.

He picked up his mobile and called a number on speed dial.

Mr C answered on the first ring.

'Andy?'

He replied with his mouth close against the handset in a low whisper. 'He's just left, so I'll follow.'

'You sure he didn't recognise you?'

'Nah, the last time he saw me I was wearing a mask.'

'And you said he was meeting someone. Do we know who?'

'Not yet, but I will.'

The line went dead and Andy made his way to the exit, pretending to stretch for his next run as he put on a show for the cops waiting by the counter.

Chapter 8

Saturday 16th December, 8:06am

Molly woke from a restless night, covered in sweat. The sour remnants of the schnapps burning the back of her throat.

She sat up and the world swam before her eyes.

Memories of last night slammed back into her brain: the brick through the window, the police arriving and telling them to sort a glazier before taking a statement and issuing what they called an incident number. The guy turning up an hour later to put boards on the window frame without hardly saying a word, and then her and Gemma finishing the bottle together. Everything after that was a little fuzzy.

Running to the bathroom, she stuck her head under the tap and let the water fall on her face before taking huge gulps of the lukewarm flow. She had never been able to get the water to run properly cold—just one of a list of things the landlord was supposedly addressing, including a shower that did no more than dribble, the heating which made horrendous clanging noises when the boiler got too hot, and now some boards up at the windows until the glazier finished the job. She wondered if the landlord's insurance would cover that or if she'd have to pay for it herself.

She heard coughing coming from downstairs and remembered Gemma.

'Oh God, my head,' Gemma said by way of greeting as Molly appeared in the front room.

Her mascara had smudged panda-like around her eyes, and for some reason the dress looked two sizes too big for her, hanging off her tiny frame like a trapeze swing.

'I've got to get going,' Molly said, breezing past her to the kitchen, pouring water in the kettle and flicking it on. 'You can have my bed if you like and sleep it off?'

Gemma didn't need asking twice, as she'd disappeared upstairs by the time Molly appeared back in the living room with a mug in each hand. She finished them both, checking her phone again, relieved there were no more messages.

Amazed she'd managed to wake on time, she wondered when the hangover would kick in properly. Maybe it was in the post, or perhaps she could work through it. She'd showered and got dressed in the dark as Gemma lay passed out on her bed.

Leaving the house, she posted the key and looked back, surveying the damage from the outside for the first time. The place looked like a squat: the front garden already a mess of thorns and broken brickwork, and now the boarding on the window. Anyone could imagine a group of junkies shooting up inside.

The landlord's face came to her mind again, and then the unwelcome reappearance of Stewart and those pictures. She hadn't deleted them; she might need evidence in the future.

She checked her watch. It read 8:32. The shop had to be ready by 9, which included navigating the complicated security shutters, the even more bewildering alarm code and setting out the stock in the cabinets. It was a twenty-minute walk, so to have the shop open on time she'd have to run. It was at moments like this she was grateful to live in the city—no cars or public transport to negotiate—but it had made her lazy, leaving everything till the last minute.

She'd just got to the end of her road when she stopped to catch her breath, feeling dizzy. The memories of last night, the schnapps, and the worry about the brick through her window were going to tip her over the edge.

A hand fell heavy on her shoulder and she spun around.

She saw a large man towering over her. She didn't give herself time to get a good look; all the anguish flooded her until she felt she would burst right there and then. She punched him hard with her fist—an involuntary swing which made instant contact with pudgy flesh.

The man let out a feminine yelp, at odds with his build and stature, and fell backwards, landing heavily on the ground while clutching his face.

'What the hell?' he said, and before she could run and get help she heard him add, 'I just wanted to give you your keys.'

'What?'

'Your keys.' He held them out with one hand while clutching his bloody cheek with the other. 'You dropped them on the pavement.'

'Oh my God, I'm so sorry,' Molly said, reaching down to help the unfortunate man to his feet.

He still had a hand tight against his cheek, and blood was oozing through his fingers. Molly assumed her clenched fist had made contact while her ring had gouged a chunk of skin with the punch. Her keys lay at her feet, so she scooped them up and threw them into her bag. 'I may have a plaster in here somewhere.'

'I'll probably need stitches, you crazy b… idiot,' he quickly corrected himself. 'I was only trying to give you your keys.'

She was about to apologise again when a familiar face appeared. It was one of the police officers from last night—the one who'd given her the incident number.

'Well, well, well,' he said in a voice that could have come straight out of central casting. 'You again. Not often I get the same person for two separate incidents in a twelve-hour shift. Lucky I was passing—I'm just about to head back to the station.'

Molly followed his arm and saw the patrol car parked by the traffic lights with the other cop from last night behind the wheel.

'She attacked me, officer,' the bleeding man spoke in an affected voice, like a child telling on a friend in the playground.

Molly noticed his cheek had stopped bleeding, but there was still a nasty gash.

'I thought he was going to attack me,' Molly insisted.

The police officer looked back at the victim, waiting for a response. It seemed he had all the time in the world and was content to let this play out.

'I was just trying to give her the keys she dropped,' he insisted, the pathetic voice still in play.

'Did you get your keys, Miss?' the policeman asked.

'Yes, thank you, and I'm ever so sorry.' Molly looked at the man, whose body language gave no sign of letting this go. She looked at her watch: it was almost 9—she'd be late opening up now anyway.

'I want to press charges for assault,' he said.

The policeman looked from him to her for a few moments before speaking.

'I think the lady has apologised and has been through rather a shock in the last few hours. Do you think you may have it in your heart to let this go?'

From the beetroot colour of his face Molly could tell he didn't want to drop it, but he also knew the cop had already made up his mind.

'Alright then,' and with that he stomped off down the street, clutching his cheek again and muttering under his breath.

'Thank you,' Molly said.

'Well done,' the officer replied with the faintest of grins.

'What for?' she laughed.

'Well, for one, not letting the man antagonise you into an argument and causing me a lifetime of paperwork, and for another, getting that window boarded over so quickly.' He pointed down in the direction of her house. 'I take it you're in a hurry.'

She explained about opening the shop and being late.

'Let's drop you off there now, shall we?'

And with that she was escorted to the police car and helped into the back seat. As they set off into town, she could swear she spotted one or two curtains twitching. All her neighbours would assume she'd just been arrested for common assault.

'Thank you for being so nice to me,' Molly said as they navigated along the Tything before taking a right down Castle Street.

'I work with Gemma's dad,' he said, as if no other explanation were necessary.

'Oh, I see,' she said. 'I'll tell him how good you've been to me.'

Both officers laughed at this, and Molly knew better than to ask what the joke was.

Chapter 9

Saturday 16th December, 8:53

The windscreen wipers were flinging from side to side, fighting valiantly against the downpour hitting the glass.

Danny could drive these roads with his eyes closed, but that wouldn't be the best idea with some flooding already closing stretches and yellow diversion signs popping up, befuddling his highway knowledge and causing the Sat Nav to sulk.

He drove in silence, deep in thought and worry, his mind as packed as the boxes stacked in the back of the van.

All his attention was on Charlie. Many of his stories for the podcast had ended with him doing some kind of detective work, a way to put things right. He just hoped he hadn't raised his old friend's expectations too high.

He hit a pothole and the van bounced. It had great suspension, so the feeling was like jumping on jelly. Some of the boxes clattered and, as he always did, he wondered if there were any badly wrapped breakables among his cargo today.

He was doing a steady fifty miles an hour along the Bromsgrove Road and reckoned he'd arrive in Droitwich in ten minutes. He had twenty deliveries there and should have them all done by lunchtime, then back to Worcester and his meeting with Charlie, where they could hopefully swap back the real ring before anyone noticed.

The magnificent Chateau Impney loomed on his right and a memory of a party came back to him. It was when he and his ex were still in the throes of early love, still learning about each other, until they discovered too much and that was that. One minute you're sipping champagne, whispering into each other's ears about future plans to see the world together while the DJ belts out Bryan Adams; the next you're back living on your own, pushing unnecessary online purchases through people's letterboxes while she's sunning herself in Italy, snuggling beside the next big hope.

Dragging himself from the past, he focussed on the present. He had a job to do and then someone to help later.

Part of his recovery was keeping away from what was called 'stinking thinking'. Whenever he over-analysed his life or started to wallow in regret, there was more danger of him picking up a drink again.

If he stayed positive and helped others, the chances were slimmer. Anything that weighed down the odds of him going back out there and starting that insane cycle again was always to be welcomed.

He turned on the radio and Bryan Adams was playing. What were the chances?

Chapter 10

Charlie's coat was still damp. His waterproof had the absorbency of a paper sponge.

Stepping through the door, he could hear his wife coughing upstairs.

'Alright, Kaz?' he called, while shaking off his coat and draping it over the radiator.

'I thought you were in work today?' she yelled down. She may have been frail, but her voice was still strong.

'Hang on, I'll come up. Do you want a brew?'

'Ooh, breakfast in bed, how can a lady refuse?'

She still had her sense of humour, and by the time Charlie had gone upstairs holding two steaming mugs, she was out of bed and seemed to be looking for something in her bedside drawer.

'Hey, I thought you were resting. I told the kids to be quiet. Where are they?' He sat on her side of the bed and put the mug in front of her.

'Maisie's popped out to see a film with one of her mates and Dylan's in his room playing something or other. I was just looking for my engagement ring box. I don't want to lose it.'

Charlie noticed the ring on the bedside table and felt a queasy pang. One worth ten times its value was stuffed in a butter dish downstairs.

'I'm losing so much weight off my fingers,' she explained while rummaging through a lifetime's worth of trinkets. 'I'm having to take it off and put it back in that lovely box it came in.'

Charlie remembered buying it and wished he could turn back time and start again, erasing all his bad choices and ungovernable situations.

She found it and slipped the ring inside before slamming the drawer shut, bringing all conversation about the ring to a close.

'Thanks for the tea, love,' she said, taking a sip, fluffing up the pillows and sitting back on the bed. 'Why are you home from work?'

'I haven't been yet. I'm only covering a couple of hours till one. Just popped out to meet an old school friend for breakfast.'

'Do I know him?'

'Don't think so, we were mates up till we left sixth form.'

'What's his name?'

'Danny Wade.'

She took another sip and seemed deep in thought for a while.

'Danny Wade… the name rings a bell.'

'Well, you might have known him from when we were kids.'

'No, it's not that.' She stared at the ceiling, waiting for inspiration. 'Danny Wade, Danny W…' She suddenly stopped. 'I've got it. Isn't he the guy that does that podcast you've been listening to?'

Charlie was stunned. 'Yeah. I didn't know you listened to it.'

'I didn't, but I've heard you with it on in the kitchen, and I've listened to a couple of episodes since.'

'Yeah, well, that's the guy.'

She was on the verge of asking another question when her pallor changed and Charlie knew the signs straight away. The bouts of nausea from the chemo would creep up on her unexpectedly, and she excused herself as she ran to the en suite.

Charlie said nothing—she hated fuss—and instead he got his uniform from the wardrobe and got ready for work.

When she returned, she was ghostly white and seemed to have forgotten about Danny Wade. Charlie was relieved that she hadn't pursued it further and was straightening his tie in the mirror when he felt her hands around his waist.

He stroked her fingers. 'Do you need anything before I go to work?' he asked.

She shook her head. 'You're a good man, Charlie Burrows,' she said, before pulling aside the duvet and getting back into bed.

If only she knew, he thought, as he blew her a kiss and left the darkened room.

By the time he'd got downstairs and grabbed his bag, he knew he'd have to get a move on. He could have stayed in Worcester and gone straight to work, but he wanted to get the ring and have it ready for his next meeting with Danny.

Reaching over the fridge, he moved aside objects, fumbling around for the butter dish.

It was gone.

Panicking, he pulled out a kitchen chair so he could lean further in. His heart was racing as his imagination played cruel tricks on him. Had his wife found it? One of the kids? Maybe someone had broken in and—

His fingers touched the butter dish, which had been wedged behind a cheese grater, and relief washed over him as cold sweat prickled down his back.

Taking the ring out and closing the door, he almost dropped it when he felt the phone buzz in his pocket.

He grabbed it without looking at the screen, assuming it was Danny or the hospital asking when he was going to be in for work. He was running very late.

It was neither.

Bring the ring and ten thousand pounds cash to a time and location to be designated in the next twenty-four hours, which should give you enough time to come up with the money. Don't be smart. Remember we know what you did.

Charlie dropped the ring on the floor. It rolled to a stop and for a second he wondered if he should just bend down, pick it up and throw it in the bin.

Instead, he put it in his pocket and sat on the sofa while his world fell down around his ears.

Chapter 11

The police had driven down the pedestrian zone and parked the squad car right up to the door of the jeweller's.

Then an officer stood guard while Molly opened the shop, in case she had any more bricks through windows or well-meaning members of the public handing over dropped keys.

She hadn't thought of the link between her home life and work, but now the kind constable had given her almost fatherly warnings about staying safe, and the fact there was another police officer guarding the shop until she'd unlocked the shutters had been a relief.

Now she was pulling the stock out of the safe, feeling unsteady and vulnerable. Last night had shocked her, and the amount of schnapps still brewing in her system didn't help her paranoia. She hoped the police hadn't smelt it too badly in the car.

As she wound up the display clocks, she pondered the extraordinary luck of the police officer recognising Gemma when they came to the house last night, and him knowing her dad from his job at the police headquarters at Hindlip.

Molly had always liked Gemma's dad. When they were growing up, she'd often stay at hers for a sleepover and they'd all eat together at the table, something her parents never did as her father was always away and her mother hardly ate anything anyway, being on some or other constant diet.

He would crack jokes about the people who'd called him at the police contact centre, and she believed him until he got to the end of his story and said the name of the caller. There would be a Robin Banks, a Corporal Punishment, or her favourite, N.O.C. Neighbour reporting on the naked window cleaner.

The police had gone, and she was starting to feel like herself again.

Having finished her chores, she popped into the staff room and switched on the kettle, then thought better, remembering there was still a Red Bull left in the tiny fridge.

She pulled it out, cracked the tab and took a long pull, nearly finishing it in one.

She heard the shop bell and left the can on the side by the sink. Company rules stated you weren't allowed to take anything more than water onto the shop floor.

A couple had shuffled in and were both focused on the rings under the counter. They looked to be somewhere in their mid-twenties, both wearing matching bobble hats. They probably thought it was a cutesy couple statement, but it made Molly want to barf up the Red Bull onto the glass counter.

'Can I help you with anything?' she asked in her customary chirpy tone, the one she could turn on at the flick of a locket clasp.

'We were just browsing,' the man said, but the woman wanted to speak for him.

'We like the look of that ring,' she said, pointing to the one she'd reserved for the man called James yesterday.

'Could we take a look?' the man said, sighing in resignation, realising that more than half of his yearly wage packet could be blown before he left the shop.

'This one's reserved,' Molly said, sliding out the drawer and plucking it free.

'Can you get some more?' the girl asked, taking it in her hand and studying it.

Molly had that bad feeling again. There was still no glow to the ring.

'Not a problem,' she said. 'I'll just check what stock's available.'

The door had opened while they'd been talking, and she'd hardly noticed the tall man in the corner studying the watches. It wasn't until he spoke that she recognised him straight away.

'Don't buy anything from here, it's all knock-offs and fakes,' Stewart said before leaving as quickly as he arrived.

Once the door had slammed shut, there was an icy silence.

'Don't worry, we'll come back later,' said the man, snatching the ring from his girlfriend, placing it back on the counter and hustling her to the door faster than her feet could carry her.

Molly was a bundle of nerves all afternoon, waiting for Stewart to come back, her finger poised to hit the panic alarm, which was discreetly placed under the counter.

She saw the police car pull up outside the shop and wondered if there had been news about the brick through her window, or maybe the guy she'd punched earlier had decided to press charges after all.

But it was just a friendly call to make sure she was OK.

It seemed that Gemma's dad had quite a bit of sway down at the station.

Chapter 12

Saturday 16th December, 1:30pm

Santa looked at me and I looked at Santa.

It was like 'gunfight at the OK Corral', Lapland style.

Even his little elves seemed to sense trouble when they stood back from this throne thing he was sitting on.

He might have been merry old St Nicholas to those excited kids waiting in line, but to me the guy behind that hook-on beard and oversized outfit was somebody I'd been wanting to catch up with for six months.

There was this little lad around seven or eight stood by him, looking up with that awe that kids have.

He reached into this bulging sack by his feet, pulled out a present and gave it to the boy. He'd been looking at me on and off for ages and only took his eyes away for a few seconds while he said his goodbye to the kid with that ridiculous Santa voice.

By the time one of the elves had whisked the boy away, I'd barged right into the front of the queue, ignoring the angry parents and the kids squealing that I was pushing in.

I marched right up to him and pulled him out of his chair by his beard. It came off in my hand and I could hear screams and cries from everybody, including my daughter, who I'd left at the back of the queue.

There was no denying it. Ian (or Richard in the podcast) was a brilliant storyteller. Whether it was the years of sharing this tale for the newcomers in the many rooms of recovering alcoholics, or maybe he was just a natural, it was hard to tell. But one thing was for sure: it was a great way to round off the year's podcasts.

Danny was tempted to finish it tonight but didn't want to rush the edit. He knew he was a little behind, but he had to reserve the rest of today's energy for Charlie, who'd be at his door in half an hour.

The morning deliveries in Droitwich had taken longer than he'd thought: a couple of mixed-up addresses, a troubled customer who was waiting at the door with his arms folded, telling him he'd been expecting the package three days ago and he'd missed his wife's birthday.

Danny listened with a patient smile as the man went through a tirade of how the delivery services in this country were completely unreliable, and how his sister-in-law, who lived in Germany, got hers on the same day without question.

He'd been driving for nearly two years now and had learned never to argue with a customer. Best to nod, apologise, pretend to make notes and give them the email address for grievances.

But that did mean the old goat's diatribe had put Danny back, and by the time he'd finished his shift he only had half an hour to work on the podcast.

At times like this he remembered HALT, which stood for hungry, angry, lonely and tired. If Danny ever felt any of these, he had to take action.

He saved and shut down the computer, grabbed a towel from the airing cupboard and took a hot shower, listening to ten minutes of a motivational app he'd just subscribed to, then made himself some herbal tea, slipping into chinos and a fresh T-shirt.

His hair was still wet when the doorbell rang.

Opening it straight away, Charlie was on the doorstep with a Morrisons carrier bag in his hand.

'Come in,' Danny said.

'Shall I take off my shoes?' he asked, noticing Danny in his socks.

'No,' Danny laughed, 'these are the closest I get to slippers. Shoes are fine.'

There was no entrance hall. The front door opened straight into the living room, and Charlie looked around, taking in the small area.

Danny wondered if Charlie was surprised that he wasn't living in some kind of Tudor mansion in the rolling countryside rather than a tiny townhouse in the ever-expanding suburbs of Warndon Villages.

Maybe he thought podcasters made millions. Most months (even with his ever-expanding subscriber numbers) he barely made enough to cover a week's grocery shopping.

'Have a seat,' Danny said, pointing to the two-seater sofa he'd got from his ex's shop for employee discount. It was the only memento of her existence in the whole house.

'I brought this as a thank you.' Charlie pulled a bottle of Moët & Chandon and handed it over to Danny with ceremony before sitting down.

'Thank you,' Danny said, and took it into the kitchen, placing it alongside a couple of other bottles he kept for guests. Many recovering addicts were reticent to have any alcohol in the house, but Danny was comfortable enough these days—though never complacent, or at least he hoped he wasn't.

'I've just made some tea, can I get you anything?' Danny hoped he wouldn't ask for a glass of the stuff he'd just given him.

'A coffee would be great,' he shouted. 'Two sugars, white.'

While the kettle boiled, Charlie went through the details of the latest disturbing text.

The kettle clicked, and by the time Danny had appeared back in the living room with Charlie's mug, the ring was on the coffee table.

'Oh my,' Danny said breathlessly, peering at it while he distractedly put the coffee down, almost missing his target.

Charlie grabbed the cup and smiled. 'She's a beauty, isn't she?' he said.

'She certainly is. I don't think I've ever seen something sparkle like that before. But I have to say I'm no expert.' Danny lifted it carefully and spun it around between his fingers.

'So whoever is blackmailing you wants the ring and ten thousand pounds cash?' Danny said more to himself as he carefully placed the ring back down.

'Yep, that's the gist of it.'

'OK.' Danny looked at Charlie and waited till he had his full attention. This man wasn't great with eye contact, but it was imperative that he understood the implications of what they were about to do together.

It was something that frightened Danny, and if it went wrong they'd both be in serious trouble. On the other hand, what was the point of vowing to spend the rest of your life helping others and doing the right thing if he baulked at the first tricky one?

'I'm going to suggest something that you might not like,' Danny said.

Charlie's head shot up from where it had seemed to be tracing the patterns in the carpet. Now Danny had his attention.

'What do you mean?' Charlie asked, his voice sounding faint and worried.

'I mean,' said Danny, leaning forward and picking up the ring again, 'we are going to smuggle this ring back into the jeweller's.'

Charlie almost knocked over his coffee as he jumped back. 'Smuggle it back in? It's impossible.'

Danny shook his head and waved the ring in front of Charlie like a hypnotist with a client. 'You got it out, now you can take it back.'

Charlie thought for a moment. Danny could almost hear the cogs turning in his brain as he went through all the variables.

'But how?' he said at last.

'Well, that's where my plan comes in,' Danny replied. His eyes glinted and he felt a welcome wave of adrenaline coursing through his veins.

He'd lived on the high of alcohol for so many years that this substance-free inspiration was all he needed to know that he was doing the right thing—even though this could all go very wrong.

'And what about the ten grand they want?'

'They can't blackmail you if the ring is back at the jeweller's,' Danny reasoned.

'But they said they'd message me back with a location to take the money and the ring in twenty-four hours.' Charlie looked at his watch unnecessarily. 'That could be any time from now.'

'So we'd better get the ring back sooner rather than later,' Danny said with more confidence than he felt.

'Alright,' Charlie said, throwing back the remnants of his drink as if courage might lie at the bottom of the cup. He slammed it down on the table and wiped his mouth with the back of his hand. 'Maybe we should open that champagne and have a glass for Dutch courage?' he suggested.

'Best to keep a clear head,' Danny replied. 'We'll have to drive back to yours so you can get changed.' Charlie was still wearing his uniform from the brief couple of hours he'd done at the hospital that morning.

Charlie nodded but seemed transfixed by the ring that was still on the table, as if he could transport it back to the safety of the shop by the sheer power of his mind.

When he eventually looked up, Danny forced a reassuring smile while holding back the nervous hurricane going on inside as he contemplated what they were about to do on Worcester High Street.

Chapter 13

Saturday 16th December, 3:03pm

'Beautiful, isn't it?' Danny's voice gave a deep echo as they walked under Edgar's Tower, strolling together with their hands in their pockets as if they were everyday tourists, just taking in the Cathedral and its surroundings.

'Amazing,' Charlie agreed. 'I only live a few miles down the road and yet I haven't been back here since that school trip.' They both stopped to admire the stonework.

Danny nodded. 'Yeah, you find that — people come from all over the world to see this place, but when you live round the corner you hardly bother. I think it's something to do with the fact you reckon you can visit anytime, but "anytime" never comes.'

'When I get myself out of this mess I'm going to get Karen out of the house more, if she's up for it.' His eyes clouded over while he spoke, as if the possibility was draining out of him the moment he thought about it.

Danny put a reassuring hand on Charlie's arm.

His mother and father were still alive and in pretty good health; being with Charlie had reminded him to pick up the phone that weekend and invite them over, or he could go to them.

They'd parked over at Diglis Basin as the Cathedral car park was full.

It gave them both the chance to clear their heads as they walked past the new-build flats along the canal side and took a short cut through the Cathedral gardens.

They were wearing baseball caps pulled low. Charlie had been the one to remind Danny of the CCTV, which had never crossed his mind. This did not bode well if Danny had ever considered a life of crime.

Charlie had a New York Yankees logo while Danny had plumped for reindeer antlers, his thought being that he looked less like a criminal wearing novelty headgear.

The high street loomed. Edward Elgar's statue seemed to be watching from his perch, judging them with one eye while mentally composing his next musical masterpiece with the other.

They had now reached the top of the high street and, as the jewellers came into sight, they both stopped walking at the same time.

There was a police car pulling up outside.

Danny's head spun around, convinced someone was following them. But no one was nearby — the closest were a group of school kids in yellow jackets drawing their own artistic interpretations of the Cathedral on massive pads.

Danny pulled Charlie to one side, away from the flow of pedestrians walking aimlessly into each other.

They hunkered under the awning of a Zizzi restaurant and watched events unfold.

'Do you reckon she's spotted the fake?' Charlie whispered.

'Why else would the police be with her?' Danny replied, never taking his eyes off the shop.

'Let's get out of here,' Charlie said. 'She saw my face up close; she'll know it was me who made the switch.'

'Let's just wait a bit,' Danny said, sounding braver than he felt. Deep down he was all for Charlie's plan — running away, going back home and finishing the podcast. Life back to normal.

But when he looked at Charlie, swaying backwards and forwards with his hand thrust deep in his pocket checking the ring, how could he leave him to sort this out on his own?

'Danny!' a loud voice yelled from the other side of the street, and a tub-shaped man wearing a huge jumper with a Christmas pudding on the front lolloped over and, to Charlie's surprise, threw his arms around Danny in a massive bear hug which seemed to envelop every bit of him.

'Good to see you, Bernie,' Danny said, although it was hard to hear the muffled words coming from his woolly cocoon.

As Bernie let Danny back up for air he turned his attention to Charlie and held out a pudgy hand.

'Nice to meet you mate, I'm Bernie; that's my wife Tracey over there.' He waved in the direction of a tiny woman holding a ridiculous amount of shopping bags, who waved back but stayed where she was, continuing to scroll on her phone. 'And you are?'

'Oh, sorry,' Danny said, shaking himself back into consciousness. 'This is my mate Charlie.'

They shook hands and, before Bernie could ask any awkward questions, Danny continued, 'Yeah, Charlie and me are just meeting up for a coffee and a catch-up.' Danny realised he was over-explaining himself; luckily Bernie didn't seem to care.

'This man,' Bernie said, pulling Danny up close, 'saved my bloody life — turned things around for me. Have you heard his podcast?'

'Oh yeah, I'm a big fan,' Charlie replied, smiling up at Danny with shared admiration.

'Did you hear that episode about me coming out of the army?' Bernie asked; his tiny eyes seemed to glitter inside a rosy-cheeked round face.

'Oh, I'm just catching up,' Charlie admitted.

'Well, I won't spoil it for you, but this fella turned my life around,' he repeated.

The wife had evidently grown bored of scrolling through her Instagram feed and was waddling over with her bags.

'You alright, Danny?' she asked with a smile, which she half gave to Charlie before saying, 'Come on, love — she'll have finished at the hairdresser's by now.'

'My daughter,' Bernie explained, a sense of pride bleeding through, 'old enough to go for her haircut on her own these days as long as we're around to pay at the end.' He finished with a booming laugh and slapped Danny on the arm before being pulled away.

'He seems like a...' Charlie searched for the word, 'passionate guy.'

Danny laughed. 'Yeah — Bernie's great. I'll tell you about him sometime, or you can listen to his story. I think it's episode five.'

'Well, when I'm in prison I'll have plenty of time to listen to all of them,' Charlie said, trying to laugh at his own gallows humour.

'It won't come to that, look,' Danny pointed over at the jewellers, 'the cops are gone.'

'I still can't go in there,' Charlie said, taking a couple of steps backwards and almost colliding with a Big Issue seller.

'You're not going to,' Danny replied firmly.

'I'm not?'

Danny shook his head. 'You're not, but I am. Give me the ring.'

Charlie shook his head vigorously. 'No way — you can't do this on your own; you'll get into trouble and I can't have that on my conscience. You've been so good to me already; I can't expect you to risk your life too.'

There was a scraping noise behind them and they both jumped as if they'd been stung.

'Sorry, fellas — just need to move these tables.' The Zizzi waiter smiled through gritted teeth.

Charlie apologised and they moved back under the Elgar statue where the crowd of kids who'd been sketching the Cathedral were congregating and checking out each other's work.

'Let me just give it a go,' Danny said, holding out his hand discreetly. 'I'll just gauge the lay of the land. If the ring's gone, then we'll know the cops have the forgery; if not, I'll try and switch it back. You're right — she'll recognise your face and, if she's reported it, you won't get out of the shop before she's alerted someone.'

'How will you know which one to switch?' Charlie asked, plunging his hand into his pocket and handing over the wrapped package.

'Believe me — I've done my research on that ring. Try not to worry. Go and get yourself a coffee or something; I'll call you when I'm done.'

Charlie was about to protest some more, but Danny was already walking towards the shop, his reassuring stride giving him the air of someone without a care in the world.

As Charlie watched him he wondered with silent awe how he did it and, more interestingly, why.

It didn't feel right going to a café when his old friend was about to risk something of this magnitude, but if he stood there much longer he might become obvious. After all, the police could well be looking for him if the girl had given his description.

He walked away and, after a few yards, noticed the Talbot Hotel, its doors invitingly open.

Stepping inside he ordered a coffee and found a quiet table by a Christmas tree.

He just sat there, watching the fairy lights twinkle and letting his coffee go cold as he contemplated the rest of his life.

Chapter 14

Molly had been so preoccupied with the events of the last 24 hours that she'd forgotten to greet the customer when he'd first come through the door. It was rule one in Graham's training guide: make sure people are seen and acknowledged when they enter the shop but never pestered.

She only became aware of his ridiculous hat when he spoke to her. She had to do a double take.

'It's not this, is it?' He pointed up at the reindeer antlers protruding from the top. 'I think I've already traumatised several babies and a sensitive barista.'

She laughed, and it felt so good. 'No, your hat is great – well, not great,' she laughed again, 'I mean, it's really bad.'

He smiled, and when she looked at him again the first thing she noticed was that he wasn't wearing a wedding ring.

It was an odd thing to spot so early, but she'd been chatted up by so many married blokes over the years and was always on her guard – particularly with those who had a tell-tale white indent where the ring had probably still been in place when he'd left the house at breakfast that morning.

Cute and baggage-free. Check, she thought to herself.

'I'm looking for a ring,' he said.

Please don't be an engagement ring.

'It's an engagement ring.'

Bollocks.

'It's not for me,' he added quickly.

Great.

'It's for my friend. He's a bit useless when it comes to choosing, and he's roped me in to find the right one.'

'Well, they're all here,' Molly said, pointing at the trays in front of her.

Danny made a show of studying each one carefully and had to hide his relief when he spotted the fake. It still had the reserved tag on it.

This meant she hadn't mentioned anything to the cops.

'What's that reserved one there?' he asked, pointing, and could swear he heard her sigh. Had he gone for that ring too quickly? Should he have taken more time browsing to allay any suspicion?

But time was not on his side. God knew when the blackmailers would call Charlie again, and he wasn't certain they hadn't been followed today.

He imagined Charlie right now, sat in a café somewhere, checking his phone every five minutes.

'This is really popular,' she said, bringing it out and laying it on the counter.

'Can I hold it?' Danny held out his hand, and as the girl's fingers lightly brushed his he felt a jolt of electricity between them. She sensed it too, breathing slightly faster while he made a show of admiring it.

She'd leant in closer to him now; he could smell perfume and the faint aroma of alcohol on her breath. He could trace booze from a mile away and felt a despondency at having to explain to her that he didn't drink, if they ever went on a date. Then he reminded himself that he was here to do a job and any romance would be highly unlikely with this girl. He needed to get a grip before he blew everything.

Danny smiled with fake appreciation while trying to work out an opportunity to make the switch – the real ring burning his leg from the inside of his pocket.

'Look, you seem like a nice guy to me,' she lowered her voice, looking round the shop before continuing, 'so if you take my advice you won't touch this ring.'

Danny stopped, and at the same time his heart skipped. 'Why not?' he asked, in as close to a normal voice as he could muster.

'Because there's something not right about it.' She took it from his fingers, and that electrical buzz returned for a second. He had to hold back the urge to take hold of her hand properly to see how long that feeling would go on. He wanted it to last forever.

'What do you mean, not right?' he asked, and for the briefest of moments their eyes met, and there was definitely a connection.

She shrugged her shoulders and, to his dismay, put the ring back on the tray and slid it into the display cabinet.

'Let's find something else for your friend, shall we?'

She'd said the word 'friend' with her fingers either side of her head.

'No, really, it's not for me,' he said hurriedly, picking up her point and not wanting to waste a second. 'I'm not getting engaged – in fact, I don't even have a girlfriend right now.' Danny blurted it out before he could stop himself.

He turned bright red and tried to hold back from saying anything else stupid. What was the matter with him? He thought he'd grown out of all this romance stuff. Why had this feeling come at the very moment he was about to carry out a felony? Then again, his podcasts were full of stories where people had done absurd things at the most inopportune times. Maybe this would be his own episode at some stage?

Thankfully she had turned away and was busying herself with another tray of rings from a different shelf, bringing one out and running her finger along the row, explaining carats and prices.

They didn't resume eye contact. It was just business now, and Danny was grateful to get things back on an even keel.

He feigned interest for a while and then tried a new tack. If he couldn't get the ring, it would be good to know more about the police car they'd spotted outside the shop earlier and what, if anything, she'd said to the authorities.

'I hope you don't mind me asking, but I saw some police here earlier. Has something happened?'

The eye contact was back, and he hoped he hadn't overstepped the mark.

She smiled again, and mixed emotions seized him. There was no doubt he was already smitten. He'd love to get to know more about her, but here he was, clumsily trying to gouge information with the subtlety of a Stanley knife.

'Oh, I had some trouble at home last night with a brick through my window, and then I accidentally punched a guy in the street this morning.'

Danny burst out laughing; he couldn't help it. The thought of this beautiful woman involved in brick-throwing and street brawls seemed bizarre beyond words.

She began to laugh too, before explaining her life in the last twenty-four hours, right up to the ex coming through the door trying to put customers off buying anything.

'I'm sorry, I really shouldn't laugh,' Danny said after a while, and without realising it he had his hand in hers over the glass counter. He didn't recall when it had happened, but neither of them seemed in a hurry to let go.

'Would you like to go for a drink sometime?' she asked.

'I really would,' he replied, and then added, 'but I have some good news and some bad news.'

She let go of his hand and took a step back.

'Oh God, you are married, aren't you?'

Danny smiled. 'No, nothing like that.' He held up his hand, hoping she'd grab it again soon. 'The bad news is I can't drink alcohol with you, but the good news is I'm a very cheap date.'

Her eyes lit up, and she grabbed his hand again.

'Tomorrow night?' she asked.

He nodded, relieved she was taking the lead.

'I've just realised I don't even know your name. How's that for fast work?' she giggled.

'I'm Danny,' he said without hesitation, before realising why he'd come into the shop – his anonymity now blown.

'I'm Molly, and it doesn't look like we need to shake hands,' she said, looking down at their entwined fingers.

Any talk of rings completely forgotten.

They spent the next ten minutes arranging a venue and time, and as he reached the exit he looked up to say another goodbye.

The CCTV camera was pointing right into his face.

Chapter 15

Charlie had left the Talbot Hotel with his coffee cup half full.

He didn't know whether it was his imagination, but the guests all seemed to be looking at him. Every time he'd glanced at one of the tables he'd seen someone giving him an uncertain glance.

It wasn't until he'd stepped outside and was buttoning his coat that he reasoned they were checking out the glittering Christmas tree beside his table rather than snooping at him. Paranoia was playing its party tricks now. His hope was that Danny had swapped the ring and he could get back to his normal life again.

How many times in the past had he wished for adventure, something different to happen to break through the monotony of his routine? At this moment the 'be careful what you wish for' mantra had never been more apposite.

He retraced his steps back up to Cathedral Plaza, which was even busier.

The kids' roundabouts had started spinning, and a small stage was occupied by a young girl in a snowman outfit singing 'Rockin' Around the Christmas Tree' to a small but appreciative audience huddled under a canopy belonging to a wooden stall selling hot chocolates and doughnuts. The sugary smell mixed with the diesel coming from the generator powering the rides took Charlie back to his innocent childhood days.

The travelling fair would come to the local common with all the rides and flashing lights, and it was at one of those he and Karen had their first dates.

As they screamed together on the waltzer, grasping each other's hands and trying to kiss while the car spun, he would never have believed that the vivacious young woman would become such a frail lady within only a few years.

He looked at his phone, wondering if Danny had already done the deed and was just waiting for the right time to message.

Then the gremlin appeared and started to whisper in his ear. What if the police had come back, arrested Danny, and at this very moment he was sat in a police station interview room being interrogated?

He decided to walk back to Cathedral Gardens and wait there. No point hanging around at the end of the High Street waiting to be spotted.

He found a seat overlooking the river bridge and tried to breathe while he watched the swans gathering on the far bank – white waves of feather fluttering in from all directions as if receiving word of some avian get-together.

His phone pinged, and he instantly grabbed it.

Hi Charlie. We hope you've managed to find the ten thousand pounds in cash as we need it by tomorrow.

You will leave it in the first waste paper bin as you enter from the Grandstand entrance at Worcester Racecourse. We will mark it with a yellow X in chalk.

Make sure the ring is in the package.

You will do this at 10pm.

Remember no police or you end up in jail.

Your family needs you so the last thing you want is us knocking on your door.

He tried to collect his thoughts into some kind of order.

Even if Danny had managed to swap the ring back, they still wanted ten grand – but, as Danny had said, without the ring what could they blackmail him on?

The worrying part was they said they knew where he lived. They could still cause trouble.

His phone rang, and Danny's name came up on the screen.

'How'd it go?' Charlie asked breathlessly.

'Where are you?' Danny replied, avoiding the question.

'Cathedral Gardens, at the back.'

'See you in five minutes.' Danny hung up while Charlie still had his mouth open with the next question.

To say that Danny had left the shop without switching the rings would seem like a failed mission, but as he walked down the High Street, the spring in his step suggested something different.

The last thing he had expected when planning his day was to bump into someone he'd be going on a date with. The twist was that woman was the person he was trying to distract to switch the rings.

Sometimes things just happened that way. Fate – or call it what you want – takes charge, and there's nothing you can do about it.

As he walked round the back of the cathedral his mood changed when he saw Charlie's outline.

He made a sad, lonely figure sitting on his own on the bench. He looked lost, and suddenly Danny felt guilty, but reassured himself it still wasn't too late to turn this all around.

Charlie heard his feet on the path and stood up quickly.

'Hey Danny, how did it go, did you…?' He looked around at the scattering of people all within hearing distance as they snapped away, taking photos of the river and then kneeling to get the full majesty of the cathedral spire into a portrait shot.

'Let's walk,' Danny said, and led the way down the stone steps which ended at the riverside.

'So?' Charlie snapped with a hint of irritation in his voice once they'd got some privacy. They'd reached a wall which had carved inscriptions of how high the river had risen during the many floods dating back hundreds of years.

Danny looked around, double-checking they were alone before he spoke. 'So, I didn't swap the ring. There just wasn't the chance, but…' He held up his hand as Charlie looked ready to protest. 'The girl in the jeweller's hasn't mentioned anything to the police.'

Charlie's shoulders sagged. 'Well, that's good,' he mumbled under his breath as he weighed up the situation.

'But she knows there's something wrong with the ring, so we have to swap it back soon,' Danny warned.

'That's gonna be a problem,' Charlie said, and began to explain about the text message and the cash-and-ring drop.

'So we've got till 10pm tomorrow?' Danny asked, his mind buzzing in time with a flock of ducks who were telling each other jokes while skimming the water on their way to Diglis Basin.

'I haven't got ten grand,' Charlie said.

Danny was about to offer some reassuring words when a group of tourists – who, by the gaudy clothing, he reckoned must have been American – all crammed into the nook by the wall where they were standing.

Sure enough, their leader, who was holding a clipboard, began to read out some Faithful City history in a transatlantic drawl.

Charlie looked at Danny and managed a smile as they walked away from the eager sightseers.

They walked in silence towards the Diglis Bridge, then took a left through a maze of new-build apartments until they hit the car park and both knew they were alone again.

'Look, I have a plan,' Danny said as they reached Charlie's car, 'but I need you to trust me.'

'Of course.' Charlie unlocked the door with a key, which amused Danny. He didn't know you could still do that – he thought all cars had some electronic alarm on the key fob these days.

He got in and unlocked the passenger seat with a button.

Danny pulled the handle, and the rusty creak sounded like the door could fall off at any moment.

'This car is quite a classic,' Danny said kindly as he slid into the seat and tried in vain to find a catch that would let it move back a few inches for his legs to stretch out. His nose was almost touching the windscreen.

'It's a rust bucket,' Charlie sighed, 'but it still runs,' he added with an almost fatherly pride as he tapped the dashboard.

'So, what's the plan?' he asked, turning to face Danny.

He looked tired and worried.

Danny didn't know if it was just his imagination or if Charlie had aged a year since yesterday. He supposed getting a message threatening you and your family, as well as having to find ten grand out of nowhere, could do that to anyone.

'You know when I said you have to trust me? Well, that's what I mean. I don't want to say any more. Just go home and I'll meet you at the racecourse tomorrow night. There are parking spaces by Sabrina Bridge – let's say 9.30, give ourselves half an hour before the drop?'

Charlie nodded. 'Are you sure you can't tell me anything else? I'm gonna be worried sick.'

'As I say, I have a plan. It might work, it might not, but either way I'll cover this for you.'

'You mean the money?' Charlie looked startled.

Danny nodded.

'If we need it, I can get it, but don't worry about the cash right now.'

'I don't know what to say.'

'You don't need to say anything. Just get back home and be with your wife and kids.'

'I've got to work another few hours tonight. I don't know how I'll cope.' Charlie raised his fingers to his face and was about to bite a nail, but noticing how gnarled they already were he plunged his fist back into his lap.

'Probably a good thing. Keep yourself busy, try not to think too much.'

Charlie reached across and, to Danny's surprise, hugged him, his big jacket crackling as the embrace tightened.

Danny's only experience of man hugs was at the end of meetings where people, emotionally drained from sharing the worst parts of their lives, fell against one another like collapsing deckchairs before embarking on the real world outside the doors. This had the same intensity.

They said goodbye, and Danny got out of the car to make his way back to the van at the other side of the car park.

Getting into the driver's seat, there was just one more thing he needed to do, and he hoped he hadn't blown this date before it had even started.

He thumbed through his recent contacts and found Molly's number – she'd only sent it to him a short hour ago.

His finger hovered for several seconds before he hit dial and waited with bated breath.

She answered almost immediately.

'Hiya.' Her voice was breezy; he could almost feel her breath coming down the line in a sweet audio perfume.

'Hey Molly, remember me – the bloke with the reindeer ears?'

'I think you'll find they're called antlers, David Attenborough.'

A giggle followed.

He ploughed on before he lost his nerve.

'You know that ring you showed me earlier? The one you said didn't look right – bring it with you. I might be able to help.'

Chapter 16

Saturday 16th December, 6:22pm

Molly couldn't believe her eyes when she reached her door; at first she thought she'd got the wrong house number.

The boards the glazier had hammered crudely into the frame last night had been replaced by shiny new windows and, what was even more incredible, the illuminated inflatable snowman sitting in the garden was rocking from side to side, welcoming her home.

She opened the door with the latch key and made a mental note that it might be a good idea to get the locks changed too — another one for her landlord's list.

She stopped in her tracks as she entered the lounge. It looked immaculate and there was the aroma of pine air freshener.

On the wooden crate–slash–coffee table was a note written in Gemma's unmistakable handwriting.

Hey Mol. Thought I'd spruce up the place a bit.

The bloke came to put the window in while I was in your pyjamas — I was totally crushed as he was well lush.

Oh and sorry about the snowman, popped to the Range and couldn't resist; thought it would cheer you up a bit. Take him down if you want.

Love ya babe, Gem xxxx

Molly smiled as she imagined her best friend flirting with the window man, swinging round her tiny house with a feather duster — did she even have a feather duster? — and then popping to get Christmas decorations to cheer her up.

Most people only messaged these days, but Gemma loved notes. Most of her expendable income was spent at Paperchase buying gel pens, paper and envelopes.

So it was no coincidence she ended up working there; the limited staff discount barely covered her monthly fix.

The bedroom had also been given the Gemma treatment — she'd even changed the bedding. How had she found the spare duvet cover? Molly had been looking for it for ages.

She poked her head around the second bedroom, which was just a mess of unpacked boxes and black bin bags of clothes she'd never wear again but promised herself she'd take to the charity shop.

At least Gemma hadn't tried to sort this mess out. The prospect of tidying in here would make Stacey Solomon shudder.

Her bed looked really inviting but she knew if she lay down for the briefest moment she'd fall asleep. She badly needed a shower.

Passing her wardrobe, her thoughts turned to what she would wear tomorrow. It had to be something smart but not too formal; fun but not too flirty. Although it was obvious there was an attraction between them, she didn't want to jump in with her size-seven Jimmy Choos too soon.

She was still reeling from Stewart and said a silent prayer that his stalking and messaging was no more than a rebound reaction.

She soaped her hair, letting the water from the shower cleanse away the stresses of the day; she massaged her scalp, kneading out what remained of the day-long hangover which had been broken by Danny's appearance.

She thought of his smile, the hat with the reindeer antlers, the perfect antidote to Stewart's sudden appearance in the shop. She allowed herself the daydream that if she started to date Danny he'd finally take the hint and leave her alone once and for all.

Stepping out of the shower cubicle she wrapped a towel around her that Gemma had left draped over the rail as if in readiness.

The mirror above the sink was steamed up so she rubbed it with the flat of her hand and saw her face looking back; she looked flushed from the hot water and was glad to see a new light in her eyes.

She brushed her teeth and wondered what tomorrow night would bring. They were meeting at a bar and restaurant in the park she'd recommended. Her thinking was if they had drinks and it went well they could move on to dinner; if it got awkward they could call it quits and leave earlier.

Then she remembered him saying he didn't drink. She couldn't remember ever dating someone who was teetotal and wondered if he'd be able to relax. Maybe she shouldn't drink either?

'Oh, for God's sake,' she said out loud as she padded back to the bedroom. 'You haven't even been on the date yet.'

With that stoic thought she asked Siri to play Adele, which always calmed her down, and slipped into her well-worn pyjamas that Gemma had last worn while flirting with the workman. From the smell of fabric conditioner they had been washed, dried and folded back on the bed. The woman was a wonder.

She paused Adele midway through 'Someone Like You' and considered the ring. Danny's call had come less than an hour after he'd left the shop. He'd asked her to bring the reserved ring with her on the date. He said he had a friend who was an expert in the jewellery trade and could take a photo of it and ask his opinion.

It hadn't seemed odd at the time but now she couldn't help worrying if this was the reason he wanted to meet her tomorrow. Then she consoled herself when she remembered it was her who'd asked him out.

She resumed Adele and blow-dried her hair, thinking about the possibilities of a new chapter in her turbulent life.

She was on the last episode of the first season of Grey's Anatomy, which everyone she met seemed to be recommending, and was trying desperately to concentrate. It wasn't that she found the show dull — quite the opposite — it was just she was really tired and knew if she went to bed any earlier than eleven she'd wake up at four and not be able to go back to sleep.

There was also the prospect of getting another brick through the window or another obscene text from Stewart pinging on her phone. She wished Gemma was here again. They had considered moving in together many times but life seemed to get in the way of progressing any further than drunk conversations about big plans, or the occasional heart-to-heart over FaceTime.

She'd rung earlier just to check in. Molly had thanked her for tidying the house and the inflatable snowman in the front garden. Gemma had said there was no need to thank her as she'd enjoyed having time with the 'gorgeous glazier', as she called him.

As the credits rolled she heard the phone buzz and was reluctant to look at it. She imagined more nude snaps, a threat, or maybe her mum saying she wasn't invited for Christmas dinner as her father would still be away till the new year. It had happened before.

She picked it up and smiled instantly. It was Danny.

Really looking forward to seeing you tomorrow x

Perfect — just a confirmation and the one kiss. Organised and not too pushy.

She switched off the TV before season two started automatically (one of her pet hates) and gave a stretch, clicking her weary bones into place.

She pulled out the plug on the fairy lights — another of Gemma's magical additions to her dreary abode — and then switched off the main light.

Just before she went upstairs she looked around at the curtains, surveying the neighbourhood. The snowman continued to wave in the slight breeze as the rest of the street twinkled with bulbs of all varieties. No one was loitering around her house this evening, and knowing that — and the prospect of a good day tomorrow — was all she needed.

As she pulled back the curtains a shadow moved across the pavement before running back towards the city.

Chapter 17

Charlie was wheeling a trolley from the operating theatre back to a private ward. The patient was still woozy from the anaesthetic, but he chatted away to her because that's what he always did. To him it was part of the job. Talking meant they weren't thinking about the operation they'd just had and, for him, it was the perfect distraction from the clandestine ring and cash drop at the racecourse tomorrow.

He'd arrived back at the hospital at 7:30 after having a quick tea with Kaz and the kids, leaving them all watching something on the telly together. Everyone was laughing, but he hadn't taken a thing in.

The squeaking wheels of the trolley, the tannoy announcements drifting around the corridors, and the smell of sanitiser gel were all a familiar blurry soundtrack that felt as natural to him as his own home. Even the winding layout of corridors, wards, consultation rooms, waiting areas and toilets were burned into the back of his retinas.

It felt a little better knowing Danny had the ring. He'd been sure Karen would find it in the kitchen cupboard at some stage. How did he ever think he'd be able to sell it somewhere? He'd hoped he could flog it to the guy who'd done the forgery, but since completing the transaction his number was no longer available. Charlie had considered going back into Birmingham to the shop where he'd picked up the forgery, but it seemed too much like returning to the scene of the crime.

The patient said something to Charlie, sweeping him out of his thoughts.

'Sorry, love, what was that?' he said, leaning closer and catching the pungent aroma of the anaesthetic.

'You're going to hell?' mumbled the patient.

'I'm sorry?' Charlie moved even closer.

'All going well?' she mumbled again, and it registered that the patient still thought the operation was happening rather than predicting Charlie's ultimate damnation.

'Yes, it's all done now,' he smiled at the weathered face with tubes sticking out of her nose. 'I'm just taking you back to your room.'

'You're a good person,' the patient said before nodding back into slumber. Charlie didn't feel very good, but for now he'd just take the compliment and get on with his job.

Back at the staff area behind reception he nudged the coffee machine and rested his head on the glass. It felt cool against his forehead and the gentle hum of the mechanism as it whirred and poured provided a kind of aural meditation.

'How's Karen?' one nurse asked as he took a sip of what was no more than chicory essence in a Styrofoam cup.

'She's doing OK,' he lied, as he did most of the time these days. When you work around serious illness and life-changing operations every day there's little room for your own trials and tribulations.

'Send her my love,' said another, who to Charlie's recollection had never even met her. But then he reminded himself that most people are good, just like it says at the start of Danny's podcast every month.

He slipped off his trainers and massaged his feet before the next job, thinking about Danny. Why had he been so good to him after all these years? It wasn't like they'd stayed in touch, but the look in his eyes when he gave him the ring told Charlie he genuinely wanted to help.

'Could you pick up someone from A&E?' a voice bled from nowhere. At first he didn't realise he was the one being addressed.

'Yeah, sure,' he said once he'd tracked where the question had come from. A senior doctor, looking harassed and on edge, had barely said more than a couple of words to him in all the time he'd been working at the hospital. That's what porters were good for: taking the edge off.

'Yeah, lad in A&E needs an X-ray, could you wheel him over?'

Charlie slid his shoe back on and strode briskly towards the lift. He didn't spend much time around accident and emergency. Most of the cases there were in and out with triage treatments, but just occasionally someone needed taking to another department.

As he entered the waiting area the real world appeared. Every plastic chair was taken; clusters of people leaned against the wall while, through the glass outside, he spotted a scattering of the addicted standing around smoking or vaping away the waiting time.

There were a couple of babies crawling across the floor, a man holding his head with a cloth covered in dried blood, and a woman sat next to him who seemed to think nursing involved rubbing his back with one hand while scrolling on her phone with the other. A grizzled individual was swaying from side to side, trying to focus on the snack machine. He reached in his pocket and spilled change all over the floor.

A no-nonsense nurse charged over to Charlie, thrust a file into his hands, and pointed at a man in a wheelchair sat by the wall, taking in the show.

'X-ray are expecting you,' the nurse said curtly, before disappearing down the corridor and back behind the curtain he'd first appeared from, like a magician making his exit.

Doctors and nurses were never rude to porters, but used as few words as possible and usually dispensed with pleasantries. There wasn't enough time for a please or thank you when someone was bleeding out after getting hold of the wrong end of a chainsaw.

'Hello, mate.' Charlie called everyone mate — man or woman, boy or girl. It seemed to add a cheerful ring to a greeting, although he always used sir or madam for the older generation, which he felt was only respectful.

It didn't matter what he called this patient as he didn't seem keen to talk. That was fine by Charlie, who had plenty on his mind. He wheeled him towards the lift and stopped to press the button. In the chrome reflection he caught a good look at the patient's face.

Charlie did a double take and then dismissed the thought — it couldn't be. His gaze focused downwards. The tattoos that ran down the man's arms were the big giveaway.

This was the person he'd met on the day he'd taken the photo of the ring into Birmingham. He may have been wearing a mask at their last meeting, but as their eyes met there was no denying this was the guy he'd been trying to contact.

Chapter 18

Saturday 16th December, 9:14pm

I told him I knew him and at first he continued this Santa act, giving a booming laugh, even though I'd ripped off his beard, revealing nothing but a three-day-old grey stubble.

One or two nosy parents joined in, laughing, thinking this was all part of some elaborate Christmas stunt.

He whispered under his breath that this wasn't the time or the place and I should think about the kids.

He couldn't have said anything worse.

I told him that my kid nearly didn't have a Christmas because of him, and if he thought he could hide behind what he'd done playing Father Christmas he had another think coming.

I think he must have sensed his number was up, because the next thing was he jumped to his feet and ran towards the exit, his great big boots clomping their way past parents and crying kids.

I ran after him and caught his collar with my outstretched fist. I felt the jacket rip and I brought him down on the rebound.

I landed the first punch, but whether it was just panic or the fact he was normally handy with his fists, I don't know. But he walloped me one with the back of his hand and I saw stars.

That's when I heard sirens.

Danny had the stock sound effects of a police car, which he now added, hoping that it was the correct make, model and era.

Listeners were quite picky when it came to convincing sounds. Whether it was the authentic car engine, train whistle or even coffee machine hiss, there was no end to the pedantry of the sound-effect elite.

He was pleased to have got another section edited, and even though he'd be a couple of days late sending it out (what with Charlie coming into his life and an unexpected date tomorrow night), it would still be a great edition.

Particularly the end of the story.

All his podcasts needed some kind of resolution, which was the hardest part. Finding stories was easy; there were enough tales of good people doing bad things to fill many thousands of hours.

But resolving it, that was the pivotal moment.

He saved where he'd got to, snapped his laptop closed and texted Molly.

He wanted to keep the message simple, just reminding her of the date tomorrow night in case she got cold feet. After all, she had asked him out very quickly.

He hated having to bring the ring into the evening, but it needed to be done. If he could make the swap tomorrow, all she would be taking back to the jeweller's the next day would be the original. He was doing her a favour really.

Hopefully she'd never know.

In his kitchen he peeled back the sleeve of microwave curry and rice, blasted it for five minutes, then clicked on the TV and tried to relax.

As he aimlessly flicked the channels with a steaming curry resting on his lap, his thoughts turned once again to Charlie. He imagined him working a late shift in the hospital while wrestling with all the worry barrelling around his brain.

It was the sound of gunfire that woke him up.

Danny jolted upright and his plate fell onto the carpet, mercifully empty.

He looked at the TV and saw Bruce Willis in his torn vest crawling around the floor, shooting sporadically at a bunch of terrorists.

He'd seen Die Hard dozens of times but never woken up halfway through it before.

Checking his watch, he realised he'd been asleep for a good couple of hours.

He reached down to retrieve his plate when he noticed missed calls on his phone.

There were three; the last one had been left an hour ago, so he immediately dialled the number while walking into the kitchen to pour some water.

It connected after a few rings and a hospital receptionist was waiting on the other end.

Within ten minutes he was slamming the front door, jumping in the van and heading to the hospital.

All the traffic lights were against him and what should have taken no more than twenty minutes had been more like forty.

One of the big complaints that was always making the front page of the Worcester News was hospital parking: the cost and, even more importantly, the fact you could never get a space.

No such problems with availability at just after midnight. Danny pulled up in the first space he saw and sprinted to the entrance where a machine stood guard. He pushed the button for a ticket, slipped it into the back pocket of his jeans and stepped inside the foyer.

This felt more like an airport terminal than a hospital.

To his left was a coffee bar, which still had quite a few customers, and to his right a couple of shops with the shutters down.

There were signs leading to stairs and corridors and, as Danny stood to take it all in, it dawned on him he had no idea where Charlie would be.

The girl he'd spoken to had said to come and pick him up, but he'd put the phone down before getting specific instructions.

He'd tried calling Charlie's mobile quite a few times on the journey over but couldn't get through.

There was a loud yell and Danny's head shot around to the source of the noise. He'd envisioned all kinds of scenarios on the drive over so his nerves were jumpy. It didn't help that he'd had enough caffeine to fell a rhino. He'd drunk at least a pint of coffee before filling his travelling cup to combat his lack of quality sleep. Dozing in front of Bruce Willis didn't count as rest.

The noise was coming from a hooded youth of around twenty who seemed worse for wear and was having some kind of argument with the unfortunate girl behind the counter of the coffee bar.

Two burly men in security jackets hastened over and, with the precision of people who'd handled many of these moments over the years, approached him, one either side in a human barricade.

At first the youth was aggressive, barrelling out expletives over an incoherent narrative that, as far as Danny could work out, had something to do with the number of immigrants coming into the country and the price of a Diet Coke.

They'd tossed him out in seconds.

Danny took his chance as one of them swept by him.

'Excuse me, but you don't happen to know if Charlie Burrows is still on duty, do you?'

The man closest to him shrugged his huge shoulders. 'Sorry mate, never heard of him,' he said bluntly, and was just about to march back to get the swooning praise from the girl at the counter when his partner grabbed his arm and said something in his ear. They both marched back.

Danny thought he may have said the wrong thing and prepared himself for bad news.

'Do you mean Chaz?' the smaller of the two asked.

'Maybe,' Danny said, his voice high-pitched with fatigue and worry.

'Porter here? His lovely wife's got the big C,' the big man clarified. Danny didn't think he meant any harm being so direct; this was just his way.

'Yes, that's Charlie,' Danny said.

'Yeah, he was on tonight but finished ages ago. Saw him in A&E a while back.'

'Oh, where's that?' Danny asked, hoping this would be their last interaction. Both men looked like they were losing patience with him even though he'd done nothing wrong.

The smaller one pointed to a map on the far wall and they both marched back towards the coffee shop, job done.

Danny studied the complicated diagram of the building with its wards and zones, tracing the route with his finger a couple of times before setting out again.

It was getting cold outside after the heat of the foyer and Danny dashed in the direction he'd studied.

There were a couple of ambulances idling outside A&E, so it was easy enough to spot in the end.

Inside, the noisy youth from the coffee bar was in an animated conversation with a police officer and there were still quite a few people waiting around.

He made his way to the reception desk and once again asked if Charlie Burrows was still on shift.

Up to that point the girl behind the desk hadn't looked up, but the mention of Charlie got her full attention and she instantly stopped typing whatever she'd been working on.

'Are you the friend of Chaz I called?' she asked. Her accent was somewhere from the Caribbean and had a gentle tone with it, the kind of voice that had probably calmed many an agitated patient.

'Yes I am,' Danny said.

'He didn't want us to call his family.' She leant over the desk and whispered, 'His wife's very ill and he doesn't want her upset.'

Danny wondered if the whole hospital knew about Charlie's domestic situation. If so, at least this woman was more subtle than the security guys.

'Yes, I understand,' Danny whispered back.

She clicked on a mouse and then said, 'He's in with the doctor now, but he may have to stay overnight for observation. Head injuries are always tricky.'

'Head injuries?' Danny said loud enough for an elderly couple who were pretending to read a battered copy of Gardener's World magazine to look up.

'Oh, sorry, I thought you knew and that's why you'd come?'

Danny replied with careful consideration, 'Yeah, I knew he'd been hurt. That's why I'm here — to take him home if I can.'

The nurse nodded. 'Take a seat and I'll give you a shout when he's been examined.'

Danny found somewhere to perch closest to the admissions desk and checked his phone again, not that there was anything he wanted to see, just to give the impression of normality.

He didn't like the presence of a police officer; he'd seen way too many of them today.

Every time a curtain was swished open he got ready to stand in case it was Charlie.

The first time, an elderly woman lumbered towards the desk being held tenderly by someone who looked the same age.

The next curtain revealed someone who, at first glance, had an intricate pattern on their shirt. It wasn't until they headed past Danny he saw it was dried blood.

Third time lucky, as Charlie appeared and, not noticing Danny, walked straight to the desk.

He was talking to the girl when she said, 'Ah, here's your friend to take you home.'

Charlie's head turned and Danny saw a bandage on the side of his head.

Danny spoke quickly in case Charlie spoilt the pretence. 'Hi mate, I heard what happened and came straight over. I've got the van outside; we can leave your car here.'

'That's great, I'll let them know.' The receptionist pointed her pen at the ceiling, which Danny assumed meant management of some kind. 'Take it steady.'

Charlie didn't say anything until they got out of the building.

'Thanks for coming. You're the only one I asked reception to call, but I just wanted them to tell you I was OK in case you were worried. You shouldn't be here, the police...' Charlie blurted in one messy sentence.

'Come on, get in the van, we need to talk.' Danny took his elbow gently and led him to the car park. They walked in silence for a few seconds, then Charlie stopped.

'You haven't called Karen, have you?'

'No, I just came straight here.'

'Thank you,' he said. 'I think I've just made everything ten times worse.'

Chapter 19

Sunday 17th December, 1:13am

Danny drove as carefully as he could on the way to Bromsgrove.

His knowledge of the local routes meant he knew to slow down for a row of potholes along the A4440 and the resurfacing work going on through Upton Warren. He was aware he had fragile cargo on board, and this wasn't the usual glass chandeliers or light fittings — it was Charlie, holding his bandaged head to one side while slightly swaying as the effects of the painkillers they'd given him kicked in.

'What are you going to say to Karen?' Danny asked, not expecting much of a cohesive reply. Ever since he'd got out of the hospital car park Charlie had looked ready to nod off at any second.

But the mention of his wife's name made him start. He sat up straighter and cleared his throat.

'I'm going to say I slipped and fell. She'll probably be asleep when I get home, so hopefully I won't have to say anything till tomorrow.'

Even in the darkness of the van cab he could sense a wave of worry pass through as Charlie mentally ticked off his domestic checklist.

Danny hated having to interrogate him after all he'd been through, but at this point he had no choice.

'Do you feel up to telling me what happened?' Danny asked eventually, 'And what you said to the police?'

There was silence for a while and Danny wondered if he had indeed fallen asleep.

'I messed up,' Charlie blurted, holding his head even tighter.

'There's nothing we can't put right, mate,' Danny said, hoping his words conveyed more confidence than he felt.

'I just couldn't believe it was him,' Charlie said, his voice sounding distant as he reluctantly began his story.

He told Danny about getting the job to collect someone from A&E, stepping into the lift and recognising the guy in the wheelchair straight away.

'I knew it was him because the ring has been on my mind so much, it seemed incredible the guy I'd been trying to contact was in the lift with me.'

'So you confronted him?'

'Yeah, I tried to be as subtle as I could, considering. I just asked him if he was the guy who'd done a job for me in Birmingham. I didn't mention a ring or anything.'

'And then what happened?'

Charlie sighed and gave his bandaged head an involuntary rub. 'He stood and hit me.'

'Stood up? But I thought he was in a wheelchair?'

'He was, but that didn't seem to stop him. I fell on the floor and hit my head against the panel on the way down. Next thing I remember is the door pinging open and the guy hopping away.'

'Hopping?'

'Yeah, so his foot injury must have been genuine.'

Danny thought for a moment while ditching his earlier theory that the guy was there pretending to be hurt and was waiting to get to Charlie.

'I tried to get up but everything was spinning. The door closed again and the lift went back down. I must have passed out then, because the next time I opened my eyes I was lying on the floor by the lift with a pillow under my head and a crowd around me.'

'I suppose if you're going to get attacked there are worse places than a hospital A&E department for it to happen,' Danny laughed weakly.

'It could have been worse,' Charlie agreed.

'What about the police?'

'There are always cops hanging round the hospital and there'd been some trouble with a bloke at the coffee shop earlier, so there was an officer already there. She took a statement but I told her next to nothing.'

This was the part that worried Danny the most, and he let the air settle before asking. He turned the heater down slightly — the last thing he wanted was for Charlie to fall asleep before he'd found out everything. 'What exactly did you tell the police?'

Charlie rubbed his eyes and was about to speak before he suddenly shouted, 'I need to stop, quickly.'

They were close to the entrance for Webbs Garden Centre and Danny took the turning before braking hard as Charlie pulled the passenger door handle and hardly made it to a hedge before he violently threw up.

Danny resisted the urge to get out and help him. He knew from many blurry experiences it was the worst thing in the world to have someone watch you puke.

'You OK, mate?' Danny asked stupidly through the open door.

He could see Charlie's outline bending over and a hand raised in acknowledgement.

The cold misty air was creeping into the van, so he reached over and closed the passenger door, giving Charlie more privacy.

He quickly Googled what to do if someone was sick after a head injury.

As he read it became clear that vomiting was quite common, but if it persisted or there was a change in personality then it could be serious.

There was no way he could take him home to a sleeping wife and children.

Charlie got back in the van and in the pale interior light he was giving Marley's ghost a run for his money.

'Sorry about that,' he said, wiping his chin. 'I feel a bit better now.'

'I can't take you home, mate. Let's turn around and you can stay at mine. That way I can keep an eye on you till I'm sure you're OK.'

'What about Karen and the kids?'

'You can send a message saying you've had a fall and didn't want to disturb her, so you called me.'

'You've got it all worked out, haven't you.' Charlie gave Danny a dim smile.

Danny reversed back down the entrance road which, in a few hours, would be a trail of queuing cars. Eager shoppers looking for last-minute Christmas trees or a sneaky trip to Santa's grotto.

That thought reminded Danny of the podcast he needed to finish. Add to that a date to get ready for, a ring swap and cash drop and nursing an old school friend — it was a wonder he wasn't the one throwing up in the bushes.

As they headed back to Worcester Danny asked again about Charlie's statement to the police.

'I said to the officer that we were in the lift and the guy seemed agitated. I asked if he was all right and the next thing I knew he punched me and legged it.'

'Did she believe you?' Danny asked, holding back any relief until he was sure.

'Yeah, I reckon so. We get quite a few violent characters at the hospital. Drugs, booze and family arguments...' He smiled in recollection for a moment. 'They can be the worst.'

'I hear you,' Danny laughed. It felt good to have a lighter moment.

'I've sent Karen a text,' Charlie said drowsily as they turned into Danny's street. 'Hopefully she won't see it till morning.'

'It is morning,' Danny said, pulling into his driveway and turning off the engine.

Danny unlocked his front door and saw Charlie standing at the end of the drive looking up into the sky.

'Are you coming in?' he asked, holding open the door.

'Yeah, just waiting for a bird to crap on me,' he smiled. 'Isn't it supposed to be good luck?'

Danny laughed and ushered him in, thinking that Charlie was right — they needed all the luck they could get. This was going to be one extraordinary day.

Chapter 20

Sunday 17th December, 3:12am

Sure enough, Molly woke up way too early.

A good-girl early night meant she'd automatically rouse in the early hours.

She rolled over and squinted with bleary eyes at her clock radio; the red neon digits read 3:12am.

She rolled over again and swiped through her meditation and sleep apps (she'd downloaded and subscribed to dozens) to try and focus on her breathing and then imagine each part of her body from the tips of her toes to the top of her head until Morpheus took possession.

Not this morning.

She tried lying on her back, pulling the duvet up to her chin, and just settling with her thoughts.

First Danny came to mind, which made her giddy and nervous, and then she kicked the image out of her head like a bully at a ballpark — Stewart's tight grip on her arm and his outburst in the shop.

Now she really wasn't going straight back to sleep.

Heaving a huge sigh, she swept the duvet aside, reached down to slip on some bed socks and went downstairs.

She flicked on the lamp in the lounge and then went into the kitchen, searching for her favourite camomile tea.

It took her a while to find the box. Gemma's big tidy had been a slight rearrangement of the kitchen cupboards — nothing major, but not her organised chaos, which was confusing as hell, particularly at three in the morning.

She poured steaming water into a cup, walked back through to the dining room and picked up the book she'd been reading.

Molly loved to get lost in a novel, but with shifts at the shop and all her emotional turmoil, she'd hardly had the time. She'd been reading the same Marian Keyes for the past three months and although it was brilliant, she always had to go back a few pages to remind herself of the characters after leaving it so long between sittings.

She opened the dog-eared paperback, adjusted the light, and had just got back on track with the latest happenings in the Walsh family when she noticed something in her peripheral vision.

There was something lying on the doormat that she must have missed on the way downstairs.

It looked like a Christmas card and she was certain it wasn't there when she'd gone to bed.

Who delivered cards in the middle of the night?

For a while she tried to ignore it, but eventually curiosity won the battle and she popped a bookmark in and went over to examine it.

There was no stamp, just a picture of Santa on the front.

She wondered if it was safe to open. You heard of all kinds of poisons that could be put in envelopes.

She laughed at her overactive imagination and blamed it on confused thinking in the middle of the night, reassuring herself that at least it wasn't a brick through the window.

Taking a deep breath, she peeled open the envelope and took out a card.

It was a couple of snowmen hugging with the Hallmark sentiment of 'Wishing you a warm Christmas'.

She opened it up and knew who it was from before she read the name at the bottom.

Hope you have a lovely Christmas and maybe there's still room for me on your Santa list. I've been a very good boy. Stu xxxx

She ripped it up immediately, letting the pieces fall to the floor. She resisted the urge to stamp on them as if exorcising the dripping, manipulative words.

This man who texted her intimate pictures he'd sworn he'd deleted, tried to get her sacked from her job — maybe even thrown a brick through her window.

Did this guy seriously think he could win her back with some shitty Clinton's card and a crass message?

Molly was now in the agitated state that not even camomile tea could touch.

Slumping down on the couch next to her unread book, she imagined Stewart sliming his way to her door while she was asleep upstairs and slipping that card through her letterbox. It was a wonder he didn't bang on the door first, but then she remembered that bricks were more his style.

She desperately wanted to text Gemma.

She'd been there all through Molly meeting Stewart right up to the messy split. She was also the only one she confided in whenever things got nasty.

Gemma would never tell her directly to leave him but carefully helped her to make the decision for herself.

Molly reflected back to Stewart's very first violent outburst. He'd grabbed her arms so hard after a drunken argument at the Slug and Lettuce when he'd accused her of flirting with the DJ.

She was still living with her mum and dad in those days and as her father was away again she stayed at Gemma's parents' that night instead of going home, telling her mum she was having a sleepover. They spent the entire night talking it through, Gemma whispering sage advice from her bed while Molly lay on the blow-up mattress on the floor next to her, massaging her bruised arm.

Gemma was seeing a guy called Gareth back then, although 'seeing' was a term she used for all her boyfriends. Even now, none of Gemma's relationships had ever got serious, even with ones who Molly thought were strong 'keeper' candidates.

Men would appear and disappear like head colds and there was never any fuss.

Molly put it down to Gemma's large family. With three older brothers looking out for her, a doting younger sister who Gemma felt she had to set an example for, and not forgetting a dad who worked for the police and may have put some potential suitors off when they found out.

Whatever the reason, Gemma always seemed in control, uncontaminated by the trivialities of romance. Molly envied her that, particularly now as she sat on the sofa looking at the confetti of a Christmas card on the hall carpet.

She gave in and went upstairs to get her phone. There was no way she was going back to sleep now, so she might as well turn on the outside world.

Back in her bedroom she unplugged the charger and heaved a sigh of relief as there were no new messages.

She scrolled up to the last one that Danny had sent reminding her of tonight's date, and her finger hovered over it.

Should she reply that they could meet another time? Did she need to get Stewart out of her life first, get Christmas over with and start afresh in the new year?

She could join a gym, finish reading the novel, spend more time with Gemma doing stuff they wanted to do.

Then she thought of Stewart and the card.

Why should he once again ruin everything for her?

She didn't know much about this Danny guy, but he seemed really nice. She had an English teacher who used to scald the class every time the word 'nice' came up, saying it was lazy, but Danny was nice.

She closed the messages app and did something she'd promised herself she wouldn't do till they went on the date, but her insecurities had got the better of her. She stalked him on Facebook and it didn't take long to find him.

What she saw stunned her. She had no idea.

The profile picture was the same smiling face she had seen in the shop (minus the reindeer antlers). His casual, effortless smile revealed the dimple on his left cheek and eyes that had the same knowing glow that caught her off guard in a single moment yesterday.

She looked at the 'about' info, but there wasn't much to be gleaned as this page seemed all about his podcast.

A podcast?

She scrolled down the entries and each one was a picture or story referring to an episode, underneath a link to the audio.

She paired her phone to the HomePod and started listening from episode one.

The sun was peeping around the curtains by the time she'd finished episode three and she stopped, bookmarked the page and got ready for work.

Now she'd heard his podcast she felt she knew way more about him, and with what she'd learned there was no way she was going to miss tonight's date.

Chapter 21

Sunday 17th December, 9:45am

The police officers grabbed each of us by the collar and I felt like a naughty schoolboy in a playground fight.

Whoever had called the cops must have sensed some kind of trouble from the moment I set eyes on Santa, because it only took a matter of seconds from the first punch to us both being hauled away.

As I was being frogmarched to a police car I still had the image of all those parents staring at us like extras from a freak show, while my poor daughter was sobbing in her mother's arms.

I'd never felt more ashamed in my life. Any alcohol that was in my system dissolved in despair.

I think that was the moment I came to realise I needed help before I lost everything that was dear to me in this world.

Danny stopped and pulled off his headphones.

It didn't matter how many of these stories he recorded, how many people bared their souls to him — the moment they hit rock bottom and realised the mess they were in, that was the part that got to Danny every time.

He remembered his own moment when the line had been crossed. A line that had cost him dearly. God knows he'd paid the price and was now on the other side. But he knew it was only a small hop and he'd be back where he was.

He could hear the muffled conversation of Charlie through the thin walls, talking to his wife, no doubt explaining why he hadn't come home last night.

He sat back in his chair and let his spine crack. It wasn't the most ergonomically friendly seat, but the best he could afford along with a small desk for his Mac computer, some decent editing software and a second-hand mic that would have cost a fortune new.

This was his studio, all crammed in at the back of his bedroom. Many people assumed he'd have a state-of-the-art mixing desk and production area, but these days you could communicate with the whole world on a limited set-up like this from a two-bedroom house in Warndon.

He waited till the muffled chatting stopped before knocking on the door of the spare room.

Charlie was sat in his boxers and an XXL T-shirt that Danny had given him last night. The phone was lying on the bed where he'd just thrown it.

'Everything OK?' Danny asked, poking his head round the door but not entering.

'No, not really.' He went to scratch his head, then stopped himself suddenly, remembering the bandage. 'Karen is mad as hell at me, she didn't believe my story about having a fall and staying at yours.' He gave a humourless laugh. 'I think she's got it into her head that I'm having an affair or something.'

'Surely not.' Danny stepped inside but stopped short of sitting beside him on the bed; that would have been too weird.

'Oh, I don't know, the story sounded rubbish while I was saying it. I think I need to go home and clear things up. It's so annoying, I stayed here to stop her worrying when I came home in the middle of the night with this.' He patted his head gently. 'But now I've made things worse and she's worrying even more about things that don't exist.'

'Look, there are fresh towels in the wardrobe over there. Go and get a shower and I'll drive you home.'

'Oh Danny, this is all too much, I feel terrible. I should never have got you into any of this, or my wife, or the kids.'

Danny abandoned protocol and sat beside him. 'Look, I'm going to sort all this tonight. You leave it to me from here and by tomorrow things will be back on track.'

'How can you tell? What about the ring and the ten grand? How can I be sure whoever's blackmailing me aren't going to come back and frighten Karen or the kids?'

All this came spilling out and Danny remembered his mantra.

'Listen to me.' Charlie's head lifted. He could see by the bags under his eyes that he hadn't slept a wink, even with painkillers percolating.

'Me and many of my friends have a saying, "one day at a time", and that's what I want you to think. Today is out of your control when it comes to all the things you can't do, but what you can do is be with your family. See Karen, explain that you were attacked by a random drunk patient and you didn't want to worry her, which is why you stayed at mine. I can verify all this when I drop you off.'

Charlie nodded slowly but said nothing, just taking it all in.

'Do whatever you do normally today and I'll call tomorrow and tell you how I got on.'

'But…' Charlie said, but Danny came back quickly.

'But nothing, just for today, OK?'

Charlie nodded again.

'Let me hear you say OK.'

'OK,' Charlie said after a moment.

'Great. Now go and get a shower, but don't nick my expensive gel.' Danny winked and left the room for Charlie to readjust.

In the kitchen Danny threw a few rashers of bacon in the air fryer and flicked on the radio.

To his childish delight, BBC Hereford & Worcester were announcing a snow alert — flurries to come into the county by early evening.

Every time he thought of snow it reminded him of days off school and hot chocolate. He and his sister having snowball fights that always ended with her thrusting handfuls of ice down his back before he went running inside to tell his parents he was being bullied. Poor Liv got into so much trouble from him grassing her up over the years — the way that big sisters do when their innocent younger brothers play the victim.

'You should know better at your age, Olivia,' his father would say to her, even though she couldn't have been more than fourteen herself at the time. The seven-year age gap meant she was always forced to lead by example. He made a mental note to give her a call before Christmas Day.

Then he remembered his date tonight and his clandestine business at the racecourse. He said a silent prayer that the snowfall wouldn't be too heavy to stop his arrangements.

'Something smells good,' Charlie said, walking into the kitchen.

He looked transformed, even though he was still wearing what he wore last night.

'I'm making bacon sarnies to get your strength up,' Danny said, holding aloft prongs to demonstrate, 'unless, that is, you're vegetarian.'

'Do I look like a vegetarian?' Charlie pointed to his ample belly.

'No, but you have the look of a butcher.' Danny waved the prongs in the direction of the dried bloodstains on his T-shirt. 'You'll need to bin that and wear the sweatshirt I gave you last night.'

'I'm surprised you had something to fit me.' Charlie laughed.

'It's nightwear — the baggier the better. Now have a seat and I'll bring it through.'

There was a small dining table set up at the back of the living room, enough to seat four at a squeeze.

Danny brought in the toasted sandwiches and a cup of coffee for both of them.

They ate in silence for a while, letting the food do its work, both with enough on their minds to keep them mentally busy.

As they chewed in silence, Danny heard an alien message alert and Charlie almost spilled his coffee mug that was halfway to his mouth.

'That's mine,' he said, pulling his iPhone out and studying the screen.

Danny leaned over.

Hello Charlie. This is just a reminder about tonight 10pm at the racecourse. Hope you've managed to find the ten grand otherwise…

'What are we going to do about the money?' Charlie sighed, slipping the phone in his pocket.

'What did I say earlier about leaving it to me and just concentrating on what you can do today?'

Charlie lapsed back into silence, leaving his sandwich untouched.

After a while he spoke again. 'Speaking of things I can't do myself, can I ask you another favour?'

Danny looked up after finishing his sandwich.

'Could you give my phone a charge?' He held it out for Danny to take. 'I get the feeling I'm going to need it for the next few hours.'

Danny took it up to his room where there was a charging dock amongst all the wires on the floor by the small studio set-up.

He plugged it in and saw the screen light up with a picture of Charlie and his family all together.

It was obviously taken before all of life's detritus had fallen down on them.

There they stood on some holiday or other, not a care in the world, thinking this was the way it would always be.

As he left the room Danny vowed to himself that one day, when all this mess was over, he'd take a picture of that lovely family again, somewhere that worries couldn't reach.

Chapter 22

There was an unusually large queue for a Sunday morning at Tesco Express. By the time Molly got to the front of the self-checkout line, she was running late.

With all that had been going on, she hadn't got anything in to make lunch at home, so she'd decided to splurge on a Christmas sandwich from the supermarket. She'd also got a box of Heroes to share; that way she could keep grouchy Graham happy. Her boss had a sour countenance but a sweet tooth.

When Graham made the rare decision to put her in charge of the jewellers yesterday afternoon she'd begrudged him at the time, hating the fact she'd be by herself on a busy Saturday. But now, remembering she wouldn't have met Danny in the same way if he'd been there lording over the shop, she felt a new warmth towards him for unknowingly helping fate play its hand.

She zipped the items through the scanner and pulled out a bag for life she'd folded into her pocket without a second thought. How had she become someone to carry around something so adult and organised? It was only a couple of years ago she and Gemma would have forgotten their shoes when stumbling out of a nightclub. Maybe it had something to do with her thirtieth birthday next year; perhaps she was becoming a grown-up. What next, a subscription to Saga magazine and a secret stash of Tena pants?

She gathered the shopping, pipped the contactless pad with her phone and headed for the exit, checking the time on her watch.

She looked up and almost dropped her bag as Stewart's hulking frame was coming towards her.

He'd just lumbered through the automatic door and she motioned a sidestep to avoid colliding with him.

'What are the chances?' he beamed at her while reaching out to get a basket from the pile.

'Oh for God's sake, Stewart, can't you just leave me alone?' Molly shrieked, unsurfaced anger and stress bursting out of her.

'Woah.' Stewart put his hands in the air, the basket dangling from his thumb in surrender. 'I've just come for some milk.'

There was a small crowd gathering in the nearby cleaning products aisle, pretending to study washing powder boxes but in reality enjoying the show.

'Milk?' Molly spat. 'You've got to stop following me, coming into the shop, sending photos and cards.'

'Look, calm down,' Stewart said, putting the basket down and moving towards her, holding out a hand.

She slapped it away; it wasn't as aggressive as the poor guy she'd floored yesterday but forceful enough to leave the impression she desired.

His mouth was wide open as she marched out of the supermarket and power-walked her way across town.

She marched down the high street oblivious to anything but her searing hate of Stewart as the bag swung ferociously by her side.

Graham stood up from behind the far counter as she arrived, thinking she was a customer. When he saw it was Molly he sat down again.

'You're late,' was all he said, and that was when Molly burst into tears and ran straight for the staff toilets, dumping her shopping in the middle of the floor on her way.

She locked the door, pulled down the toilet lid, sat down and unspooled yards of tissue as she rocked back and forth.

The weight of everything crashed down on her.

After a few minutes there was a soft rap on the door.

'Are you OK, Molly?' She had never heard Graham's voice so light before; it was effeminate and high-pitched. This was obviously an area he had little experience of and he was uncomfortable with it.

'I've made you some tea with a couple of sugars. I'll just leave it in the staff room — take your time.'

She'd never really warmed to him as her manager; she'd thought him slimy and career-motivated. This was a new Graham and it helped to know that people could surprise you.

She wiped her face, stood up and checked her reflection in the cracked mirror above the tiny sink. She had panda eyes from her smudged mascara. Running the tap she dabbed it away and reached for her handbag.

She reapplied make-up and squirted perfume behind each ear, tried a smile and then unlocked the door, all ready to face Graham's questions.

Surprisingly, he didn't require any further information apart from asking her if she needed anything. He'd put the shopping bag on the side in the staff room beside a steaming mug of tea.

She took a grateful sip and pulled out the tin of Heroes, unpicking the seal round the sides.

Walking back into the shop, Graham was busy polishing the glass counters, humming something to no doubt ease his own discomfort at witnessing such an outpouring of distress.

She opened the tin and offered him a chocolate.

'For being so nice,' she said.

'Thanks, I'll save it for later,' he replied without emotion, slipping it into his suit trouser pocket.

The morning passed by quickly — not many buyers but a lot of browsers. Most of the purchases were young men frantically trying to butter up girlfriends with charm bracelets or cheap rings which, secretly, Molly thought were a bit vulgar. She would never do a Gerald Ratner and say some of their stuff was 'total crap', but there were parts of the shop that were nothing more than gaudy gifts.

The most expensive rings were in the show cabinets by the counter and a scattering on display in the window. She remembered her promise to take the reserved engagement ring with her tonight and secretly hoped that the guy wouldn't come back to buy it today.

She was already nervous about her date and seeing Stewart this morning had thrown her off balance. Having the ring analysed by Danny's friend would be something for them to talk about — a way to establish the conversation in those early tricky moments that came with all first dates.

She had lunch in the staff room and used the time to slip on her headphones and listen to another of Danny's podcasts.

This one was about a woman who'd been a charity worker most of her adult life until a road-rage incident had led her to criminal prosecution and a suspended prison sentence.

As the story unfolded she marvelled at Danny's ability to get to the bottom of why this woman had done what she had — how somebody whose work had been about helping others had the capacity to resort to violence in a split second. As Danny said at the start of each of the podcasts, sometimes good people do bad things.

She was also impressed by how freely he talked about his own struggles with addiction and she wondered what incident had occurred that had caused his epiphany. Maybe it would come up later in the series? She certainly wasn't going to ask him tonight.

She was only halfway through when Graham put his head round the door, still treading carefully after the morning's outburst.

'I'm taking my lunch break now — are you OK to man the shop?'

She had never heard him so polite; she could almost detect the eggshells crunching underneath his shoes.

'Of course,' she said, winding up the cord from her earbuds and slipping them back into her bag. She felt a little like she'd been caught doing something naughty listening to a podcast at work — she'd never done anything but read a magazine or pop for a walk round the Crowngate shopping centre at lunchtimes; this felt too immersive to be a work-time hobby.

She also worried that she'd found out too much about Danny before the date. Everybody did a little cyber-stalking before meeting someone new these days, but the fact that Danny was something of a podcast superstar gave her a tiny thrill and the last thing she would want to come across tonight was a demented fangirl.

'Take your time,' Molly said as she stood up, brushing crumbs from the Christmas sandwich off her skirt.

'If you're sure?' he gave the faintest of smiles.

'I really am.' She took a step closer and he inadvertently took a step back — he wasn't good with any physical closeness. 'And to show my gratitude I'd like to lock up tonight.'

'Really? But you're due to finish at three.' He glanced at his watch. 'You covered yesterday afternoon.'

'Please let me show my appreciation.' She gave him her best smile, the one she reserved for customers who were most likely to tip. 'Call it a Christmas present.'

Graham thought for a moment as if this were some gargantuan mathematical problem. 'Well, in that case I accept,' he said at last, 'but what say you come in later tomorrow morning to make up?'

'It's a deal,' she said, resisting the urge to shake his hand — this wasn't his style at all.

He left with a nod and Molly sighed in relief as she heard the bell indicate his exit.

This was a result. Him leaving early meant she could borrow the ring without him asking questions, and coming in late meant she could enjoy a late night tonight, if the date went well. Just thinking of it made her stomach flip.

Maybe she was putting too many wishes on the night ahead. Was she just hoping to rid herself of the ghost of Stewart? Had she put all her eggs in the Danny basket? He'd been in her ears quite a bit since yesterday.

She resolved to herself that it was worth the plunge.

Her nervousness was tripled by the time the clock reached four and she was locking up the shop — thank heavens for Sunday opening hours.

Every time the bell over the door had rung she'd expected to see the man coming in to buy the ring he'd reserved, but he never did.

This gave her mixed emotions. If he'd come in she wouldn't have to take it away with her tonight, which was breaking just about every company rule, but now he hadn't come back she felt compelled to take it and let Danny show his friend.

She pulled it from the display case and slipped it into her bag.

Turning out the lights and locking the door she had the niggling feeling she was being watched, and the ring in the bottom of the bag felt as heavy on her conscience as a gold bar.

Chapter 23

Sunday 17th December, 2:28pm

Together they had rehearsed what they were going to say to Charlie's wife as Danny drove him back to Bromsgrove, so by the time they arrived the story was note perfect.

She was standing at the door waiting for them when Danny pulled the van up outside their house. Her slender frame looked imposing in spite of her illness.

Once inside and with the kettle on, they both explained why he had gone back to Danny's, only leaving out the fact that the man who attacked him was the bloke he'd used to forge a ring and was no doubt part of a violent gang who were blackmailing them.

'I've said it so many times to him, Danny,' she said. 'It's too dangerous doing all those shifts at night with the drunks causing trouble.'

'But we need the money,' Charlie said, leaving Danny fumbling with his coffee cup, feeling like he wasn't even in the room anymore. This domestic conversation was private and he needed to get going.

'Thank you for looking after him,' Karen said as he made a move to leave.

'Please don't get up,' Danny said, noticing her struggling to free herself from the embrace of her upright chair, cushions arranged around her in a cocoon.

Danny sensed the reason she'd warmed to him so quickly, in spite of bringing her husband home with a bandaged head wearing one of Danny's old sweatshirts, was she'd heard his podcast. He could always tell those who'd experienced the stories he'd helped to tell.

'I'll see you out,' Charlie said, and walked him to the door.

They stepped outside and both looked up simultaneously. A flurry of snow was starting; it felt refreshing to be out of the overheated house.

'The kids will go crazy if they ever leave their rooms,' Charlie said, looking up. 'They've hardly seen any snow.'

'Just concentrate on them tonight,' Danny said, putting a hand on Charlie's shoulder, 'and Karen.'

'You'll let me know how you get on?' Charlie asked, looking back to make sure he'd closed the door firmly away from Karen's super-senses.

'It won't be till tomorrow, so try not to think about it.'

Charlie nodded and was about to say something but couldn't think of any more platitudes.

Without another word Danny walked to the van and started up.

Turning on the wipers, he could see Charlie standing in the garden getting covered in snow but hardly noticing.

He pulled away and drove home, lost in thought.

His first was the plan, then turning to the more appealing prospect of the date. Meeting Molly would be a welcome distraction, but he couldn't help but feel nervous about the two biggest events of the year happening on the same night.

He turned on the radio to distract his busy mind.

There was a phone-in and the subject was the weather. Good old Blighty espousing on its favourite topic.

Danny loved phone-in shows. Hearing what people cared about gave him great inspiration for his podcast and he'd already made several notes on future stories he could chase up, particularly the ones involving people with unresolved issues.

The current caller was Carole from Ombersley, who wanted to know why the gritters weren't out where she lived. She claimed it would be almost impassable in a few hours.

He looked through the windscreen at the light fall of sleet and marvelled at the exaggeration of the British public fuelled by media goading.

He could see tomorrow's Worcester News headline: WHITE HELL or COMMUTER CHAOS. When in reality there'd be little more than an inconvenient dusting and a couple of train delays.

Meanwhile John in Claines wanted to talk about how snow was nothing today compared to when he was a kid, walking to school without a coat in three feet of snow.

'Kids today are soft, that's the problem,' he ranted. 'Soon as the heating's on the blink they get a day off. We didn't have heating at our school, it was so cold there was ice inside the classroom windows and…'

Danny turned it off. He needed a touch more positivity, so slid in the CD of Queen's greatest hits, which had a permanent place in the slot, and sang along with 'Don't Stop Me Now' for three blissful minutes.

Pulling into his drive, he waited till 'We Will Rock You' had finished before turning off the ignition.

He reached for his phone and sent Molly a quick text. He was aware that he didn't want to bombard her but just needed to double-check she'd still be up for tonight and that the weather hadn't put her off. He wasn't sure about the two kisses he'd typed at the end, but sent it before he could overthink.

By the time he'd got inside and taken off his jacket she'd replied with the same number of kisses and a thumbs-up emoji.

Taking this as a good sign, he pulled a Diet Coke from the fridge and sat down at the lounge table. It was time to check the plan.

He laid the ring on the table, once again bewildered at how it glistened. He could understand how something like this could cause so much trouble. It indicated many things.

As an engagement ring it was a token of commitment; as a piece of jewellery it personified wealth. Both were just surface, really. At this moment it only meant trouble and worry. The sooner he swapped it back for the original the better.

A myriad of thoughts bashed his brain as he stared at the stone, transfixed.

What if Molly didn't bring the forged ring from the shop with her? What would he leave for the blackmailer at the racecourse? He couldn't take the real one; it would be lost forever and Molly or someone else at the jeweller's would eventually work out that the one she took back was a forgery.

He couldn't think about that. Once again his serenity prayer came to mind: 'Change only the things I can.'

Then there was the subject of the money. They wanted ten grand in cash, and although he'd told Charlie he'd cover it, that wasn't entirely true.

He wrapped the ring in several sheets of paper like preparing a crude pass-the-parcel and then set about composing a note that he hoped would settle things once and for all.

He finished writing, slipped it into an envelope and then wondered who to address it to.

His pen hovered, and then he thought READ ME would be the only option.

He ordered an Uber for an hour's time and took another look out of the lounge window.

It was postcard pretty outside, the street lights glowing orange over the white surface. It still didn't look like a heavy fall, but it was settling now.

He could see the outline of a couple of kids wrapped up in big coats and bobble hats, running up and down the pavement, pretending to slip in their oversized wellies.

He thought about Charlie's kids doing the same thing about now, or was his eldest daughter too cool for that kind of thing?

Danny had never considered having kids. It wasn't that he had a problem with young people, it was just that the women he'd dated were far from mummy material.

He wondered if Molly liked children, then stopped himself immediately. He'd only met her once and already they were having babies together.

It was time to get some perspective, so he climbed the stairs and got ready for the most eventful night he'd had in years.

Chapter 24

Sunday 17th December, 4:22pm

Molly was feeling nervous and decided that retail therapy was the only answer.

She had some Boots vouchers that had been burning a hole in her purse, so as she walked by and found the store still open, she slipped through the doors and straight to the cosmetic department, where all the staff smelt like they'd just fallen out of a vat of Chanel.

The assistant pounced at her like a lion on a wildebeest.

'Can I help you?' she smiled. Deep red lipstick parted to reveal the kind of teeth Molly could only acquire with a deep Instagram filter or thousands of pounds' worth of dental implants.

'Just browsing,' Molly said cheerfully. She was well aware of the annoying customer who came in just as you were wanting to lock up, particularly late on a Sunday afternoon.

She'd had her eye on the Good Girl Blush and picked up the display bottle, giving her wrists a gentle squirt.

It smelt devine, and although it would probably be half the price after Christmas, she wanted something to boost her confidence for tonight's date.

She pointed out the bottle imprisoned behind the glass and did a double take when she saw the price. 'I'll take the small one,' she said, realising that she'd need to add cash to the vouchers even for the tiniest option.

She paid at the till and tried a little gentle banter.

'I don't know how perfume got so expensive, do you?' she asked.

The girl smiled, sensing she had found a kindred spirit, replying in a full Worcester accent which she'd hidden on her arrival, 'I know what ya mean, bab, and I heard somewhere it's all made out of whale vomit.'

They both laughed as she wrapped it in an oversized paper bag. 'I hope he's worth it, bab,' she said as Molly left the shop, narrowly avoiding colliding with a girl who was in the process of moving a six-foot cardboard stand-alone while some of the other girls were laughing at her efforts.

The cold air hit her full on as she continued down the high street, reflecting on the laughter she'd left behind and wondering if a change of job, where she had more interaction with girls like that, would be a good New Year's resolution.

Did Danny have a resolution of his own? Maybe that was something else they could discuss on the date tonight.

She suddenly felt happy as she strolled by the pubs and bars, music bellowing the same Christmas songs as every year, lights breaking through the darkness and promising fun and friendship.

Crossing over the bus lane towards Lowesmoor, she could see all the shops selling exotic foods and ingredients, giving the city a cosmopolitan feel.

A homeless guy was wedged up against the gate of St George's Church, his worldly belongings on a threadbare sleeping bag and an empty Costa cup with a few coppers inside placed hopefully by his outstretched foot.

Molly tossed a pound coin in the cup and wished him a happy Christmas. It felt like an empty gesture, but the guy looked up and gave her a lost smile before letting his head fall downwards again, as if the world were just too heavy for him.

The inflatable snowman waved limply at her as she walked through her tiny ramshackle garden to the front door. She wondered if he needed blowing up already and how she'd go about doing it. It seemed a shame for all of Gemma's hard work making her home look Christmassy to dwindle already due to a flaccid decoration.

She opened the door and shivered. Her goodwill had just taken its first hit of the evening.

Why hadn't the heating come on?

She walked to the thermostat and studied it. She had no idea how it worked, only that you turned a dial till it clicked if you wanted to increase the heat.

The timer had been set by the landlord when she'd moved in, and she hadn't touched it since for fear of breaking it.

She couldn't worry about it now. Maybe it would magically work by the time she came back tonight.

Taking the stairs at a pace, she threw the bag for life with her perfume, handbag and coat on the bed and went to the bathroom.

She turned on the shower and said a few 'Hail Marys' for heat to materialise. The Almighty answered when she felt the temperature warm through the pathetic dribble of the shower head, so she stripped off and got under straight away before the hot water ran out.

Back in her bedroom she selected Danny's podcast and started to play it through her speaker, picking up from the moment she'd left off at lunchtime.

It was the final part of the episode where the charity worker had been involved in road rage. She told her story, and now Danny was doing what he had done at the end of the other episodes she'd heard. He was helping her to make amends.

Although the incident had happened quite a few years ago, Danny had managed to track down the woman she'd attacked and he had them both together in a room. It was powerful stuff.

It was so engrossing that Molly had just sat on the bed, hair still wet from the lukewarm shower and towel wrapped around her, listening intently to the two women talking it through.

She was close to tears when they parted as friends.

How had Danny managed to track down the woman who'd been attacked and then to get her to agree to meeting up with her attacker?

The end music was just fading in when she heard something rattle against the window.

She stood up so abruptly her towel fluttered to the floor.

Reaching down, she wrapped it around herself again and pulled the bedroom curtain to one side.

She was convinced she'd see Stewart or some hooded figure running away after throwing something at her window again.

Her heart was thudding but soon levelled out and was replaced by a warm glow.

There was a covering of snow on the ground. The noise she'd heard had been flakes against the glass.

She opened the window slightly and put her hand out into the elements. It felt hard, like hail rather than snow, as the small pellets hit her hand, leaving an icy sheen on her palm.

She shivered, closed the window and concentrated on getting ready, hoping that it wouldn't snow too hard. She didn't want Danny to cancel because of the weather.

Her phone buzzed and Gemma's smiling face lit up her screen.

'Hey, Gem,' she gushed.

'Wow, you sound like you're in a good mood. Has the inflatable snowman perked you up, or has the dishy window man swung by again?'

'Not the window man but…'

'Jesus, Molly, have you met someone?'

Suddenly Molly felt bad for not updating her best friend sooner. She was always the first person she'd call when she was in trouble or scared, but it seemed she hid the good news.

She told Gemma about all that had happened in the last 24 hours, hoping that she wouldn't put a damper on her excitement by telling her to be careful.

'Be careful,' Gemma said.

Molly was pleased she hadn't mentioned anything about taking the ring from the shop. She still wasn't sure about it herself.

'And you say he has a podcast?'

'Yeah, it's really good. I'll send you a link.'

'So you've got a date with a celebrity tonight?'

'I wouldn't say "celebrity", but he's got quite a big following.'

'I bet Stewart's going to go ape when he finds out.'

This stopped Molly short. She hadn't mentioned Stewart to Gemma since the brick incident, and it felt odd for her to mention him now when Molly was feeling so positive. It was so unlike her.

'I wish you hadn't mentioned him. He's still following me around,' Molly said after a few moments' uncomfortable silence.

'Oh God, I'm sorry, it's just…'

'Just what?' Molly felt the unwelcome return of nerves, and not the good kind she associated with snow and Danny.

'Oh, I wasn't going to say anything but I think I ought to.'

'What is it, Gem?'

'I don't want to spoil your evening, that's all.'

'Too late, come on, spill.'

'Well, it's just Stewart has texted me now. Says he's worried about you and wants me to arrange a get-together as you won't talk to him.'

'Of course I won't talk to him, he put a brick through my window.'

'You don't know that was him.'

'And he followed me to the supermarket this morning.'

'He said he just bumped into you and wanted to apologise for something he said in your shop.'

Molly stopped, the blood draining from her.

'Gemma, why are you defending him?'

'I'm not defending him, I just think the sooner you sort out the loose ends with him the sooner you can move on, and from what he's said to me he seems like that's what he wants too.'

Molly was speechless.

'I can't believe this,' she said, and for lack of something else to say she did something she'd never done to her friend in all the years they'd known each other. She put the phone down on her.

It rang again, Gemma's beaming face on the screen making the situation even worse, as if she were mocking the seriousness of what had just happened.

She let it go to voicemail and fell back on the bed, trying to make sense of everything.

Was she overreacting? Was Gemma just trying to help? She'd never taken sides before during her and Stewart's difficult relationship, so why was she doing it now?

Her phone buzzed again and she wondered if she were being childish by ignoring her.

But it wasn't Gemma this time, it was a message from Danny.

Hope the weather hasn't put you off? See you in the park at 7.30 xx

All thoughts of Gemma disintegrated like melting snowdrops.

She messaged back straight away and matched his two kisses, followed by a thumbs-up emoji.

Her night would not be spoiled before it had even started.

Chapter 25

Sunday 17th December, 5:27pm

As Charlie had predicted, both kids were excited by the snow once they'd left their rooms.

For the first time in months, Dylan powered down his PlayStation halfway through a game when Maisie informed him of the white phenomenon accumulating outside her bedroom window.

Dylan clumped downstairs in highly inappropriate clothing he'd just pulled out of random drawers.

'You'll catch your death if you go out wearing those,' Karen had said from her chair. She'd just woken from a nap and was still a little drowsy.

Maisie, on the other hand, tried to play it cool when Dylan asked, 'You coming out with us? I'm gonna get the sledge out of the garage.'

'Yeah, I might catch up,' she'd said, never taking her face from her iPhone screen. 'Just gotta have a quick Snapchat with Immy. She's well into this boy and he's like waaay sketchy.'

Charlie held back a smile. Sometimes he thought his daughter had developed an alien language that only she and her friends understood. He sure as hell didn't.

Karen made to move but Charlie stopped her by putting a gentle hand on her arm.

'You stay here, love, keep warm, I'll take them out.'

'But you can't, what with your…' She pointed at her own head to demonstrate.

Dylan looked up from the floor where he was having a battle with a green Wellington boot and losing.

'Oh yeah, Dad, what's happened to your head?'

'He fell over, daft thing,' Karen answered for him, and he snuck her a grateful smile.

On hearing this news Maisie unglued herself from the screen. 'Wow, Dad, that looks well bad,' she said before returning to her world.

'I'm fine,' he said to the room in general before bending down to help Dylan.

When Maisie had put her friend's romantic world to rights and spent the best part of fifteen minutes trying to decide what to wear (much to Dylan's annoyance, who was hopping from one foot to another like a coiled spring), they were all bundled up and ready to go.

'Be careful out there,' Karen said from her chair.

'We will,' the kids said in unison.

'Won't be long,' Charlie said, giving her a gentle kiss. He noticed that her skin felt thinner as his lips met her cheek. She was dropping weight on a weekly basis as the drugs were taking their toll.

He badly wanted to stay with her, thinking how unfair it was going out and having fun without her.

'Please go and enjoy yourself,' she said weakly, as if reading his mind — something Charlie was convinced she'd been able to do since they'd first met.

He hoped she didn't know everything that was going on in there at the moment.

Walking down the road, Charlie saw several other families doing exactly the same as them. He said hello and exchanged pleasantries with people he hadn't seen in ages, not since the pandemic when everyone was going for their 'daily exercise' and there was the kind of community spirit not experienced since the war years.

He was pleased to see that quite a few had gone for the same cheap and cheerful sledges that Dylan was dragging behind him, the kind you could buy from an opportunistic corner shop, while others had more classy affairs with shark fin designs and artistic graffiti on them. Then there were those that Charlie liked the best — merely pimped-up tea trays or sheets of polythene.

They reached what was known to the locals as the Old Rec, which was no more than a field waiting to be developed into more housing. There was a scattering of people all sliding down the hill like ants, the sodium lights casting an orange glow over the snow.

They reached the top of an incline where the queuing system seemed to depend on the kind of bringing-up you'd had.

The good kids waited in line to slide down, making sure the coast was clear before taking the plunge.

The rough kids just went for it, deliberately blocking any path and, given a chance, pushing people over or just running in a feral attack at one of their clan.

All life is here, thought Charlie as he pushed his son down the hill till the sledge got traction, while his daughter seemed to be just filming everything — including herself — as she angled the phone in different directions, doing pouts for the camera.

It felt strange to be out in the dark but you never knew if the snow would disappear before sunup. A truly British attitude — to make the most of extreme weather while it lasted, like when you couldn't get near a beer garden when the temperature rose above fifteen degrees.

'I think we need to go now,' Charlie yelled to Dylan hopefully after half an hour had passed. 'I don't want to leave your mum alone for too long.'

He thought of her sitting in that chair, thinking of what she was missing while she watched the falling snow through the window.

'Just one more,' Dylan shrieked, sounding more like an eight-year-old than twelve. Snow brought out the kid in everyone — except for Maisie, it would seem.

Thinking of his daughter, he started to look around. The last time he'd seen her she was posing by the entrance gate. He scanned the area but couldn't see her — it was hard to distinguish anything in the artificial light. Shadows moved like ink blots across the landscape.

He was aware of someone stood close by. He'd spotted him before but hadn't really paid much attention.

Sensing he'd been noticed, the man walked slowly towards Charlie.

He was wearing a beanie hat pulled low over his ears and forehead. His brows seemed to protrude, giving him a Neanderthal look.

'Alright, mate?' he asked, avoiding eye contact. He just kept focused on the horizon.

'Yeah, just looking for my daughter,' Charlie said.

'Yeah, you gotta be careful with girls her age.' He looked down and kicked some snow from his Doc Marten boots. 'Never know what they get up to, or who can get to them. Very impressionable, these young girls.'

Charlie shivered and made to move away but stopped dead at the next words.

'She's a pretty girl, your daughter. You want to make sure nothing bad happens to her because of something stupid you do, right, mate?'

Charlie was stunned. Words froze in his mouth, his fists clenched, but he could do nothing with them.

The guy walked away and Charlie was about to grab him when he heard his daughter's scream.

It was coming from the bottom of the hill, so he ran in that direction.

He'd only gone a couple of paces when he fell head first onto the ground, which mercifully was a soft landing in the sludge and snow.

He was dizzy with the cold, his head still spinning from his earlier injury, but more importantly the sound of his daughter.

He felt a hand reach for him and was about to slap it away, thinking it was the creep who'd just been talking to him.

Looking up, he could see the shadow of a woman in a pink bobble hat holding out a gloved hand.

'Are you alright, love?' she asked. She had a strong northern accent — the North East somewhere — and for some reason he found it instantly calming.

'Yes,' he said, stumbling to his feet and then falling flat on his backside again. 'It's my daughter.'

At that moment he saw Maisie running towards him, closely followed by Dylan heaving the sledge behind him.

'Dad, are you OK?' Maisie said, kneeling down beside him. There was a small crowd gathering — the last of the sledge stalwarts coming in force.

'I'm fine,' Charlie said, heaving himself up successfully this time, and the crowd moved aside and dispersed. The show was over.

Once they were alone, Charlie moved closer to Maisie and whispered, 'I heard you scream. Did somebody do something to you?'

Maisie looked up at him and screwed up her face. 'Urgh, God no, Dad, it was just me falling over. I was being a bit dramatic for the video — get more likes that way.'

Charlie would normally have found this annoyingly amusing, but after the comments from the guy stood next to him there was little humour left.

'I fell over loads,' Dylan bragged from behind them, trying to keep up as they trudged back to the entrance.

'Big woo-hoo,' Maisie said before pulling out her phone again.

Charlie let her walk a pace ahead and picked up the sledge for Dylan, tucking it under his arm.

From now on he wasn't letting the kids out of his sight.

There had to be a connection to the guy at the hospital and this.

Back home, the smell of domesticity hit them the moment they opened the door. Something was cooking.

'Make sure you leave those boots by the door,' Karen said, appearing in the hallway wearing the flowery apron he'd bought her as a joke for their wedding anniversary one year and she'd used ever since.

'Dad fell down,' Dylan said before running upstairs, no doubt to catch up with whoever he'd missed online during their rare trip into the outside world.

'Dylan, you grass,' Maisie shouted at him as she followed him upstairs, her coat and shoes still on and her face magnetised to the phone screen. 'Dad said not to say anything.'

Both bedroom doors slammed and Charlie fell into the lounge chair and heaved a sigh.

'You told the kids not to tell me, eh?' Karen said, luckily with a smile on her face.

Charlie took solace in the fact she hadn't linked the head injury from last night to the fall in the snow, which was great.

'No cookies for you then,' she said, disappearing back into the kitchen.

While she fussed with plates and turned on the kettle, he had time to regroup.

The memory of the ape man giving him the warning about his daughter, the message saying they knew where he lived and that bloody ring. He didn't even have it any more — it was all in Danny's hands now.

Remembering Danny's words of only doing what he could, he turned his attention to his wife.

He entered the kitchen to the smell of cookies fresh from the oven and hot chocolate being poured.

He held his wife as tight as he dared and didn't want to let go.

His children safe upstairs in their rooms, his wife in his embrace and the ring somewhere he didn't know.

For now, that would have to do — and for now, that was enough.

Chapter 26

Sunday 17th December, 6:45pm

The Uber pulled up outside Danny's house bang on time and hooted twice.

He double and triple-checked he had the ring and note, zipped up his winter coat and, locking the door, made his way to the cab.

It was getting slippery underfoot.

The repetitive boom of dance music greeted him as he opened the door. This was instantly followed by the distinctive smell of cinnamon air freshener, which cab drivers the world over must buy in bulk.

'Town, mate?' the driver asked.

'Yes please,' Danny answered politely, having to raise his voice over the beats.

'Music too loud for ya, bro?' the driver enquired, while pulling out onto the street.

'No, it's fine, honestly,' Danny replied, reckoning that the louder the music, the less chance there would be for trivial chit-chat. He needed the time to mentally prepare for the night ahead and the soundtrack of drum and bass was fine by him.

The track playing took him back to his clubbing days; it was where he first met his ex. He was a little worse for wear (not unusual in those days) when she came up to him and shouted in his ear that he'd just won a prize.

'What for?' he'd slurred.

'Best dad dance,' she'd laughed, and he'd swung round to see a petite brunette in a short white dress and, just beyond, a group of girls all laughing hysterically by the bar.

She'd obviously been sent over on a bet.

It was a couple of weeks later that she'd spotted him again at his local pub. This time he was unusually sober, as he had an early start the next day.

'Sorry about the other night,' she'd said, 'my mates put me up to it.'

She'd been about to leave but he offered to buy her a drink and said she'd have to accept, otherwise she would hurt his feelings twice.

That was how it started, and at the time it seemed like they were going in the right direction.

They moved in together and it was quite a sweet arrangement.

She'd leave for the furniture store where she worked just as he was heading out to his office, and they'd arrive home at pretty much the same time every night.

The stone in their domestic shoe was that she had the same relationship with alcohol that he did, and although she was probably still living that same life right now with someone else, Danny was in a very different place these days.

What he'd done that fateful night was hard for her to ever truly forgive.

There was a sudden jolt pulling Danny out of his reverie.

The driver hit his horn and said something that Danny couldn't quite understand. It was obviously a swear word of some kind but in a language he wasn't familiar with.

The driver turned his head, looking briefly at Danny through the gap in the beaded headrests. It was the first time he'd seen his face and he looked barely old enough to shave, let alone drive a taxi. 'Sorry, mate, bloody bike pulled up right in front of me. Shouldn't be out in bloody weather like this, man,' he said before mercifully twisting his head back to concentrate on the road.

Danny thought, with a rant like that, he belonged on the BBC phone-in he was listening to earlier.

He could hear the topic tomorrow morning: 'Should pushbikes be banned in the snow?' Better still: 'Should pushbikes be banned from roads completely?' That would get the calls flooding in.

Eventually the taxi swerved into the car park and Danny got out, thanking him, though not sure he even heard over the volume of 'Groove Is in the Heart' blasting from the speakers.

The entrance to the bar and restaurant was directly in front of him, but there was an illuminated pathway to the side which led into the park.

He walked unsteadily, listening to the crunching under his boots as he walked to their meeting place.

He glanced at his watch and was pleased to be ten minutes early.

There was a fountain just past the tennis courts. It had been empty of water for many years but had always been a good meeting point.

As a kid he'd sat on this low wall, dangling his chubby legs in the water. But his reminiscences blasted into particles when he saw Molly walking uncertainly towards him.

Was it the ice underfoot or was she having second thoughts about this date?

She was bundled up in a large coat and there were flakes of snow in her hair.

Whether it was the magical weather or the anticipation he wasn't sure, but he'd never seen anything quite as beautiful in his whole life.

Danny held open the door and Molly stepped through into the warmth as 'I Wish It Could Be Christmas Everyday' was playing under a soundtrack of laughter and clinking glasses.

The place was rammed and at first Danny was worried they wouldn't get in, but the queue they collided with turned out to be for the restaurant to the right of them, where a young girl wearing an oversized Santa hat was holding a clipboard and ticking off bookings.

They nudged past the couples and families to the bar area on the left, which still had a few free tables.

They found one overlooking the park and sat down opposite each other.

There was a candle stuck in a Chianti bottle in the middle of the table and, after dusting down their coats and hanging them on the backs of chairs, they picked up the drinks menu and were silent for a second or two, pretending to study it.

Molly wondered what Danny would order, as the majority of the selection were cocktails, beers, ciders or wine. She'd already made up her mind that if he ordered a soft drink she would do the same, even though she was nervous enough to down a large vodka and coke and just keep them coming.

They'd both got the awkward small talk out of the way on the walk from the park, so the scene was now properly set and the location couldn't have been better.

The smell of garlic from the restaurant area made Danny wonder if he should have booked a table, then he remembered he had to get to the racecourse to drop the ring and envelope at ten, so he'd have to make some excuse to leave before that anyway.

Molly took a sneaky look at Danny over the top of her menu and thought he looked a little tense. Maybe he was as nervous as she was; she hoped so. That would make things even to start with.

It was all very well flirting over the shop counter, but now the date was actually happening it felt more awkward than she'd anticipated.

He looked good, though. She'd only seen him in the reindeer cap up till now and was pleased to notice he had a full head of dark hair mussed on top and shaved at the sides. For all she knew he could have turned up with a comb-over.

He was wearing jeans and a shirt that could have done with an iron. That also boded well — a man who wasn't too vain, unlike Stewart, who was designer everything right down to his socks, which he would happily pay twenty quid a pair for just to have the Ted Baker monogram.

She mentally slapped herself for thinking about her ex again. Even when he wasn't physically there, he was still stalking her brain in one way or another.

'What do you fancy to drink?' Danny asked, putting down the menu.

She looked into his hazel eyes and tried to gauge what he wanted to hear.

'I'm not sure, there's too much to choose from,' she said coyly.

'Well, there are some impressive cocktails,' he said, 'or maybe wine or beer, whatever?'

'I'd love a glass of Zinfandel if they do it. If not, a glass of house rosé would be fine.'

'Cool,' he said, and disappeared to the bar.

Molly let out a breath she hadn't realised she'd been holding, feeling that the first obstacle had been removed.

While he was queuing at the bar she fired up her phone in the hope that Gemma had sent a message. They had only had the fall-out a few hours ago, and it already felt like an age. They never argued like that before.

There were two notifications: one from a scammer saying that she owed money on a package that needed delivering, and the other from her mother asking if she'd help her set up a Slimming World Facebook page for the new year.

Typical mother, she thought, only texting when she needed something. She was probably her second choice anyway, as her dad would have obliged her but was away again till Christmas Eve.

She always looked forward to seeing her dad, even if it was only over FaceTime when he got back from his travels.

As she watched Danny leaning over the bar, trying to be understood by a harassed youth who was clearly struggling to keep up the pace of the orders, she wondered what her dad would make of him. She thought he may just approve.

He turned round clutching two glasses and gave her a brilliant smile while pretending to drop them. Yes, her dad would like him very much, if only for the dad jokes alone.

He slid the drink in front of Molly and she took a nervous sip.

He'd ordered himself a large coke with enough ice to sink a rhino.

Leaning close enough for Molly to smell his expensive shower gel and toothpaste, she thought for a split second he was going to kiss her. She was in no way ready for that yet, but instead he whispered in her ear conspiratorially, 'I managed to secure us some olives, but keep it to yourself or everyone will want some.'

She giggled and took another sip, the wine already doing its magic, and Danny's confidence was spreading over her like the warmest of blankets, juxtaposing the cold, harsh winter night outside the window.

'How did you manage to "score" the olives?' she asked, playing along.

'Well, don't tell everyone, but there's a guy called Bernie who works security here sometimes. Mention his name and it carries a lot of sway in the olive department. You can even blag up to dry roasted peanut territory, but that's another conversation.' Danny tapped the side of his nose.

'How do you know Bernie?'

'Well, he was a guest on a podcast I do,' he said, and then, almost catching himself halfway through a boast, waved a hand. 'It's just a little project really.'

'I think it's great,' Molly said without taking a beat.

'You've heard it?' Danny was stunned and a little worried. He remembered part of the reason he was here: things were supposed to be casual, and she'd obviously been doing her research. He was flattered and concerned all in one.

'Yeah, I've heard the first three episodes and they're really interesting,' Molly squirmed at her use of the last word. She'd made it sound like a wildlife documentary.

'Thanks, I appreciate that,' he replied modestly.

'What made you want to start a podcast?'

'It's a bit of a passion project, to be honest,' Danny replied, then just as quickly switched tack. 'How about you, what are your passions?'

She told him about her love of books which, although not a lie, hadn't seen her wearing out her library card recently. She thought of the Marian Keyes lying dog-eared on the sofa.

She was going to talk about Gemma and how they had adventures together, but after the row it hurt too much to bring her into the conversation. Apart from that there had only been Stewart in her life, and she certainly wasn't going to chat about him in the flickering candlelight.

It suddenly struck home how much of her life she'd devoted to him and, since they'd split, how she'd tried to rebuild her life with interests of her own.

'Excuse me, I'm afraid you'll have to leave.'

Molly's head shot up and saw a large man in a monkey suit glowering down at Danny.

'Am I in trouble?' Danny asked, looking up at the same time.

'Big trouble, sunshine. You know what you've done and I'm afraid you and me are going to have to go outside and settle this like gentlemen.'

Danny scraped his chair back and stood face to face with the monster man. He must have been at least a foot shorter, so Danny's face looked directly into his double chin.

'What's this all about?' Molly said, her heart racing at the prospect of another fight. She'd witnessed a couple of drunken brawls involving Stewart, but Danny didn't seem the type. He didn't even drink. How could she have got him so wrong?

'Before I abandon this lovely girl,' Danny said, looking down at Molly, who was seriously contemplating finishing her drink in one and legging it out of the door, 'I'd like her to hear what the problem is.'

She glanced at the bar to see if any of the staff had noticed what was going on and, to her shock, instead of calling the police they were crowded together laughing.

The big man spoke: 'For ordering olives using my name,' he boomed, and then gave a hearty laugh that could only have come from someone who had been smoking since the age of ten.

Then both men embraced in a bear hug.

'Sorry about that, but it's a running joke between us,' the big man said, wiping his eyes with the back of his hand. 'I'm Bernie.' He held out a meaty hand which Molly shook. It was like plunging her fist into Play-Doh.

'I've heard about you,' she said, releasing her hand, which felt limp and damp.

'Ah, heard me on his podcast, have you?' He nodded at Danny with the eyes of a proud father watching his son ride a bike for the first time.

'Not yet, but it's on my list.'

'She's a keeper, and beautiful too,' Bernie said, turning to Danny and making a slight bow. 'See you later, olive-nicker,' he said before disappearing back outside, the doors slamming behind him and the bar staff just stopping short of giving him a round of applause.

'I'm so sorry about that,' Danny said, settling back down and adjusting his shirt which had ridden up during the unexpected embrace.

'It's fine, he obviously loves you,' she said.

'He's a good man but...' he leaned forward again, 'he gets a bit over-excited.'

'Like a puppy?' Molly suggested.

'A Doberman at the very least.' Danny gave a laugh and Molly liked it. It wasn't forced or nervous, just natural. She could see why people warmed to him — from the road-rage woman on the podcast to big Bernie and his little jokes.

'Let me get you another,' Danny said, getting up and taking her glass. She was a little ashamed at how quickly she was drinking but, with her nervousness and then the shock of Bernie's joke, she'd barely noticed the glass draining.

There was a queue at the bar so Danny used the time to mentally prepare himself for the next part of the evening.

He needed to mention the ring, which he hoped she'd brought with her as promised, but he had to be subtle. Then he'd do the swap with the real one in his pocket and end the evening before ten so he could do the drop-off at the racecourse.

It suddenly seemed like a huge ask. He had to help Charlie and not lose Molly.

No matter how hard he tried, he found it hard to imagine that this evening was going to end well.

Chapter 27

Sunday 17th December, 8:44pm

When Danny got back from the bar with the next round of drinks he was all ready to bring up the subject of the ring. He needn't have worried.

'Thank you,' Molly said and reached for her bag as if she was about to pay him. Rummaging around, she pulled out a small velvet box and slid it across the table. Anyone observing may have been under the impression she was preparing to propose to him.

Leaning closer she whispered, 'I got you the ring for your friend to look at,' her head rotating in all directions, expecting someone to leap on the table and steal it at any moment, 'but I'll need to take it back with me.'

'Of course,' Danny said, taking the box and putting it into his pocket away from the public gaze. He could feel it brush against the paper towel the genuine one was wrapped in.

'Is it OK if I take a picture in the loo, there's more light in there?'

'Yeah, no worries,' she said, hoping her confident tone would hide any suspicion.

Danny could see the unease in her eyes, which had thinned slightly. He gave a smile and headed to the gents while Molly sat back in her seat and took another healthy pull from the glass, wondering if she'd ever see him again.

A scenario crossed her mind of him dashing out the back door fire escape with the ring (and her future employment prospects) gone with the wind. Then she remembered he was known here and, more importantly, his coat was still hanging from the chair opposite. She really did have to learn to trust people again before the spectre of Stewart ruined the rest of her life.

The gents' toilet was empty, even though there had been a queue for the ladies. That always seemed to be the way. He took the first cubicle and turned the lock. It was pretty dark but it didn't matter; it wasn't like he was really going to take a picture.

There was no lid on the loo, only a seat, so he carefully pulled the box out of his pocket, putting it on the ledge of the cistern. He reached into his pocket and pulled out the paper tissue with the genuine ring inside. Unfolding the tissue, he took out the ring ready to swap with the forgery in the box.

One moment he was studying the beauty of it between his fingers, the next he heard a plink and saw something glittering from the water below. The ring had come loose and fallen from his grasp into the toilet basin.

'Left you for another woman has he?' Bernie had appeared from nowhere and was towering above Molly. She noticed how his suit jacket was a little too small for him, making his shoulders bulge. But then again, she reasoned, maybe that was the whole point.

'Just gone to the loo,' she said and turned towards the window, hoping he'd take the hint. She didn't want to be rude but there was something a little too—she searched for the word—'much' about him. He had kind eyes that betrayed the hulking figure, and that messed with all her preconceptions. She just really didn't know what to make of the man.

'Mind if I have a seat until he gets back?' he said, sitting down anyway.

Molly just nodded resignedly as the chair creaked under his weight.

'I just want to say that Danny's a really great bloke,' he said, those kind eyes meeting hers, 'he's been really good to me over the past years and he helps so many people.'

'Yeah, I've been hearing his podcasts,' Molly said.

Bernie smiled. 'After all he went through with his struggles,' he pointed to the Diet Coke to signify, 'and that terrible accident.'

'What accident?' Molly asked, her voice cracking slightly.

'Oh, he hasn't told you?' Bernie held up a palm the size of a road shovel. 'It's not for me to say anything,' he shook his head, 'me and my big mouth. Just be good to him, will you? He deserves it.'

Without another word he lumbered away back through the door, bringing in a small flurry of snow in his wake.

Molly pulled out her phone to check the weather, wondering if she'd be walking home in a snowdrift. It was hard to tell through the window. There was an almost full moon which gave a faint illumination of the park, and she could see the outline of the tennis courts and beyond, trees that had an icing-sugar dusting of snow on them.

The weather app promised moderate snow showers for the rest of the night, but from the look of the flakes it was thin and a little sleety.

She'd played in this park as a kid. Her dad had brought her to see the brass bands playing 'Una Paloma Blanca' to residents from the nearby flats, some of whom had brought their own deck chairs.

Molly recalled a vague memory of her dad dancing with her on the newly mown grass while the elderly crowd 'awwwed' at the free show.

She was just about to put her phone away when it buzzed in her hand. To her relief it was a message from Gemma.

Hi Mol. Can't stop thinking about the row. Please don't let it spoil your night and let me know how your date goes. I promise I won't mention 'him' again. Xxxx

Relief flooded through. The one thing that had been nagging at her was resolved for the moment, so she could concentrate on Danny more now. If he ever came out of the toilet. How long had he been in there? Then she thought maybe he had sent the photo of the ring to his friend and he had called straight back; it wasn't going to be a quick conversation.

She sat back and finished her second glass. It was definitely her round next and this time she'd have a Coke as well. If she had any more wine she might get a little too giddy.

She'd always been a happy drunk; if she had one too many she got the giggles and usually fell over at some point. Stewart was the opposite. She used to dread the long sessions when he'd turn charm into harm in the space of a couple of hours. There were occasions when she'd swear he was actively looking for a fight.

She'd once challenged him on it while they were having one of their heart-to-hearts the morning after a particularly embarrassing evening. With his head in his hands and a glass of impossibly orange Berocca fizzing beside him, he'd apologised for any upset he'd caused, blaming it on his father's influence. He'd been a professional boxer in his youth and, by all accounts, used to practise on his son when a bout hadn't gone his way. He'd left Stewart and his mother when he was just thirteen years old to take up with a woman who worked behind the bar at the Working Men's Club.

She couldn't imagine Danny having any such problems, but the story of the 'accident' Bernie had almost blurted out must have been serious. What had happened to him then, and more importantly, where was he now?

Danny looked down into the toilet bowl, which thankfully had been flushed. It could have been a lot worse. Pulling up his sleeve, he closed his eyes and began to fish around with his fingers. He could feel the edge of the ring but every time he tried to grab it, it slipped again. Forcing himself to look down into the toilet, the ring had now completely disappeared.

Chapter 28

'Goodnight, kids,' Charlie said as he reached the top of the stairs.

To his left was Maisie's room where he could hear the sound of the TV, probably one of those teen shows that Netflix churns out about boys falling in love or supernatural vampires falling in love or zombies falling in love. Whatever it was, both he and Karen were past telling her to turn it off at bedtime; she was old enough to suffer the pain of getting up for school on just four hours' sleep — hopefully she'd learn by experience.

Dylan, on the other hand, had always slept well, even as a baby. Charlie remembered when they first brought him home from the hospital, checking his breathing every half an hour; he slept so soundly.

He had a blue projected night light that was bleeding under the door and by his muffled reply of 'night, Dad' he was already under the duvet, probably knackered from all the sledge action earlier. He must have been up and down that hill forty times at least.

As he brushed his teeth he could hear the faint tapping of sleet against the bathroom window. He wondered how Danny was getting on. While he rinsed his brush he looked up at the damp patch on the ceiling; it seemed to get bigger every day and would need looking at sooner rather than later. He'd been on Facebook to look for local tradesmen and he'd planned to get one or two in for a quote once he'd sold the ring.

He felt stupid now after all the trouble he'd caused, the worry that prompted him to look out of the window every few minutes expecting someone to be lurking near the house. The guy on the field had shaken him and it had been hard sitting with Karen pretending to watch TV while all this was going through his head, which still throbbed from the attack.

She'd come up to bed straight after Antiques Roadshow so he was surprised to find her awake when he walked into the bedroom. She was sat up straight, a pile of pillows behind her and a Kindle on her lap. Sensing his presence but not taking her eyes from the screen, she patted his side of the bed.

'Come on,' she whispered, and he pulled off his slippers and slid under the duvet, feeling her warmth as he snuggled beside her.

'Thought you'd be asleep?' he said, brushing a stray hair from her forehead.

'No — I couldn't get comfy without you so I thought I'd wait. Besides,' she pointed to the Kindle, 'I'm quite enjoying my book.'

'What is it?' Charlie asked.

'Just romantic rubbish, you wouldn't be interested.' She gave him a playful pinch.

It was fair to say he wasn't much of a reader at the best of times.

'I can be romantic when I want to be,' he insisted.

She smiled. 'Oh yes — the headwear is very sexy.' She stroked the bandage and her face turned serious. 'Does it still hurt?'

'Only a bit,' he lied.

She looked deep into his eyes and Charlie saw the flame of kindness and love that had always been there since the first moment they'd met, only now it had been dampened by pain and worry, like ice thrown onto the flames.

'What's going on, love?' she asked.

Charlie's heart stopped beating for a few seconds; lying was not an option now. The woman he loved more than anything in the world had asked him the question direct and there was no way out of the cul-de-sac. She still had her hand on his head, her eyes never leaving his.

'I've done something really stupid,' Charlie said and felt the force of his emotion get the better of him. The tremors started at the pit of his stomach and worked their way up until he began to let them out, crying but trying to stifle the tears into his pillow to avoid disturbing the kids.

Karen let them pass without saying a word, all the time stroking the side of his bandaged head. Eventually the tremors stopped; he cleared his throat and told her everything he'd done, the confession spilling from him like a rip in a bag of sugar.

It was only when he'd run out of words and the energy to say them that Karen spoke.

'I want you to listen to me very carefully,' she said. Her voice was clearer than it had been in months. 'You have done something incredibly stupid but it has come from the purest intentions. Look at me, Charlie.' She pulled his chin up from the pillow; his red-rimmed eyes looked up at her.

'We are going to sort this, you hear me?'

Charlie could only nod; even if he had wanted to say something he couldn't — the words constricted in his throat, they seemed inadequate anyway.

'We will beat this the way we'll beat this cancer, the way we'll sort out our money problems. And do you know why?' Once again Charlie could only shake his head.

'Because we have each other and we are strong people. Maybe one day we'll look back on this and laugh.'

Charlie nodded again, this time having to hold back more tears which was taking the last of his emotional energy to keep at bay.

'What time did you say Danny's doing the swap at the racecourse?'

'Ten o'clock,' Charlie croaked, plumping his pillows upright to match hers.

'Nothing we can do till tomorrow — time to get some sleep, I think,' Karen said firmly, and with that she pulled the string for the bedside light.

Charlie lay still for a few moments, not quite sure what to say next. It was only when he turned off his own light and snuggled behind her that he found the courage to speak again; the blanket of darkness was the perfect hiding place.

'Please tell me what you're thinking now,' he whispered.

She grabbed his hand and pulled it tighter round her waist. She felt slimmer every time he'd done this in recent weeks but tonight there was more warmth to her, like his confession had somehow given her a shot of something that doctors couldn't prescribe. To his surprise she laughed; he could feel her body shaking as she tried to stifle the giggles.

'What's so funny?' he whispered in her ear.

'Oh — it's you,' Karen whispered back, turning her head slightly in his direction.

'Me?'

'Yeah. I'm just imagining you as a mastermind forger and it's about as bizarre as I can think.'

'Doesn't it worry you about the threats — that guy who talked about Maisie while we were sledging?' Now she turned around again. He could only see her faint outline from the streetlights bleeding through the crack in the curtains, but he didn't need to see her to know she was deadly serious.

'Now you listen to me, Charlie Burrows. Nobody threatens our family, nobody blackmails us and gets away with it. I won't let that happen — not till it takes every last breath in my body. If I have to leave you guys early, then I'm going to make damn sure you're all sorted before I go.'

Charlie was stunned. It was like someone had taken Karen from a few hours ago and replaced her with a different version — some kind of upgrade.

'Either Danny has done the switch or he hasn't; either way there's nothing we can do right now,' Karen said.

Charlie kissed his wife on the forehead. 'I love you.'

'I love you too, you daft bugger,' she said. She fell asleep almost immediately, leaving Charlie staring at the ceiling trying to comprehend what had just happened.

Chapter 29

Danny stared down into the toilet and wondered if he should just go back to Molly, who was probably worrying about where he'd got to.

The genuine ring was probably floating away down the pipes; this was a lost cause.

The door had kept opening and closing over the past ten minutes and Danny had just waited, hoping nobody wanted to use the stall next to his.

He was about to give it one more go, getting ready to plunge his arm down the pan and contemplating the unthinkable—wedging a hand under the bend itself—when the door squeaked open again.

'Danny, you in there?' Bernie's voice boomed in the echo, followed by a bang on the cubicle door.

'Yeah, I am, a bit of privacy please,' he said, grabbing the box with the fake and stuffing it back in his pocket.

'You alright, mate?' he said, his voice closer to the door. 'That lovely girl is getting worried about you out there. I reckon she thinks you've done a runner.'

'No, I…' Danny was about to make an excuse about a bad stomach but then a moment of inspiration entered his mind.

'Could you do me a huge favour?' he asked, suddenly feeling foolish talking to a man through a closed toilet door.

'Sure, mate, are you ill?'

'No,' Danny replied, 'but I need you to tell Molly I'll be another five minutes—say I'm just on the phone.'

'Yeah, no worries mate, take your time, I'll sort it.'

'And one other thing.'

'Yep.'

'I need you to ask someone behind the bar for something, but keep it discreet.'

Molly had got herself and Danny a Diet Coke and asked for the bar menu. It turned out the restaurant was fully booked but they could order small meals at the table.

She was studying the selection, looking for something that wasn't too filling but sociable. She wondered if they'd reached an intimacy that would accommodate a sharing platter or if that would be too presumptuous.

'Nothing for me, I'm on a diet.'

Bernie was stood there again, his shadow blocking out the overhead light. She looked up at him, initially miffed at his reappearance uninvited, but his kind eyes and rosy cheeks stopped annoyance in its tracks.

'Oh, hi Bernie, I was just wondering if we should eat?' She put the menu back on the table. 'That is, if Danny hasn't got stuck down the toilet.'

Bernie gave a rumbling laugh. 'It's OK, love, he's still in the loo but told me to tell you he'd be out in a minute—he's just with someone on the phone.'

Molly instantly relaxed. Things were back on track. He'd obviously sent the picture of the ring to his friend and they were chatting about it. She knew that authenticity was not something that could be explained in a sentence. In fact, she'd been on a few courses where she'd sat through PowerPoint presentations and corporate videos explaining in tedious detail how to spot fakes and forgeries.

'I'll try not to bother you both again,' Bernie smiled and left her, walking straight to the end of the bar.

She watched him lean over and ask for something.

The guy he was talking to became quite animated and then disappeared. She saw him looking over at her with his usual smile and she felt bad for spying on him, so picked up the menu to hide her face.

The door banged open, bringing in another flurry of snow as a gang of elves filled the entrance.

They'd really gone to town on the costumes and were frantically looking for a large enough table to accommodate them all.

Bernie breezed past them, holding a yellow sign in one hand and what looked like a long stick in the other, saying hello to a couple of elves he knew on his way.

There was a small cheer as he said something to one of them before disappearing in the direction of the gents.

'Mind if I take this chair?' one of the elves asked. He had an impossibly deep voice at odds with his green tights and floppy hat.

'Of course,' Molly said, stifling a laugh. He nodded his thanks and dragged it across, joining his friends who'd managed to push a collection of recently vacated tables together.

On the Christmassy night there was now definitely no room at the inn.

Danny heard the door and then a bang on the cubicle.

'Let me in, mate,' Bernie said, 'as long as you're decent.'

'Of course I am,' Danny replied, unlocking the door. 'I'm hardly going to actually use the facilities at a time like this.'

'Thank God,' Bernie chuckled. 'Come on, out you come, leave this to me, Romeo.'

'What if someone comes in?' Danny said, squeezing past Bernie and standing back.

'I've put a sign outside saying the toilet's closed for cleaning.'

He took off his jacket, passing it back to Danny, and inserted the plunger down the toilet.

'You're a lifesaver,' Danny said, watching his huge back bend over.

'Don't thank me yet,' his voice echoed as the words disappeared down the pan. 'I can't believe you'd drop your engagement ring down the loo like that. I didn't even know you were serious about this girl, I've never seen you with her before.'

'Well, there's lots you don't know about me,' Danny said, hating himself for the lie—but if that's what it took to get the ring back, so be it.

'That's not fair, you know everything about me… ahhh,' he stopped suddenly and let out a breath. 'There's gold in them there hills,' he said, turning round and dropping the ring from the plunger into his pudgy palm, 'or should I say in them there toilets.'

'Oh, mate, thanks,' Danny said, taking the ring and a swathe of tissue paper from Bernie.

'My pleasure, mate, now you're free to propose,' he said, flushing the loo and taking his jacket back from Danny.

'Yeah, about that—please don't say anything to Molly. I don't think tonight's the night, I'm too on edge now.'

'Mum's the word.' Bernie tapped the side of his nose and disappeared through the door as quickly as he'd arrived, followed by a gang of elves who'd been waiting impatiently outside.

Danny went back in the cubicle and switched the newly salvaged original with the forgery in the box before flushing the loo again for effect.

'Sorry,' he said to an impatient elf who was hopping from one foot to another waiting outside, 'it was a bit of an emergency.'

Back at the table Danny could see the relief on Molly's face as he approached.

He realised he must have been gone a while as the bar was now packed and he had to manoeuvre round tables that were dragged across with extra chairs perched on the end of them.

He sat down and took a grateful gulp of the Diet Coke he'd left before starting on the second one Molly must have bought.

'I'm sorry it took so long,' he said, settling down at the table.

'Must have been hard work—you've still got your sleeves rolled up.'

Danny looked at his shirt and gave a nervous laugh, rolling them down. He hoped she'd never find out where his hands had been that evening.

'What did your friend say?' she whispered.

Danny reached into his pocket and he almost gave her the fake, which was now wrapped in tissue, rather than the original he'd put in the box.

He grimaced, thinking of the hoops he'd already jumped through for the swap, and to give her the forgery back again would be ironic, to say the least.

He handed her the box.

'He reckons it's genuine enough,' Danny said, avoiding eye contact, 'although you have to hold it in the correct light to get its full impact—otherwise it can appear quite dull.'

'Oh, right,' she said, opening her bag and popping it back in. He was glad she hadn't checked it—it could still have been a little wet after its adventures round the bend.

'It took you ages.'

'Yeah, sorry, I had to wait for my mate to call back after I sent the photo. Anyway, are we eating?' He desperately wanted to finish with the lying and get back to where they were.

He had the forgery in his pocket and the note he was going to leave for the blackmailers. The racecourse was only across the bridge and down the hill a bit. All he had to do was make his pre-prepared excuse, do the drop and come back.

'I wondered if you fancy sharing a platter. I like all of these but nothing with fish,' Molly said, handing him the menu.

'I'll go a sharer without anything fishy if you want?' Danny replied, while taking a surreptitious glance at the clock over the bar. It was almost 9:30.

'Can I ask you a favour?' he said. This was the moment he'd been dreading. He just needed half an hour—just a couple more white lies—and they could finish their date with a sharing platter.

'Sure,' Molly said. She seemed much more at ease now she had the ring back in her bag and Danny hadn't been the subject of some sinister toilet kidnap incident.

'I promised this mate of mine, who just took a look at the ring, I'd make sure his daughter gets a cab as she's a bit drunk. She's only in a pub over the bridge. I've ordered a taxi—I just need to pop out and make sure she gets in it.'

Molly's face fell.

He'd blown it. She hadn't been taken in by his deception and was obviously aware he was talking bollocks. The first time he'd been on a date with someone he'd felt an instant connection with, and he'd stumbled at the final hurdle.

But to Danny's relief the frown turned into a smile of sympathy. 'Oh, he must be so worried. Go on and sort her out and I'll order the food for when you get back.' Molly gave his hand a squeeze. 'You really can't stop yourself helping people, can you?'

'Thanks, Molly, I'll be back in a sec.'

Relief pulsed through Danny as he pulled his coat off the chair and made his way to the door. He couldn't look into her eyes as he was bright red with guilt and would have given away his true thoughts instantly.

He yanked open the door, pulled his collar up tight as the snow hit his hot face, and ventured into the night—hopefully putting an end to this nightmare so he could go back to a life he so desperately wanted to start.

Chapter 30

Sunday 17th December, 9:47pm

Andy had parked his bike at The Hive, a magnificent library just by the racecourse.

As he strolled past the giant windows, the lights were going out one by one. Silhouettes of people in lanyards wheeled the last of the book trolleys around and a scattering of cleaning staff emptied bins and drew blinds.

The world was closing, but his job was just beginning.

For a moment he wished he was one of the library staff, locking up with a clean conscience, returning to a happy home and a warm bed.

He'd been alone for a long time; the nature of his job meant unsociable hours and the necessity to lie low between assignments, working the door at 'the shop' as Mr C was fond of calling it.

It was the furthest thing from any high street retail outlet—appointment only and a staff so close you almost had to give blood and DNA samples every day.

He was front desk and occasional operations like this one. Mr C monitored progress from his office and the guys at the worktables practised their specialist art.

Andy could handle a gun and had learned the basics of surveillance from watching suggested spy films and YouTube videos. He'd read John le Carré and wished he could have lived in an era of dead letter boxes and honey traps.

So it was no surprise Mr C had chosen him for tonight's pick-up, even after the unfortunate incident at the hospital.

His foot began to throb again. The splint was a crude affair at best and he wouldn't be surprised if he ended up in a proper hospital soon. The pain was bad and the horse pills—or whatever they were—that the quack had given him when he got back to the shop after fleeing A&E were hardly taking the edge off.

Maybe he'd go back for another check-up, but get further out of the area next time.

There was no way he could go back to Worcester Royal Hospital anytime soon. He'd given a false name anyway, but after his assault on Charlie they'd no doubt have questions if he were to darken their doorstep again.

Back on the bike, he cruised through the snow until he found a spot under a bridge overlooking the entrance to the racecourse.

Pulling up to the kerb, he kept his helmet on, hopped off the bike and walked towards the cover of the bushes, squashing himself into the damp leaves.

He pulled out his binoculars from the pocket of his leather jacket, which was insulated but hardly kept out the cold. He kept having to wipe the snow from his visor.

It was ten to ten. He wondered if Charlie had already made the drop. He was tempted to look but decided to wait a little longer.

The last thing he wanted was for them to spot each other.

There was sudden movement and he pushed even further back into the darkness, blending in with the foliage.

A man was jogging past him, leaving tracks in the snow.

The figure was heading through the main gates into the racecourse entrance. This had to be Charlie, but he seemed taller and a lot more athletic. Maybe he'd sent someone else to do the drop-off?

According to Mr C, one of the other operatives had seen Charlie earlier, out with his kids sledging, so he couldn't be incapacitated. The right hook Andy delivered as he dashed out of the hospital had caused Charlie to fall to the floor, but he hadn't hung around long enough to see what damage had been done.

Pulling out the binoculars again, he focussed on the man. A security light had come on, illuminating the footpath and part of the racecourse grandstand in the background. As he looked up Andy recognised him as the guy who'd been chatting to Charlie at the café a couple of days ago, when he was following them disguised as a runner.

Stupid idea for a disguise. It was while he was pretending to run he'd fallen and twisted his leg.

He adjusted the focus to tighten up the image. It was the podcaster, Danny something-or-other. He tried to remember what his research had uncovered; he had notes on his phone which he'd look at later.

Watching him lean over the bin, he rooted in his pocket and placed something inside before looking around and jogging off again.

Mission accomplished.

Waiting until he ran past, Andy disentangled himself from the bush and hobbled his way to the racecourse entrance.

The cold had bitten into his leg, adding to the dull ache he always got when he didn't keep moving it. He'd tried gentle yoga exercises but was worried he was doing more harm than good when he felt something creak.

He passed under the shadow of the grandstand and once again the security light flicked into life.

They'd already established where the CCTV cameras were placed at the initial briefing Mr C had given. He just had to keep his helmeted head low and grab the package.

He crept to the bin with the yellow chalk mark (something else Andy had nicked from a spy novel) and, looking in all directions, plunged his hand in. Sure enough there was an envelope on the very top. He could feel the outline of the ring within, but the thinness of the package would no way contain ten thousand pounds in notes.

Bending down, he tried to delve a little deeper—maybe a larger package bursting with currency had slipped further into the bin.

His hands landed on something soft and he gave an involuntary retch. Even though he was wearing gloves the soft, squidgy substance was disgusting. He didn't want to know what it was, just stood back and contemplated what to do next.

He had the ring in the envelope. Maybe it was a cheque? There was no way he could do a thorough examination till he got some light; the yellow security beam was not adequate.

He scraped whatever the goo was from his glove against the side of the bin, pocketed the envelope and turned to leave.

The distant sound of a siren crept into his consciousness—could someone have called the police?

He straddled the bike and kicked the starter. It coughed but wouldn't take.

Trying again, this time a harder kick, he had to be careful he didn't end up breaking his good leg. At this rate he'd be spending an early retirement in a wheelchair. Better than a prison cell, he thought, as he kicked again.

This time the engine roared into action and he sped off, skidding slightly on the ice.

Just as he turned onto the road and back over the river bridge, the police car he'd heard went zooming past him in the direction he'd just come.

He was out of Worcester city centre in a matter of minutes and headed for the M5 motorway.

Chapter 31

Sunday 17th December, 9:59pm

It had been so cold when he'd set out from the bar, leaving Molly in the warm glow of festivities. Now he was running, sweat was trickling down his back.

There were one or two brave revellers still out, but the snow was getting heavier and if you lived somewhere rural you'd probably be best to get a taxi home before you were stuck in the city for the night.

He knew Molly lived close by and hopefully cabs would still get him back to his house in Warndon.

He just had to get this drop-off done.

Almost slipping on the steps leading up to the crossing, he caught himself just in time.

He ran over the Sabrina Bridge and caught a glance of the river glistening in the moonlight, a picture-perfect image that people always stopped to snap, no matter how local they were.

He didn't have time for sightseeing right now. He jogged quickly but carefully, taking shorter steps but more of them per minute. That way a fall would be less likely if he hit an invisible sheet of ice.

He reached the racecourse entrance and slowed his jog, aware that if there was anybody lingering around at this time of night he'd arouse more suspicion running than just being another guy enjoying the snow.

He tentatively approached the litter bin and looked around. He had the sense that he was being watched, but the night played tricks on you at the best of times, particularly when you were involved in criminal activity.

He couldn't see much past the mist and snow but spotted the yellow chalk mark, so as instructed he dropped the envelope in the bin and turned around, once again fighting the urge to run as fast as his legs would carry him.

He'd only been gone fifteen minutes. Molly would have ordered the sharing platter; maybe it would arrive just as he did. Back through those doors into the warmth. He'd be less distracted when he got back.

As he walked he began to reassure himself.

Sure, there had to be some ramifications after the blackmailers discovered what was in the envelope, but he and Charlie could deal with those if and when they happened.

Molly had the ring safely back in her bag. They had nothing to blackmail him with now. Hopefully they'd call it quits and leave them alone, look for another victim.

Danny crossed the bridge directly facing the BBC building. It was a large white structure already blending in with the snow.

He'd just got to the other side when a siren wailed in the distance and was getting closer by the second.

Just as he turned onto the footpath by the river a squad car pulled up beside him.

The blue lights reflected onto the snow like an Icelandic dance party.

Danny stopped and automatically checked his pockets. Thank God he'd already done the drop-off.

Then he thought maybe the police had found the ring and the note in the litter bin before the blackmailer got to it. How would he explain that to curious coppers?

One thing at a time, like one day at a time. He said the serenity prayer to himself before he walked in what he hoped was a confident, if unsteady, strut to the police car.

An officer got out, gave a theatrical blow on his hands before rubbing them together.

'Good evening, officer. Can I help you with something?' Danny said, hating how the words sounded. He always poshed up whenever he was addressing the law.

'Can I ask what you're doing out here in this weather?' the cop asked.

The driver's door opened and another officer stepped into the cold night. Pulling her hat into place she made her way towards them, obviously assuming back-up was needed if this got ugly.

'Just on my way to meet someone.'

'Oh yes, and where's that exactly?' cop one asked, folding his arms.

'Just at Hickory's in the park.' Danny pointed in the general direction.

It was the other cop's turn to speak. 'Only we've had reports of someone hanging around looking suspicious,' she said. Her voice was lower than he'd expected. It was disconcerting but not exactly threatening.

'Well I haven't seen anyone,' Danny said.

The cops glanced at each other like they held information he was not party to.

'Why were you at the racecourse right now?' cop one asked again, this time taking a couple of steps closer. Danny noticed he had a seventies-style moustache and wondered if it was a rollover from the Movember challenge his mates at Barbertown were always trying to rope him into.

'Just getting a look at the snow,' Danny said.

Both cops looked at each other again, reaching some kind of silent agreement.

'I wonder if you'd mind coming back to the station for a few questions?' cop one said.

Danny tried to gauge what would happen if he flatly refused. Would they still be able to detain him? He hadn't done anything wrong, but then again he had…

'Could I call the girl I'm meeting?' Danny asked.

'Of course,' the woman said, making her way back to the squad car and opening the back door for him. 'Do it from in here if you like, it's a lot warmer.'

Danny felt himself guided by the moustache cop towards the car and felt a hand on the top of his head. A practised manoeuvre for anyone who'd been arrested and put in the rear of a vehicle. It brought back sinister memories. This wasn't his first time.

He found Molly's number and dialled, formulating a plan as the ringtone started.

She picked up almost immediately.

'Hey Danny, everything OK?' He could hear the sound of happiness in the background and wanted to be there so badly. Once again he'd have to lie to her, and he wondered whether the fates were just not letting them align.

He knew how he felt about Molly already and he couldn't believe they weren't meant to be.

The car had started and he could hear the two cops in animated conversation in the front. He didn't think he was being overheard.

'I'm so sorry but my friend's daughter has got in a bit of trouble, so I've got to sort it out with the police.'

'The police?' Molly gasped. 'Do you want me to help? I could meet you.'

'No,' Danny barked louder than he'd intended. Cop one's head turned round, then he continued his conversation.

'Sorry,' Danny blustered. 'I mean I don't think it would be wise, she's embarrassed enough.'

'How long do you think you'll be?' Molly asked. 'The sharing platter's getting cold.'

They'd already arrived at Castle Street. The police station entrance loomed through his window, the blue light swinging ominously from the doorway.

'Look, I don't know…' His tone was harsher than he'd intended.

'It's OK, Danny, I'll just walk home. The weather's getting pretty bad anyway.'

His door had opened and he was being led out again.

'No, please Molly, it might only take—'

But she'd disconnected, and Danny felt his heart break a little.

He was escorted through reception where a bored-looking officer sat behind a glass partition, leaning over what appeared to be a crossword puzzle.

There was a short exchange between them but he barely looked up. Business was obviously slow tonight.

'Sorry, have we messed up your date?' cop two asked, swiping a card into the reader. She didn't sound like she was bothered one way or another.

Danny didn't reply, just gave a faint smile as he followed cop one down a deserted corridor.

They passed a couple of rooms where a scattering of people were talking. There was a squawk of radios and an occasional laugh. Danny reckoned you had to have a sense of humour working the late shift in a city centre police station on a Sunday night.

They arrived at a door with INTERVIEW ROOM 3 in white letters.

He was led in and told to take a seat. He did. It was deliberately uncomfortable and reminded him of school exams.

Girl cop sat to the left, moustache cop to the right.

Danny wondered if he was about to be read his rights. His brain was burning with what-ifs and whys, but he let it play out, remembering to breathe as he shrugged out of his coat and hooked it over the back of the metal chair.

'So, Danny?' moustache cop said, and waited for a response.

'How do you know my name?' Danny asked. He couldn't recall having said who he was when he was picked up.

The girl gave a gotcha smile and said, 'Danny Wade? We have you on our criminal database. Your image from the CCTV at the racecourse was an instant hit.'

She made it sound like a compliment, like he'd just reached number one in the charts.

'I'm not a criminal,' Danny shouted, the words coming out automatically. He suddenly realised he should have called a lawyer before speaking to these two.

'Well that's not strictly true, is it?' moustache said.

Danny sat back and sighed.

They were right, and it was coming back to bite him again after all these years.

Chapter 32

Sunday 17th December, 10:49pm

Andy stopped at Hopwood Park Services and found a Starbucks.

The pain in his leg was unbearable and, although he needed to report back to Mr C and update him on the pick-up, he had to open the envelope first.

He wondered if he'd overreacted at the sound of the siren. Maybe they weren't headed for the racecourse at all. Perhaps there had been some disturbance nearby — it was nearly Christmas after all, perhaps some domestic incident. He just couldn't have taken the risk of being stopped.

Reassuring himself for the tenth time that he hadn't left behind any trace, he ordered an Americano and slid into a booth overlooking the coach park.

The snowflakes were getting thicker now and he wondered if these giant beasts of the road would be going anywhere tonight, or remain parked up like sulking dinosaurs waiting for the thaw to set in.

The table was a little sticky, so he ran a napkin over it before opening the envelope, clearing the way for the mighty gem he was about to unwrap.

He pulled out the ring and held it up to the light.

It only took him a matter of seconds to know what it was. He'd been the one who had given it to Charlie when he returned to the shop to pick it up after the forgery was complete.

There was no doubt the forger had done a good job — he always did — but there was no denying this was not the original.

'Harry?' a voice shouted across the room.

He didn't hear anything at first. The anger he felt was making his senses hum. It took a few more calls for him to realise the barista was shouting the alias he always used. Harry — after the Harry Bosch TV series. He loved the tough-guy cop and the Los Angeles locations. When he'd made enough money, he'd visit; who knows, maybe get a visa and do some detective work himself.

'Harry?' The voice of the young girl in the apron was getting more irritated.

'Coming,' he said, sliding out of the booth to the counter.

The ring lay on the table where he'd dropped it. It wasn't as if it was really worth much anyway. If someone decided to steal it while his back was turned, let them have it. In a way, he hoped they would — get the thing out of his life.

He thanked the girl behind the counter, who gave him a weary smile, threw in a couple of sachets of sugar, stirred with a wooden stick and slumped back to his table.

He took a deep drink which scalded the roof of his mouth. He didn't care. He was tired and worried. What was he going to tell Mr C when he called?

Then he remembered the envelope.

He peeled back the edge and felt a slip of paper. He hoped it was at least a cheque. Maybe the boss would be happy with a chunky amount of money that covered the ring and the ten grand they'd insisted on. Even if it wasn't in cash, it would be a start.

It wasn't a cheque he pulled out but a handwritten note.

He read it several times and couldn't believe what he was seeing.

This guy had just written a death warrant.

This was supposed to be an easy assignment for a quick stash of cash, like most of the previous stings he'd been involved with.

Charlie had come into the Birmingham shop with a picture of a ring, they'd done the forgery, followed him home and to the jeweller's a couple of weeks later, wondering if he'd actually go through with it. When he did, they played the blackmail scam the way they always had.

In the past everyone paid.

They had done the research, found out about his family — a poorly wife, two young kids — the perfect target.

And now he was looking at a note that derailed everything and would mean he'd be ordered to do something he took no pleasure in.

There was no way Mr C was going to take this lying down.

He read it one more time, absorbing every word.

Dear Blackmailers,

Please find the ring you forged inside this envelope.

By returning this, there is no more business to be done. Call it a refund on a product we are not happy with and you can keep the three thousand pounds we paid as a token of goodwill.

However, as far as ten thousand pounds in cash is concerned, we don't have it, and even if we did there's no way we'd give it to you to fund more of your blackmailing schemes.

We will not pursue this harassment any further if you agree to leave the Burrows family alone.

Any more threats and we go straight to the cops.

Take the ring and disappear from our lives.

It wasn't signed, but it didn't need to be. He knew exactly who had written this note, and it sure as hell wasn't mild-mannered Charlie Burrows.

This had to be the work of the podcast guy.

He checked the jotting he'd made on his phone: DANNY WADE – PODCASTER – DELIVERY GUY.

Combing through the note again, he noticed the term 'we' was used all the way through. It was obvious Danny had written this for Charlie.

Didn't he realise who he was dealing with?

It was much quieter now and Andy began to worry he was becoming too exposed in a coffee bar on his own. Only a scattering of weary travellers remained, roaming the shops zombie-like — even the ones that were shuttered for the night. Comatose commuters, seemingly shocked to be here. Many, he guessed, would have been caught out by the snow.

He wanted to stretch his legs too, but the pain was screaming through a bullhorn at him. He reached into his bag, pulled out a blister pack and popped a couple of painkillers, washing them down with the cold coffee.

He contemplated another drink and looked over at the bored barista, who was leaning against the counter, swiping her phone — no doubt lost in a TikTok world where her friends were posting videos of clubbing while she was stuck here scraping a living.

He admired young people who had a work ethic. He'd been the same from a young age: paper rounds as soon as he could ride a bike and then 'errands' for a local guy who lived in a big house just off the estate.

It had a swimming pool which was only the size of a large bath, but was still very exciting to an impressionable sixteen-year-old.

He'd been working for that same guy, known only as Mr C, on and off ever since. One scheme after another. The jewellery scams had been the most successful — until now.

He knew by ordering a coffee he was just procrastinating, so he picked up his phone, hit the contact known only as 'shop' and cleared his throat, ready for the verbal onslaught.

'Well?' One word. A deep voice he instantly recognised, belonging to a man who didn't do pleasantries.

He'd hoped that Mr C would be asleep and one of his crew would be on phone duty. But to get through to the main man reminded him again of what a priority this job was.

'We have a problem,' he began, and then explained in hushed tones what had happened.

He was only halfway through the story when he was stopped mid-flow.

'No more chit-chat on the phone. You know what to do. It's the option two.'

The line went dead.

Andy's phone was so sweaty it almost slipped out of his hand. He knew what option two was — he'd done it before and it wasn't pleasant.

His leg screamed in protest, imagining the effort he'd have to go to now. He could bike it along the motorway and go home, sort things out after a rest, but they'd want him to put things in motion by sun-up.

He needed somewhere private and close by.

Looking online, he found a Travelodge and booked himself in.

He was surprised there were any vacancies, but the last-minute enquiry had paid dividends.

He got unsteadily to his feet and walked past the barista, who still hadn't taken her eyes off the screen.

Good thing too, he thought. No witnesses were best.

He bought some deodorant, a travel toothbrush and paste. He'd have to live in the same clothes two days running.

The cold in the car park bit at him like a rabid dog. The painkillers had kicked in but only just, as he straddled the bike, giving a few kicks on the foot peg before it reluctantly spluttered to life.

Option two was now in motion.

Chapter 33

Sunday 17th December, 11:02pm

The snow was stinging her face but she hardly noticed.

Molly had left the bar with the sharing platter untouched; she couldn't have eaten even if she'd wanted to.

A hovering waitress was obviously eager for her to go anyway. It was closing time and she'd foolishly hung on to the table just in case Danny returned.

Now she felt like a fool.

It was obvious that Danny was lying to her. Whatever he was doing felt wrong.

Even if he was helping a friend's daughter, why was he so adamant she couldn't go and meet him?

He was hiding something, and that didn't bode well for a future relationship.

The romance car had stalled before they'd even pulled out of the showroom.

Her mind went to a different outcome: them having dinner together, maybe a stroll arm in arm through the park afterwards, snow falling gently on their heads as they kissed goodnight and made further plans to meet.

As if to ridicule her, a couple were locked in an embrace as she walked across the river bridge, clinging onto each other, jaws locked, not pausing for breath.

The girl caught sight of Molly staring and broke free.

'Take a picture, love, it lasts longer,' she said, before getting back to business, grabbing hold of her partner's head and pulling it back towards her.

Molly rushed past and almost fell, skidding on the ice.

She'd reached the other side of the bridge and noticed the sign for the police station. She had a moment of inspiration — a last chance before she tried to forget all about Danny Wade.

Molly tapped on the glass and the officer looked up as if surprised to see someone in the police station reception area at this time on a Sunday night.

She, on the other hand, was amazed to be the only person here. On the lead-up to Christmas at gone eleven, she'd expected drunks fighting and couples arguing.

'Can I help you?' he said, and gave her a smile that reminded Molly of Gemma's dad — and it wasn't just the uniform. He had the same manner, calm but with an air of authority. The kind of bloke you'd want around in an apocalypse.

'Do you have a Danny Wade here at all? He came about...' She stopped herself before she said any more. She didn't want to get the girl he'd said he'd been helping into more trouble by blabbing.

'Came about...?' The policeman wound a pen between his fingers in a circular motion.

'Well, I'm not sure actually. I just wanted to know if he was here?'

She had turned bright red and began to regret walking through the door.

He was about to reply when the reception door burst open and a youth fell onto the floor, followed by a screaming girl.

Molly could see blood on the boy's cheek and it reminded her of the punch she'd given the guy on her way to work yesterday.

She really wanted to leave.

'You gotta help,' the girl screamed at the policeman. 'Luke's had his phone nicked and someone's hit him with a bottle.'

Molly wasn't sure if these were separate events and wished she wasn't around to witness it.

'Hang on a sec, calm down.'

Suddenly the door behind the reception opened and a couple of burly-looking blokes in short-sleeved shirts and smart trousers entered the room from the office.

They took one arm of the guy each, their lanyards swinging, while they got him sorted on a bench that ran along the wall.

While the men attended the guy and his hysterical girlfriend, the calm officer behind the glass waved a beckoning finger at Molly.

She walked back over and he moved closer to the partition so he could be heard over the yelling.

'Danny's with a couple of officers at the moment. If you take a seat, I'll see when he'll be out. It could be a while.'

He smiled again and Molly smiled back.

'Thank you,' she said, and took the bench opposite the newly arrived floor show.

She reached for a Worcestershire Life magazine and pretended to read while the story of the bottle and the phone was played out in the reception.

Molly glanced up at the clock; it had gone midnight.

The crying girl and wounded youth had been taken through to the office and now she was on her own again.

She'd read the whole of the magazine but hardly taken in a word.

Glancing at her phone, she saw a text from Gemma:

Hey Mol, just checking in, how did it go???

If I don't hear back I'll know it's going very well!!!!

Xxxx

'Do you want a cup of tea, love?' the officer said from his booth.

She hadn't seen him move from there and wondered what he looked like standing up. She reckoned he'd be tall with thin legs, just like Gemma's dad.

She was about to politely refuse when the door buzzed open and Danny appeared.

He looked pale in the sterile environment; the last time she'd seen him was in the glow of candles and flashing fairy lights.

The officers must have told him she was waiting, as he looked ashamed rather than surprised.

They didn't say anything, just turned back, buzzed the door and disappeared.

'Hi Molly, you didn't have to wait.'

'How's the girl?' she asked.

He looked lost and then something seemed to ignite him.

'Oh, it's all OK. Can we get out of here?'

She found herself waving at the officer behind the glass, and he waved back. She bet he didn't do that every day. Now she'd never find out how tall he was.

Outside the snow was even thicker. It had stopped falling but the accumulation was now a good inch on the pavement.

They walked silently up Castle Street, both of them hardly knowing where to start.

'My taxi's this way, if they're still running,' Danny said, pointing right.

'Well, my house is that way,' Molly said, signalling the road ahead. 'Let's call a cab from my place, shall we?'

Molly opened the front door and, although it was a little warmer than outside, there wasn't a great deal of difference.

Any hope that the heating would have magically fixed itself was dashed.

'Sorry it's so cold,' Molly said as she led Danny through to the living room.

It felt odd having him here.

She couldn't pretend she hadn't thought about bringing him home as she was getting ready for the date. The room was tidier than it had been in months. She'd even pulled out the Dyson from the cupboard under the stairs. Her father had bought it for her as a moving-in present and she'd probably only ever turned it on a couple of times. She'd given the carpet a good going over. It had crackled and spat so much at whatever was ingrained in the fibres she'd be surprised if it ever worked again.

'It's not that chilly,' Danny lied. 'Where's your thermostat?'

'On the wall over there,' she pointed. 'Fancy a nightcap?'

'Just a coffee would be great.'

Molly cursed herself for forgetting he didn't drink. So much had happened in the past couple of days, she was frazzled.

'That should do it,' Danny said, and Molly heard the thwump of a pilot light being ignited in the boiler over the sink.

'You're a magician,' Molly yelled over the boiling kettle.

'The wheel was just stuck, I only loosened it,' Danny replied.

She returned to the room holding two cups to see Danny looking through his phone.

'Any good cab companies you could recommend?' he asked while scrolling.

'Never mind that, I think we need to talk,' Molly said, setting the cups down and sitting next to him on the sofa.

'Yeah, I think I owe you an apology,' he said, looking up from his phone screen and plunging it back in his pocket.

It suddenly felt strange to hear Danny's voice in her home. She'd only been listening to him on her speakers in the bedroom above their heads a few hours ago, and now here he was in the flesh.

Molly cleared her throat before speaking. 'I don't think you're being straight with me and I'd like to know the truth. I've heard your podcasts and I know you're a good guy, but what was tonight all about? Why did you really want the ring? What did the police want with you? Was there really a girl in trouble you had to rescue?'

All the questions tumbled out of Molly like the coins in a jackpot win.

Danny waited a beat. He managed to buy some valuable seconds by taking a sip of his coffee and deciding how much he should tell her.

He knew he'd have to stay silent about his true intentions with the ring. It was back in her bag and tomorrow it would be on display in the shop again. But what about his trip out to drop the forgery and the police station?

Weighing the pros and cons, he realised that to tell her about any of this would put her in danger too.

He recalled something he'd read about confessing to one lie but continuing another.

'There was no girl I had to rescue,' he said at last.

He glanced at Molly's reaction and she looked close to tears — no one liked being lied to.

'Where did you go when you left me at the bar then?' she said, her voice sounding strained.

'I was getting a bit nervous. I'm not used to the dating game.' He couldn't give Molly eye contact now, so he kept his gaze to the floor.

'I went for a quick walk to get some air and then the police saw me and thought I was up to no good. There'd been some disturbances and they assumed I was involved.'

'Why?' Molly asked, her voice almost pleading. 'Why you?'

'Because…' He paused, getting a breath. 'Because I've got a criminal record, Molly. That's why.'

Chapter 34

Sunday 17th December, 11:52pm

The hotel room was standard but surprisingly spacious; it even had an extra bed snuggled into the far side of the room.

Andy sat on it and winced in pain as he took off his boots and fell backwards, letting gravity do its job.

There was little chance of sleep with his mind buzzing like a bandsaw, but he could at least get comfortable.

Emptying the contents of his bag onto the bed, he stripped down to boxers and shirt, then flicked on the tiny kettle and fixed himself a tea with unbranded bags and three minuscule cartons of foul UHT milk.

Catching an unwelcome glimpse of himself in the mirror, he was shocked to see how frazzled he looked.

He felt as if his internal organs were crumbling too. Lack of sleep, too much caffeine and the dull thud of pain from his leg made his stomach broil.

Mr C. had declared they move on to Option 2, and that was not where he needed to be at midnight in a Travelodge.

He'd been sent some updated photos, which were end-to-end encrypted.

One of the team had tailed Charlie and his family and taken a few shots while they were playing in the snow.

The first three were of Charlie and his son dragging a sledge, then two more of a pretty girl who seemed to be posing for her own phone — this presumably was Charlie's daughter.

Next, he scrolled back to his own photos he'd taken when he'd followed Charlie and Danny to the café by the river, when he'd disguised himself as a runner and shortly after taken a tumble.

His leg shot out a piston of pain at the memory.

The photo showed Danny leaning close to Charlie, sharing something, oblivious to the fact they were both sealing their fate.

He'd done his best to snoop on the conversation, increasing the volume of his earbuds, pretending to listen to something when in reality recording the conversation.

He missed huge chunks of the dialogue thanks to the giant espresso machine emitting a hiss as loud as a steam train every couple of minutes, but there was no doubt that Danny was getting himself involved.

It only took a small amount of digging afterwards to discover they were old school friends.

When he contacted Mr C. after that breakfast meeting, he'd been told to keep tabs on them but make no contact.

How was he to know that he'd fall over a tree branch on his run back and end up in A&E at the very hospital where Charlie worked as a porter?

When he'd informed Mr C. about Charlie spotting him in the wheelchair and his scuffle to get away, the reply had been short, which was worse than an ear-bashing. Whatever punishment he would be doling out would wait until the end of the latest job. Andy intended to be long gone before he suffered the consequences.

The software installed on his iPhone was completely untraceable, made by a tech geek who'd been working for his boss longer than he had. He'd never met the guy but had received various coded messages about software updates over the years.

It had been known for some of Mr C.'s crew to send a message without updating the software when prompted; on one occasion someone even used their own personal phone. This made it much easier for the police to trace the source if there was any comeback from a job.

Not that the law were ever involved — there was always too much at stake for any of their victims to take the chance of reporting them.

Activating the app that jams all contact information at the other end, he carefully composed a message to Charlie, then hit send.

Throwing his phone on the bed, he padded to the window and slid the heavy curtain to one side.

His view was of the car park, where vehicles covered in snow looked like giant cotton buds.

He showered and pulled back the thick white sheets, falling asleep in seconds.

His disturbed dreams that night were nowhere near the nightmare that was to come.

Chapter 35

Monday 18th December, 12:07am

'What do you mean you've got a criminal record?'

Molly was holding his hand but she couldn't remember when she'd grabbed it. It seemed wrong to let go now and she didn't think Danny had even registered it. He seemed so far away.

'Did you call the police about a broken window?' he asked.

'Yeah, but I don't see what that has to do with anything?'

'The cops who interviewed me wanted to know how I knew you and if I had anything to do with throwing a brick through your window.'

'What?' Molly was stunned. How was this possible?

'They said they'd been doing some enquiries and my name came up from an anonymous source that I was seeing you.'

It didn't take long for Molly to link Stewart in all this. Any money she could gamble would be on a sure bet that he'd been talking to Gemma, who probably mentioned Danny, and he got jealous, wanting to pin him for something Stewart had done.

'And as I have a criminal record they were looking for me, and then I was spotted on CCTV, so they pulled me in.'

'Oh, this is ridiculous,' Molly said, clenching her fists. If Stewart crossed her path again she was going to the cops herself. The guy was a psycho, end of.

'It's not ridiculous, Molly, it happens quite often. Even when I'm helping people I meet for the podcast, the police are always suspicious if I ruffle any feathers.'

'You still haven't told me why you're a criminal,' Molly said. Now that they were spilling everything out, there seemed no need to stop. If she and Danny were to be together, she needed everything laid out.

'Are you sure you want to know?' Danny asked. He was looking at her now, his hazel eyes burning into her soul. He had to be sincere. What was the worst thing he could have done? It couldn't be that bad.

Could it?

'I really like you, Molly, and I don't want to mess this up before it's even started.'

'Then just be honest, that's all I ask.'

Danny looked at her bag, which was slung on a chair at the far end of the room.

He thought about the ring, back safely where it needed to be. Should he confess about Charlie's forgery? He didn't need to right now. She had the genuine one back safely; she might never know, never need to know. Safer that way.

But he had to tell her about what happened on that night, that terrible night when he hit his rock bottom, when his life would never be the same again.

Molly was looking at him so intently.

'OK, but once you've heard this there's no going back.'

'Please,' she said and squeezed his hand tight.

He cleared his throat, drew a breath and was about to begin when he felt his phone buzz.

Molly felt it too but didn't say anything, just waited to see what Danny would do.

He pulled out the phone from his pocket and saw Charlie's name. He'd have to talk to him, he wouldn't have rung if it wasn't an emergency.

'I'm sorry, I really have to take this, it's a friend of mine and he's quite vulnerable.'

'Sure,' Molly said, and grabbing the mugs she walked back into the kitchen and closed the door.

'Alright, Charlie?' Danny whispered, knowing all too well that it wasn't.

'No, not really. What happened at the drop-off, what have you done?'

Danny couldn't risk being overheard, so he grabbed his coat and opened the front door, flicking it off the latch so he wouldn't be locked out.

'Are you there?' Charlie asked. He sounded agitated, even angry.

'Yeah.' Danny shivered. The snow had stopped falling but it was well below freezing now.

'I did the swap,' he left out the part where he'd dropped it in the toilet, 'and I walked back,' he also chose to skip the fact he'd been questioned by the police. 'Why, what's up?'

'I thought you were giving them cash and the forgery back, I didn't know you'd be writing them a note.'

'They got back to you already?' Danny said.

'Of course they did.' Charlie was shouting now and Danny had to move the handset from his ear.

Everything sounded loud in the still of the night; a nearby cat fight was in progress, baby-like howls rebounding down the street.

'Where are you exactly?' Charlie asked. It sounded like he was walking, probably far away from Karen and the kids, who were hopefully sound asleep and oblivious to all this.

'I'm at a friend's house,' Danny said, and then realised how pathetic he sounded.

'Well, you better tell your friend that you're needed elsewhere. I've just had a terrifying message. You need to get to mine as soon as possible.'

'Look, Charlie, I'm not sure…' But his words hit dead air. Charlie had hung up and now there was only the soundtrack of feline ferocity in the Worcestershire air.

He shook his head and went back inside.

The warmth was so inviting, he'd obviously done a decent job fixing the heating.

Molly was sat back down on the sofa, cradling a fresh mug of tea.

He noticed she hadn't made one for him.

He sat down next to her and searched for the look they'd been sharing when they'd first sat down.

It wasn't there. Her head was down, fiddling with the mug as if she were moulding it into a new shape.

'I've ordered you a taxi,' she said without looking up.

'But we haven't finished talking.'

'I think there's been enough excitement for one night.'

He nodded and stood up again, feeling awkward in the tiny room, like he was taking up too much space.

He was trying to think of something else to say but the words would not come.

The thoughts of Charlie pacing up and down at home because of something he'd done were overpowering.

She must have dialled a cab the moment he'd walked out of the door to take the call, because there were a couple of horn beeps coming from outside only moments later.

They said goodbye but there was no hug, no promises, and Danny worried that there would be no more Molly either.

'Where to, mate?' the cabby asked.

Danny gave him Charlie's address.

'Might take a while, mate, roads are bloody treacherous,' the cabby explained, punching Charlie's postcode into his satnav.

'No worries,' Danny sighed, falling back into the leather seat. His head was a bundle of 'what ifs' again. How could everything have gone so wrong?

He really thought the note and return of the ring would be enough to finish this. It wasn't the first blackmail scam he'd dealt with, and he knew these people were invariably cowards. Any hint of it coming to bite them and they backed off immediately.

Glancing at his watch, he knew there wasn't going to be any sleep tonight.

He tried to plan what he was going to say to Charlie and said small thanks that he wasn't working today.

It was too difficult to think about Molly. They had got so close on the sofa, he was at the very point where he was going to share his story.

He distracted himself with thoughts of the podcast; he still hadn't finished the Christmas special and couldn't imagine doing so now this had all kicked off.

Then he thought of Ian and his Santa story. He owed it to him to finish editing and publish it.

As with all the experiences he'd collected so far, once they were out there for the world to hear, there was a sense of closure that they might not get anywhere else.

He shook his head; there was too much going on in there. He had to take it steady, he was in the danger zone when that 'stinking thinking' was coming back.

Closing his eyes, he tried breathing exercises and was a couple of minutes in when the driver announced their arrival.

He got out his phone to pay but the battery was dead.

The driver waited patiently. He always paid on his phone; his bank cards were at home.

'Sorry, I didn't check, are you an Uber?'

'No mate, private hire,' he said.

Danny exhaled. 'Sorry, could you give me a sec?'

He got out of the cab and his shoes crunched on the compacted snow.

Luckily Charlie was already standing at the door waiting for him. He must have been hovering by the window, apprehensive about waking the rest of the family.

'Have you got any cash?' Danny asked as soon as he got close enough.

'What, you want to pay them the ten thousand after all, do you?' Charlie asked. There was a childishness to the words but no smile on his face.

'No, I just need to pay the cab,' Danny said. If it wasn't three below zero he would probably have blushed.

Charlie said nothing, just disappeared back inside to get his wallet.

Standing on the doorstep of the Burrows' house on that cold December night, Danny had never felt more useless in his entire life.

He hoped things would get better. They couldn't be any worse.

Chapter 36

Monday 18th December, 1:03am

Charlie had paid the taxi and led an apologising Danny into the lounge, closing the door quietly behind him so he didn't wake Karen and the kids.

He didn't offer him anything to drink, just sat down and whispered his way through the evening, starting when the guy had threatened him while they were out sledging, followed by his fall.

'So I try to put it to the back of my mind knowing you'd be doing the swap tonight and then I get this message.'

He pulled out his phone and handed it to Danny.

So that's how you want to play it?

Trying to blackmail the blackmailers.

We have the ring but you are still ten thousand pounds light and now there's a little interest to pay.

The total has doubled to twenty thousand to be delivered soon.

We will text with a new address and time.

In the meantime something will happen to show you our intentions.

Danny gave Charlie his phone and sat back on the sofa, rubbing his eyes and letting out a huge sigh.

That was when they both looked up, the sound of movement from upstairs, the slow steps down the stairs and then Karen's appearance in the doorway.

She was swamped in a pink towelling robe but somehow she dominated the room, her hands on hips, looking from one man to the other and waiting for either to speak.

Danny was shocked that she knew all about the ring forgery and the plan to swap it back.

'At least this Molly girl has got the ring back now,' she said, followed by, 'you boys need to make a plan to get these people off our back. If you can't, I'm going to call the police myself.'

'I don't think the police are the best move at the moment,' Danny said, then explained his night in the interview room, followed by his disastrous date.

To his surprise, Karen sat beside him and put a hand on his. She still felt bed-warm and there was something so calming about her presence he had to resist the urge to envelop her in a hug.

The message from the blackmailers had been sent while Karen was asleep and now she insisted on seeing it for herself.

'Are you sure you want to read it?' Charlie asked, but she didn't need to answer. The look was enough.

An hour later Danny was back in a cab again. He needed to get home and regroup, but the car was grinding to a halt. It could hardly be a tailback at three in the morning.

He leaned over to look out of the windscreen at the white haze.

'Looks like there's been a bash,' the driver said. 'Hardly surprising, people drive like twats in the snow.'

Danny let this drop of cabby wisdom land and fell back into the seat again, closing his eyes.

He could picture Charlie and Karen huddled together, talking it over and over until the kids got up. He'd be surprised if Charlie let them go out of the house even if the schools were open.

Danny still believed these were just idle threats, but then again this wasn't his family that was being targeted.

What if it was Olivia who'd been threatened? How would he feel if it was his sister at the centre of all this?

He'd managed to recharge his phone at Charlie's. He could just call the cops now, get them to keep an eye on the Burrows' house, but then they'd have to confess to the ring forgery—how else would they spin it?

There was no way they could involve the police, not yet anyway.

The stress and tiredness engulfed him and the next thing he knew the driver was shaking him by the shoulder.

His bed was beckoning, even if it was just for a few hours, but first he had one more call to make.

'Bernie, it's me.'

The big man yawned and said, 'Danny? Do you need another plunger?'

'Sorry, I've woken you.'

'Not really, I've only just got to bed so no harm, no foul. What can I do for you?'

'I really need to see you. Can you come round to mine when you've had a sleep?'

'Nah, sleep is for wimps.'

Bernie had put the phone down before Danny could insist.

Chapter 37

Bernie was wearing the same outfit Danny had seen him in at the bar.

It had seemed like a lifetime ago that they were sharing a toilet cubicle and rescuing a ring with a plunger, so much had happened since, but his smiling face as he stood on the doorstep gave Danny a flicker of hope he so badly needed.

They shook hands and Danny invited him in but Bernie didn't move.

'We need to walk,' he said, stretching his huge body in preparation, 'otherwise I'm gonna nod off on your sofa.'

'OK,' Danny said and disappeared inside to get his coat.

'Where to?' Danny asked, slamming the door behind him.

By way of an answer Bernie walked to his 4x4 and slid open the back door.

A huge dog bounded out and immediately began barking. It sounded loud in the deserted street; even the hardiest of dog walkers weren't rousing yet.

'Hope you don't mind but Tinkerbell needs some exercise.'

'Tinkerbell?' Danny laughed, looking at the dog who was the size of a small pony and probably weighed a little more.

'Yeah, my daughter named her,' Bernie laughed, hooking a chain lead around her thick neck while her head bounced up and down, 'I call her Tank, Tink the Tank.'

'What make is she?' Danny asked, putting out a trembling hand expecting her to bite. She gave him a drool-laden lick.

'You mean breed?' Bernie laughed. 'She's a Burmese Mountain Dog, aren't you, baby?'

Danny held back a laugh watching this big man talking child-speak to the huge dog. They really did belong in each other's worlds.

They walked silently for a while, Danny taking the opportunity to get fresh air into his lungs.

The dog was pulling hard on the lead, she seemed excited by the snow although now it was mostly sheet ice, so that even a man of Bernie's size had difficulty reining her in. She was letting out pants of desperation like a small steam train.

Once they'd reached the park Bernie unhooked the lead from the dog's collar and she sprang off to freedom, barking madly, racing towards the playground at the far end of the field.

Just as Danny was going to ask Bernie if he was concerned she might run away, she came bounding back as if checking in, and then ran off again.

'She needs plenty of exercise,' Bernie said as he reached down for a stick ready to throw on her imminent return.

'So what's up, mate?'

Danny shrugged for a second, wondering where to start.

'Is it trouble with the girl last night? Did you want to propose after all? I saw her running off after you left.'

'No, it's nothing to do with the girl.' Then he stopped and corrected himself. 'Well, it is but not directly.'

'It's like having a conversation with Tinkerbell, you're making no sense, mate.'

On hearing her name the dog raced back to them and jumped up when she caught a glimpse of what he had in his hand.

'Why don't you start from the beginning?' Bernie said, giving the stick a hearty throw.

Danny watched the dog disappear again and began his story.

By the time they were reaching the tenth stick throw he'd got the big man up to date.

'I think I might be able to help,' Bernie said, after he'd mentally digested the barrage of information Danny had just fired at him. 'I need to make some calls.' His voice sounded serious, all business, like the first time they'd met in very different circumstances.

Even when they were recording the podcast together the amiable, sensitive man always shone through, but there was an edge to him that lay dormant until prodded, like a wasp's nest buried deep down.

Maybe it was his size that caught people unawares, expecting him to be more abrasive or abrupt. Instead, the man Danny had come to know had reinvented himself into a quiet life and managed to keep his dogs of war at bay.

From what he'd talked about on the podcast his time in the military had taken more than a slice of him.

'What do you need to know?' Danny asked. Tinkerbell was nudging Bernie's leg with the stick that was protruding from her mouth, inviting him to play.

He pulled it free and pitched it as far as he could.

'I'll need to know where Charlie went to for the forgery. I have some mates in Birmingham who knock about the jewellery quarter.'

'OK,' Danny said, wondering why he hadn't asked Charlie these specific details before. Maybe in reality he didn't want to know, for fear of getting himself in too deep.

'And then I can have a chat with some boys who may be able to put some pressure on.'

Danny froze. He didn't like where this was going.

'Look, Bernie, I can't tell you how much I appreciate your help with this but I need to be careful. The police have got me on their radar and all I've been trying to do is get the ring back safe and get this gang, or whoever they are, to leave us alone.'

The dog was back and this time without a stick.

She flopped down by Bernie's feet panting, her mouth wide open and her tongue lolling out like a leathery stair carpet.

'I notice you used the word "us" rather than "they",' Bernie said, reaching down to fuss Tinkerbell's ears. 'And that should tell you all you need to know. By getting involved with this guy you've rattled cages that should have stayed undisturbed. You're in as much danger as his family is now. If you want my help I may have to cross a few lines. Are you sure you're happy with that?'

'What kind of lines?'

'I don't know yet but I'll do my best to get this sorted. You've helped me, I owe you that much.'

Danny thought for a while. How could he refuse this offer? He had gone as far as he could now and the choices he'd made by leaving the blackmailers a note rather than the cash demand could have just made things worse. But what other choice did he have? Neither of them had that kind of money anyway.

This really wasn't his world.

But it was Bernie's.

'Thank you, mate. Do what you have to but please don't put your own family at risk as well.'

'Don't worry,' he said, giving Danny a slap on the back which would have been more akin to the Heimlich manoeuvre, 'this isn't my first rodeo.'

The dog didn't resist Bernie putting her lead back on and they walked in silence back to Danny's house.

He could almost hear the big man's cognitive wheels spinning alongside the rasping breath of a well-exercised dog.

Bernie refused the offer of coffee and got straight back in his 4x4, the dog hopping into the back, obviously welcoming a snooze on the journey home.

They shook hands Bernie-style.

'Try not to worry. I'll get on this, but do be careful.'

'Yes sir,' Danny said, giving a mock salute.

Bernie didn't smile. 'I mean it, mate. Be aware of everywhere you go from now on, say the same to Charlie. Don't take any chances, try to lie low. When are you back at work?'

'Supposedly today,' he said, wearily glancing at his watch.

'Call in sick, stay home and I'll keep you updated. I may need you around to help me.'

'OK,' Danny replied uncertainly. It seemed this project was being taken out of his hands and he couldn't help feeling relieved.

'Tell Charlie the same.'

Danny nodded.

'Oh, and don't be tempted to give them any money. You were right about that. It's pure blackmail and now the ring's back they've got nothing on him anymore.'

'What about the threats?'

'That's all they are for now, just threats. As long as they think there's gonna be some cash they'll keep on, but they are not going to bite a hand that pays them. Not yet anyway.'

'Not yet?'

There was barking from the car.

'Look, I've got to go but please keep safe and I'll be in touch soon.'

With that he turned on his heel and bleeped open the car.

The dog's barking stopped instantly and was replaced by some kind of country and western music he must have been listening to on his way to Danny's house.

The car reversed off the drive like a knight in a shining 4x4, leaving the strains of Dolly Parton in its wake.

Chapter 38

Monday 18th December, 6:01am

Andy had set his watch alarm for 6am. In his line of work, sleep was a necessity. Even when it was only a couple of hours here and there, any chance to recharge had to be taken. When you got tired, you made mistakes, and there wasn't room for any errors now he'd reached option 2. It wasn't until his foot hit the floor that he realised how bad the pain had got. The comfort of a mattress, his leg upright with a little help from the painkillers, had managed to keep it at bay long enough for him to get enough rest.

He stumbled to the lift and took it to the ground floor for breakfast. The painkillers on an empty stomach were a bad combination, so he spent half an hour going back and forth to the buffet, helping himself to selections served in silver containers. Piles of scrambled eggs, bacon and sausages all did their magic. Washing it down with a dozen tumblers of fresh orange juice, he knew he'd fuelled up enough to see him through the day. A day where things got serious.

Back in his room, he showered and dressed. The same clothes as yesterday, but enough deodorant to knock out Tyson Fury. Taking another peek out of his window, the ground was still a blanket of white, but there were one or two black patches where cars had already left. This boded well that the motorway was running. He was heading back to Bromsgrove. This was no longer a solo job, so another two employees of Mr C's gang were meeting him at a location they'd pinned in a message half an hour ago. There wouldn't be much chit-chat. He'd only met these guys a couple of times before, and they were like so many of the team: large, quiet and efficient. He didn't have their names either, only initials B and G, or the Bee Gees as Mr C referred to them. Nobody knew Andy's name either; he was just known as A. That way, if anyone squealed, they had no idea who anyone was. They weren't the kind of firm who went for after-work drinks or formed a lunchtime jogging club. With A, B and G on the case, option 2 would go without a hitch. Hopefully, things would be sorted by the end of the day and Charlie and his friend Danny would realise just who they were playing with.

He didn't need to check out at the hotel reception and always kept his card key. Andy knew they could get data from used door cards; he wanted to leave as little evidence of his movements as possible. He'd parked his bike under the awning near the front, so mercifully the seat wasn't too cold. He pulled on his helmet. It took several kicks to get it started, and he promised himself to get the bike serviced once all this was over. He couldn't rely on his legs right now; the last thing he needed was to lose his wheels too.

There was a bridge just before Droitwich. The kind that people commuted over and under every day but never really noticed. A concrete construction that had a footpath running under it and layers of graffiti splattering the giant posts that held it up. That was where the location was pinned on his message, and as he approached, he saw two large men standing side by side like a pair of bookends. He pulled his bike up on the path, and they didn't move an inch. They had matching padded black bomber jackets, jeans and boots. They wore flat caps, Peaky Blinders style.

He hobbled off the bike and walked up to them. They huddled together, going over notes, B and G mostly grunting as Andy went through the plan while the traffic thundered from the bridge overhead and the road by their side. A couple of hardy joggers went gasping past, not even an arctic blast putting them off getting the miles in. B and G didn't say any more than they needed to. It had occurred to him that their use of the English language would be limited anyway. It was hard to tell where they were from, as so few exchanges had been made. Andy was under no illusions; it was always serious if these two were involved.

He hobbled to his bike, watching the two men disappear back up the embankment where he guessed they'd parked. He noticed a gun hanging from the belt of G — or was it B? He hoped he wouldn't be asked to use his any time soon.

Chapter 39

Monday 18th December, 6:45am

Danny took Bernie's advice to call in sick. He knew that they'd be miffed at the office about him missing deliveries at the busiest time of year, but with the lack of sleep it would be seriously dangerous being on the road. He could hardly focus on anything apart from sorting out Charlie's problem once and for all. He made an industrial-strength coffee and took the stairs to his room where he booted up the computer. Clicking on the podcast file, he dragged his cursor along the wave file to where he'd left off, just as the brawl between Richard and Santa had started.

'By the time the police arrived we were both on the floor of the school hall. I'd pushed Santa into a nativity display and we were wrestling on the top of crushed cardboard and artificial snow. There were traces of blood on the floor where we'd both made contact with our fists. It wasn't until two coppers dragged us apart that I saw a ring of horrified parents with their arms wrapped around terrified toddlers, looking at us with their mouths open. A few were pointing iPhones, capturing an event which would end up going viral on social media.

'I remember the ride in the back of the squad car; I'd never sobered up so quickly. The thought of brawling with Santa on the floor of the hall my daughter had her school lunch in was mortifying. While I was being processed at the police station, I had images of what was going on back at school: teachers clearing up the mess while parents gossiped and speculated about the drunk father and poor Father Christmas.

'They took my name, address, shoes, belt and dignity that night. I was led into a blue-lit drunk tank that smelled of bleach

and vomit. Lying down on the hard mattress, listening to a drunken rendition of some Oasis song coming from the next cell, I stared at the cracked ceiling and swore—like many prisoners before me, no doubt—that I'd never drink again.

'The very worst part was feeling that I'd never see my kid again, and even worse, that she would never want to see me.'

Danny pulled his headphones off, letting them fall round his neck, and let out a guttural sigh. There was still the resolution to add, but he was too fatigued to even look at the screen anymore. He hit save and rubbed his eyes. He hoped that Charlie Burrows' story would have the kind of resolution Richard and Santa's had.

A phone call a couple of hours later would smash that hope.

Chapter 40

Monday 18th December, 8:23am

The street was quiet enough. There were more cars around than they would have wanted, many people using the snow as an excuse to stay at home for the day. The most important part was that the schools were open. Andy arrived on the bike first, at the far end of the road, just near enough to the Burrows' house not to be seen, while B and G parked their car two streets down. They were in place, no need to move just yet. He sat on the bike, shivering. It hadn't gone much past freezing point all morning, and he was glad he'd at least boosted his system with a big breakfast. B and G had enough bulk between them to survive the Arctic naked for a week.

It was only twenty or so minutes until the Burrows' door opened. The kids were leaving for school. Charlie was following behind, something he hadn't done since primary school days. Usually the kids made their own way to the bus stop, but last night's message had hit home. They disappeared round the corner and Andy kick-started the bike to follow them. Meanwhile, B and G marched up to the Burrows' front door, heads down, hands in pockets. They knocked loudly and waited.

Andy followed Charlie and the kids to the bus stop at the bottom of the hill and stopped on the other side of the road, letting the bike engine idle, afraid that it would stall and not start again. The kids were hugging Charlie and the girl was saying something in his ear—probably reassuring him that she'd keep an eye on her little brother. He wondered how much Charlie had divulged to his kids about the threatening message he'd received. Watching him walk away, leaving them waiting in the ever-increasing queue of over-excited brats in matching uniforms, he took out his trusty binoculars and, making sure he had the perfect shot, took something out of his pocket.

Karen opened the door a few seconds after the knock, thinking it was Charlie who'd forgotten his key. To her surprise, it was two enormous men blocking the light and filling the doorway. They took an arm each and carried her back into the living room, shutting the door behind them with the back of a boot. By the time she'd realised what was happening it was too late to scream. A bolt of panic raced through her, making it impossible to let out a sound. She was placed into a chair and one of the men pulled out a roll of black gaffer tape from his pocket. One held her down while the other wrapped the tape round and round until she was secure. She found her voice and let out an anguished cry, but neither of the men responded. They just ripped off a small piece of tape and stretched it over her mouth. Taking a step back, they looked at her like handymen admiring their work after fixing a door. Then one of them pulled out a knife with a serrated edge and walked forward.

Charlie walked back up the hill, resisting the urge to retrace his steps and fetch the kids. After the message last night, why had he given in to them going to school? It was Maisie who'd convinced him, arguing that snow days were the best at school and she'd keep an eye on her brother. She'd insisted they'd be safe on a bus that took them straight to the gate. Charlie was no fool and knew the real reason was to see her boyfriend. Although she'd denied it, saying they were just friends, she'd spent many hours in her bedroom with the door firmly shut, FaceTiming a sixth former with a ridiculously deep voice. The compromise came when he'd insisted on walking them to the bus stop, but now he knew he wouldn't rest until they got home again. What with that and waiting for an update from Danny, he really couldn't take much more.

Charlie opened the front door, stamped his boots free of snow and took off his coat, hanging it on a hook. He was about to yell that he was back but remembered he'd been away for half an hour—Karen may have fallen back asleep. These naps were important and he didn't want to wake her. He walked into the living room and had to do a double take. His wife was strapped to the chair with masking tape, her arms bent backwards and her legs fixed in place. Her mouth was taped shut and she was still as a photograph.

He rushed towards her, pulling the strip off her mouth in one tug.

'Karen, Karen, oh my God, Karen, are you OK?'

She lolled forwards and drool spilled out of her mouth. Charlie put his ear to her lips and could trace faint breathing—she must have passed out. He held her face in his hands and relief flooded into him as their eyes met. Her pupils were watery and pleading, her voice came in rasps.

'Men came and… couldn't breathe… strapped me… had a knife.'

'It's OK,' Charlie lied, forcing back the tears he felt coming as sure as a tax bill. 'You're safe now. I'm just going to get some scissors so I can cut these off.'

He ran into the kitchen, pulled open the cutlery drawer with such force items flew out all over the floor. He swiped old utensils they hadn't used in years to one side. Where were the bloody scissors? He eventually found a pair of pitifully inadequate nail scissors and started to work away at the bonds. It took a few goes but he eventually freed his wife before lifting her gently from the chair onto the sofa and running back into the kitchen to get water. He put the glass close to her lips and she took a few sips before her breathing seemed to be getting back to normal.

'What happened?' Charlie asked eventually.

Karen told him about the knock on the door and the two big guys barging in and strapping her to the chair.

'Did they say anything?' he asked, as she took another sip and let her head fall back on the mountain of cushions he'd constructed for her.

She shook her head. 'No, they just grunted a lot and looked at me with their arms folded. Then one of them pulled a knife.'

'Oh Jesus.' Charlie grabbed his wife's hand—it was still clammy from the shock. 'Did they hurt you?'

She shook her head again. 'No, just waved the knife at me and…'

'And what, love?'

'And laughed,' she said. There was no fear in her voice now, only a brewing anger. She was taking control again, the way she had with everything challenging in her life, including the cancer.

'Did the kids get on the bus OK?' she asked, trying to get upright against the cushions.

'Yeah, they were fine, surrounded by other kids.'

Karen grabbed Charlie's arm. 'But you did stay with them till the bus came?' She squeezed tight. 'You did see them get on the bus, didn't you?'

Charlie's insides turned to jelly. 'No… Maisie told me to go because she was getting embarrassed in front of her mates with her dad standing there.'

'So you left them?'

Karen didn't wait for a response, jumping up from the sofa and grabbing her phone.

Chapter 41

Monday 18th December, 8:45am

The bus was bedlam.

It seemed the whole of Year Eight, Nine and Ten had squeezed on board. The excitement about the weather and the fact that they'd be later for lessons was too much for the wild kids.

Ties hung loose, skirts were hitched up way too high and bags were thrown around, while the driver kept shouting that if they didn't sit down he'd chuck them out in the snow and they'd have to walk to school.

It was a lame threat and everyone knew it.

Normally Maisie would want to be seated a long way from her little brother, or preferably on another bus. But today, after what her dad had said, she felt responsible for keeping him safe.

'Did you see that bloke on the motorbike?' Dylan asked, as someone's school shoe went whizzing past them.

'You mean the perv taking the photos?'

'Yeah — creepy or what?'

'We've got to watch out for strange people, that's what Dad says,' Maisie warned, while giving the finger to a Year Nine who was blowing her a kiss.

'What do you think Mum and Dad are so worried about?' Dylan asked.

'Oh, I don't know — it's probably got something to do with the cancer; it's all about the cancer these days.'

They were silent for a while, watching the show on board and the snow outside the window. Whenever they dared to talk about what their mum was going through it ended with silence; neither of them could think of anything to say. It was better to leave it unsaid — that way maybe it would go away of its own accord after a while.

Maisie's phone rang; a picture of her and Mum taken in the garden last spring appeared on the display. For one terrible moment she thought she'd bum-dialled her by mistake and she'd managed to hear what they were saying.

'Hey Mais — it's Mum.'

'I know, Mum, your name comes up when the phone rings.'

'Don't be a smart arse — are you OK?'

'Yes, Mum.'

'Is your brother OK?'

'Yes, Mum, we're on the bus to school. Dad dropped us at the stop, don't you remember?' Maisie started to worry that maybe her memory was going; since she'd started chemo she could forget things easily.

'I know that, I'm just making sure.'

Suddenly Maisie felt terrible. She didn't want to be unkind; she knew how serious her mother's illness was and the thought of her not being around to pester her like this was unthinkable.

She often wondered if that was why she was always short with her mother these days, as if she'd threatened her with leaving, even though the leaving would not be her mum's choice.

'Have a good day and keep an eye out.'

'What for, Mum?'

'Just anything unusual and don't talk to strangers.'

The age-old mantra made Maisie roll her eyes but she said pleasantly, 'Will do — love you,' before disconnecting.

'You didn't tell Mum about the perv taking the photos then?' Dylan asked without looking up from his phone screen.

'Are you kidding? She'd send the police to bring us home.'

'Maybe that's a great idea — I've got double maths.'

'Shut your face,' Maisie said, and ruffled his hair the way she knew he hated.

The brakes hissed as the bus rolled into a slot at the front of the school gates.

The children piled out like lemmings, marching into the playground swinging bags and pushing each other.

In the midst of the crowd were Maisie and Dylan.

She was tempted to hold his hand but there was no way he'd allow that to happen. He'd never live it down in the boys' locker room.

So she walked close enough for them to bump shoulders until they were well into the school building and parted to their respective classrooms.

As the bell went and the school day started half an hour later than scheduled, Maisie sat at her desk and breathed easy.

Up to this point she hadn't realised how on edge she was; now in the safety of a warm classroom behind locked entrance doors she felt untouchable.

For now.

Charlie had been making a cup of tea and working out what he was going to tell Danny about how he'd found Karen when his phone buzzed in his hand.

Face recognition opened the message straight away.

It had come from an unknown number but the image was as recognisable to Charlie as the inside of his own soul.

It was a photo taken at long range and then zoomed in on Maisie and Dylan.

They were close together, looking at something on Maisie's phone screen.

It wasn't the photo that disturbed him so much as the message typed underneath.

If we can get to your wife imagine what we can do to your kids!!!

Chapter 42

Monday 18th December, 8:50am

'Morning,' Graham almost sang, as Molly walked through the door, the bell tinkling in harmony at her entrance.

'Morning,' she sang back, amazed at this new Graham. What had happened to the old, slightly morose version? Maybe her little breakdown yesterday had landed hard on him and he didn't want to provoke another one.

'The kettle's on if you want a cuppa?' he said, then added, 'I tried to put the rings out in the display cabinet but I can't find the key for the safe.'

There was nothing accusatory about the statement but she still felt guilty and a little panicked.

She remembered putting all the other rings back in the safe last night, slipping the one Danny wanted to show his friend in her bag, but in her hurry she forgot to put the key back on the hook.

She looked in her bag and sure enough it was in there alongside the ring box.

'It's OK, I put it in my bag by mistake,' she tried a laugh and looked at Graham, searching for sympathy. She would be waiting a while.

Pretending to be nice to avoid any uncomfortable encounter was one thing but going against company rules was something else.

'I'm sorry, Molly, but that is completely unacceptable.' His voice turned stuffy and toneless, he was back in charge again. 'It is against protocol to take a key from this shop into the public. Suppose someone stole your bag?'

'It wouldn't matter, there's still the combination to punch in after you've turned the key,' Molly snapped, and immediately wished she hadn't.

She was tired of men telling her what she could and couldn't do, she was sick of men lying to her — overall she was sick of men.

'I'll have to report this for the record,' Graham said, before marching off to the back office to get his bumper book. It was the one he'd been using since the last leadership course he'd taken in Swindon, the one where he'd come back with a headful of motivational phrases and a fondness for wearing waistcoats.

This was her chance to put the ring back.

She drove the key into the safe lock and punched in the combination.

There was a loud beep.

It wouldn't budge.

She tried it again.

Another loud beep.

Still nothing.

She breathed hard, trying to clear her foggy brain. After only a couple of hours' sleep with a head full of Danny she wasn't exactly in the mindset of a master criminal. Graham would be back any second and the opportunity would be lost.

Slowly this time she punched in the number; to her relief the door swung open to reveal a tray of rings winking at her.

She'd just reached over for her bag when Graham appeared in the doorway, looking down at an open page in his book.

'See here?' he said, sashaying towards her and pushing the book under her nose. 'Page ten, section three. "It is forbidden for a member of staff to take the keys to any safe from the premises unless under strict orders and supervision from their line manager."'

He snapped the book shut.

'That's me,' he half-smiled.

Molly smiled back, which she hoped conveyed some kind of sincere apology, but then replaced it with a grimace.

Her bag was wide open and the ring box was visible.

He would only have to move a couple of inches to catch sight of the borrowed ring.

She took the initiative and walked right up to him, putting a hand on his shoulder; she could feel him tense like a finely tuned violin string.

'Look, I'm really sorry,' she said, deliberately giving him eye contact — anything to stop him looking in the direction of her bag.

'You saw what a state I was in yesterday,' she said. 'You were so kind — do you think you could be kind again?'

The violin strings eased and he shrugged slightly. 'Let's just say it won't happen again, shall we, and leave it at that.'

He snapped his book closed and turned on his heel, disappearing back into the office.

The moment he was out of sight she plucked the box from her bag, took out the ring and slipped it back into the slot it had come from, the box going back in the cupboard with the others.

She did all this while trying to calm her heart, which was hammering hard enough to break her ribs.

She picked up the tray and lifted it closer to her eyes.

Did the ring seem to have its sparkle back?

She thought of Danny taking it to the loo and calling his friend about it.

Maybe he'd given it a polish or something?

No — she was going crazy. And how pathetic she was, thinking about Danny again only a few minutes since she'd sworn she wouldn't give him another thought today.

But the ring did look different.

'Everything alright?'

Molly jumped and the tray fell from her grasp. The rings tinkled onto the glass-topped counter and a couple rolled to the floor.

They both squatted down at the same time to reach for the
escaping rings, only to bash heads.

The shop doorbell went before they'd caught breath.

She really should have stayed at home today.

Chapter 43

Monday 18th December, 9:50am

Andy met B and G back at the bridge and they exchanged notes.

The big men mostly grunted and showed the pictures of their handiwork. A terrified woman tied to a chair didn't need any explanation. This was just option two in full swing; it would never be pleasant.

As they rarely spoke, Andy was elected spokesperson to Mr C.

He dialled, put the phone on speaker and waited, listening to the traffic over his head and the heavy, guttural breathing of the men towering either side of him. It was like standing at the bottom of a well.

He could smell sweat and garlic and his stomach churned.

'Well?' Mr C snapped, his tone almost cracking the speaker. He wasn't one for audible foreplay.

'It's all rosy,' Andy replied — the code they'd agreed beforehand. It was a lot more discreet than 'we've frightened a sick woman and taken threatening pictures of a couple of kids'.

'Good,' he said. This was not a word that came out of his mouth often, but there did seem to be some kind of caveat in its delivery.

Andy waited, knowing better than to interrupt the main man until it was crystal clear that he'd finished.

He hadn't.

'I've been doing my own bit of research,' he said, and then, for effect, took a deep drink of something. It was probably one of the smoothies his wife made for him — disgusting green concoctions that he offered his team on the rare occasion they were all in the same room together.

'We're going straight to option three,' he said, before letting out a satisfied belch.

'But we haven't sent a location for the next drop yet — maybe they'll come up with the money this time?' Andy said hopefully. He really didn't fancy an option three.

He'd said all this in one breath, afraid that if he didn't get it all out he'd never have the nerve to say it again. He knew he'd said too much over the phone but needed to say it nevertheless.

The silence at the other end was as impactful as a punch in the face.

'My research,' Mr C continued as if Andy hadn't spoken, 'with this podcaster guy getting involved, I reckon there's going to be more pissing around — and we haven't got the time for pissing around, have we?'

'No,' Andy replied, and the men grunted something in the affirmative. The upturn of their mouths, the closest things to a smile they could offer, said that they were looking forward to a chance to play out option three.

'Take the rest of the day off and I'll send instructions tonight.'

B and G stood away from the phone, ready to jump back in the car and get on with whatever they did in real life, but Mr C hadn't finished.

'Oh, just one more thing — you'll need to swing by the office and pick up necessaries.'

The big guys nodded with childish glee but Andy's stomach took another turn for the worse.

'Necessaries' was code for guns.

Chapter 44

'And then we banged heads,' Molly said, recalling the dropped ring tray earlier, before slurping the last dregs from an orange and passion fruit smoothie.

Gemma threw her head back and laughed.

'Only you, Mol,' she said, wiping tears from her eyes.

They'd found a table at Costa after Molly had called Gemma suggesting an emergency meeting.

They both had the afternoon off so the world, or Worcester anyway, was their oyster.

As she watched her best friend laugh she was suddenly thankful that they'd made up last night. With all that had happened with Danny she didn't know who she would have turned to.

She was due for a FaceTime with her dad that evening but she hated to burden him with her tales of woe, particularly when he was working so far away.

If she called her mum she would pretend to be interested before she got bored and managed to turn the conversation around to her problems, which, as far as Molly was concerned, were non-existent.

They finished their drinks and it took Gemma an age to get herself wrapped up again.

'God, how many layers have you got on?' Molly asked.

'Two jumpers and this,' Gemma said, wrestling her way into a pink fluffy coat she'd bought at St Richard's Hospice shop about five years ago and never left her back when the weather turned chilly. 'Anyway don't take the piss out of me when you're dressed for a summer street party.'

'I was in a hurry this morning.' She'd woken up after a fitful few hours of sleep, including a dream where Danny had come back to her house with flowers.

'At least you remembered to put trousers on, that's a start,' Gemma said, throwing her tote bag over her shoulder and leading them out into the biting cold.

'I'm gonna buy you a scarf from H&M,' she insisted, and grabbed Molly's hand.

Molly knew she couldn't argue so they set off, brushing shoulders with the rest of Worcester who all seemed to be out in force.

'Look, I'm gonna pop home and change into something warmer then we can really enjoy the afternoon,' Molly said.

'OK, but I'm still getting you that scarf. I've seen the perfect one for you.'

She gave Gemma a hug. 'See you in about half an hour?'

'Send me a WhatsApp and I'll let you know where I am. I'll be easy to spot waving a scarf around.'

Molly walked steadily up her path; it was really slippy.

The decorative snowman gave his wave. He had almost shrunk to half the size now — the air must be leaking out from somewhere. She knew how he felt.

Slotting her key in the lock, it flew open the moment she'd touched the door.

She remembered Danny leaving it off the latch when he took the phone call last night. She must have left it unlocked when she slammed the door in a hurry this morning.

She walked inside and flicked the latch back down.

Walking into the lounge she stopped in her tracks and let out a scream.

'What the hell are you doing here, Stewart?' Molly shrieked.

The noise she'd emitted had caused him to stand up suddenly, his hands held up in surrender.

'Sorry, I didn't mean to scare you.'

'Scare me? You've just broken into my house, I'm calling the police.'

'Hang on, I didn't break in. I was going to post something and when I leant on the door it opened. I thought you were in. I knocked but when I got no answer I thought you might be hurt or something.'

'What, like when someone throws a brick through the window? Did you worry about me getting hurt when you did that?'

Molly's shock had turned to anger now. She had her fists balled up and would happily strike him if he got within punching distance.

'I'm sorry about that. I had a few drinks, I didn't mean for it to go right through the window. I was missing you and venting my frustration. Mol, I told Gemma I was sorry and she believed me.'

She walked up to him now. He was a foot taller but at that moment she felt head and shoulders above him. How often had she been dominated by this man? His sheer size, the swagger of confidence when he walked, the roll of his eyes when she was talking earnestly about something that mattered, as if her thoughts were of no consequence. Well, not today.

'First of all, my name's Molly, not Mol. You lost the right to any familiarity when you last hit me.'

'Honestly Mol… Molly, I wasn't… I didn't… This new job I've got is really dangerous and I—'

'And second,' she interrupted his disjointed response with a verbal hammer blow, 'you don't get to chat to my best friend about things anymore. She's on my side, not yours. She was only trying to help me and if I told her half the things you've done to me in the past she'd go straight to her dad. And you know where he works, right?'

'Yeah, he's a pretend cop in an office.'

There it was. The real Stewart. Even though he was trying to be pious and pitiful, his true colours couldn't help bleeding through like a knife wound bound in a cheap bandage.

'Yeah, he's a cop. And I'm in a different place now.'

The eye roll happened as predicted. 'Oh yeah, and where's this place exactly? With your new podcaster boyfriend? You know he's just a delivery driver, don't you?'

'My new place,' Molly said, ignoring his taunts and brushing aside the nagging question about how he already knew about Danny, 'is the "I don't give a shit about Stewart" place. Now piss off.'

Stewart didn't move. His hands were twitching and he was biting his lip. Molly could almost hear his tortured brain deciding how he could finish this as a winner.

'Do you hear me?'

He shrugged, grabbed his coat from the sofa and pushed past her, slamming the front door behind him.

Molly fell onto the sofa and felt something under her.

It was the thing that Stewart had been going to post when the door swung open.

Another card.

This time she didn't open it, just tore it in half and half again, before throwing the pieces to the floor.

All the frustration of a disastrous date, hardly any sleep, getting the ring back where it belonged and then her ex making himself at home in a space she'd made deliberately to get away from him, all piled on top of her in a rugby scrum of emotion.

His presence here had polluted the house. She could smell his Lynx body spray, like a perfumed ghost permeating the room, still lingering in his wake.

She wouldn't put it past him to have had a nosy round while he waited for her to come home. Snooping in her drawers and cupboards.

She felt sick with the thought.

Her phone buzzed. It was Gemma.

'Where are you? It's been ages and I got you the scarf in red. Hope that's OK, they didn't have the colour I wanted. Molly… Molly, are you there?'

She eventually spoke and told her what had just happened.

'Christ, hang on there, I'm coming to yours.'

'No,' Molly shouted louder than she'd intended. 'I don't want to wallow in the house, I'll meet you back in town.'

'If you're sure?' Gemma said.

'Yeah, O'Neill's in half an hour?'

The thought of some rousing Irish music and a few drinks was just the ticket for now.

'Alright, I'll get you a Guinness,' Gemma said.

'Uggh, I hate Guinness.'

'Me too,' Gemma giggled, 'but when in Ireland…'

Molly disconnected and spent ten minutes walking round the house like someone entering a show home, checking everything was where it should be.

The kitchen was in the same state she'd left it in, same with the bathroom and spare room — all in chaos, but at least her chaos.

Her bedroom had the same clothes on the bed she'd tossed aside when hurrying to dress that morning.

She found an extra-thick jumper in the drawer and pulled out her big winter coat from the cupboard at the bottom of the stairs. It was so padded she could hardly move when walking in it.

She was transferring her phone from one coat to another when she got a second message.

An unwelcome thought passed through her mind. Had Stewart sent another photo of her from his perverted library just to get his own back for the stripping of his masculinity on the living room rug?

But it was not from Stewart. It was a message from Danny.

Hi Molly. I'm so sorry last night didn't go well.

Maybe we could try another date and see if it's any better???

I really like you. Danny. X

She read and re-read the text.

Only the one kiss?

No, she told herself as she wrapped a scarf around her shoulders and double-checked the latch was in place. She was not going to get involved any more.

She checked a few times before leaving her front door, just to make sure Stewart wasn't lingering round somewhere.

There were a couple opposite who'd just moved in. They gave her a friendly wave while she stood on the doorstep. The woman was cradling a large mug of something steaming while her husband — or was it boyfriend? — was scraping the pathway with a large spade, chipping away at the ice.

As she strolled back into town she wondered if she would one day be that woman with the cup of coffee.

Chapter 45

Monday 18th December, 2:38pm

O'Neill's was busy.

The soundtrack was perpetually U2, the Pogues and an occasional B*Witched 90s hit. Not full-on Gaelic folk numbers but enough of the commercial catalogue to at least touch a part of the Blarney Stone.

The unexpected snow day and the fact it was only two weeks to Christmas made this a party place even at 2.30 on a Monday afternoon.

There was a mahogany horseshoe bar which took up the centre of the floor, while tables and booths were scattered around it.

Black-and-white pictures of ancient Irish farmers, staring bewildered and tired, were framed on the walls, and there was the smell of frying chips coming from a kitchen at the back.

Molly squeezed between a pack of beefy blokes in tight rugby shirts, advertising the many hours they'd sweated in a gym. They were all cheering about something and clinking glasses.

Gemma waved at her from a table at the back.

She manoeuvred past the queue for the bar, which was at least two rows deep, and sank down into a leather chair opposite.

'Ta da!' Gemma sang, reaching down to a bag by her feet and producing the brightest scarf Molly had clapped her eyes on outside RuPaul's Drag Race. 'I got red to match your eyes.' She looked up from her glass knowingly and took a sip from a straw. The liquid was almost as red as the scarf.

'Not sure what you wanted so I got myself a cocktail while I waited.'

'Same again?' Molly asked as she took off her layers, letting the warmth of the pub engulf her body.

'Why not, it's a Strawberry Santa,' she giggled.

Molly jostled to the bar, which was drowning in testosterone. Where were all the girls? Maybe they'd been more conscientious about turning up for work on a Monday rather than making excuses about the weather.

She returned to the table with a cocktail for Gemma and a bottle of Budweiser for herself. She could drink a few of these without getting too drunk, and they never made her morbid, unlike gin which drove her to think about past mistakes and miss her dad.

Gemma had lined up a few purchases on the table like a stallholder.

'Thank you,' she said, raising her glass and taking a large slurp.

'Cheers,' Molly said, bashing the bottle against her glass.

'So, apart from the scarf I've also got you a few items I'm calling Molly's survival kit.'

'Oh no, you didn't have to…'

Gemma waved the interruption away; she was in full flow now. This was Gemma at her best. Gemma the fixer.

'I got you this diary so you can put all your thoughts down, good or bad.' She waved the journal in the air.

'Next I've got you a super-smooth pen to write in it with.'

'And finally,' she announced with a flourish, 'a calendar to stick on your wall. It has a quotation for each day — inspirational stuff.'

'Thank you, that's so kind.' She took the items and put them gently in her tote bag. 'You really didn't have to.'

'No worries, I get staff discount, you know?' Gemma tapped her nose. 'Oh, and I hate to say it after what's just happened, but Stewart did try to give me a cheque.'

'What?'

'When he called me and said he wanted me to tell you he's sorry, he wanted to give me a cheque to give to you for the broken window.'

'He's just playing with me.' Molly slammed her fist on the table, causing Gemma's cocktail to spill over the side of the glass. A blood-red pool started to spread.

Without missing a beat Gemma pulled a tissue out of her bag and stemmed the flow before it reached her. 'He said he wanted to help with the cost, and he was sorry.'

'Bollocks,' Molly spat.

'Hey, don't shoot the messenger.'

'Well,' Molly said, after taking a bolstering swig from her bottle, 'when I saw him sat in my house just now he didn't have a cheque with…' She stopped, as she remembered the envelope on the sofa — the one she'd ripped to pieces.

Was Stewart really being genuine, or was he continuing to play with her?

Chapter 46

Monday 18th December, 3:30pm

Charlie and Danny were sat on a bench, each one wondering when Bernie would call with an update and if their lives would ever get back to normal.

'I feel bad leaving Karen and the kids on their own,' Charlie said.

Danny had turned up at their house after getting a call from Charlie, who was on the cusp of calling the police.

He'd managed to dissuade him from doing anything rash before setting off back to Charlie's.

He'd texted Molly along the way in what he hoped was some kind of apology for last night and maybe a chance at reconciliation, if this nightmare ever ended.

When Danny had arrived at the Burrows' house the whole family were sat together watching something on TV as if nothing had happened.

Karen was staring at the screen, no doubt masking nightmarish recollections of being strapped to the very chair she was sitting on only hours earlier.

Charlie had rushed to collect the kids early after he'd received the threatening pictures of them at the bus stop. There was no way he was leaving them at school. He'd driven with his foot flat on the pedal, swerved into a reserved teacher's space in the car park and jogged to reception. A frazzled attendance officer nodded sagely as Charlie claimed a family emergency without being specific. Ten minutes later two miffed kids appeared, Dylan obviously gutted to be dragged out of snowball fights in the playground and Maisie crushed that she'd lost time with her boyfriend.

Now as Danny stood in the doorway he looked over at Karen, who was in her upright chair with her feet stretched out on a stool. The kids were sat on opposite ends of the sofa, Dylan half watching the screen while Maisie was curled up with her elbow supporting her head and a phone glued to her other hand. Charlie sat between them, on guard.

When it had become clear they couldn't talk in front of the kids, and wandering off into the garden or upstairs would only rouse suspicion, Danny suggested a stroll into town for what he called a mate's catch-up.

For obvious reasons Karen was finding it hard to settle. 'Don't be long,' she said weakly from the chair as they disappeared.

The kids didn't even notice they'd gone.

'They are going to be safe enough,' Danny reassured Charlie for the tenth time.

'Show me that text again, would you?' he asked.

Danny got his phone out and scrolled to the messages.

The last one was from Bernie. He passed Charlie his phone.

Could you send me Charlie's address? I'm going to put a couple of guys in the area to keep a look out. Bernie.

'Is this really the same guy we saw in Worcester on the day we were going to swap the rings over?'

'The very same,' Danny said, taking back the phone.

'He didn't look like someone who could handle something as big as this.'

'Well,' Danny smiled, 'looks can be deceiving.'

It was still fairly chilly but the snow had already begun to melt, leaving grey slushy trails for the market traders of Bromsgrove to negotiate.

The bench they'd chosen overlooked the stretch of stalls that were in full festive swing. Hardy tradesmen were clanking metal rods in place while others ferried cardboard boxes to eager traders all wrapped up like human Christmas presents.

'After what happened to Karen and those guys coming in and tying her to the chair…'

'It must have been horrific for her,' Danny said, feeling the reply was hugely inadequate.

'I should have called the police, especially after they've threatened the kids. It's gone way over the line now.'

Danny didn't and couldn't say anything more. He agreed, but once the police got involved this would turn into a criminal matter and Danny couldn't guarantee both of them wouldn't end up in prison.

Danny noticed Charlie watching a young girl hanging out T-shirts on a rail. She was around Maisie's age with the same colour hair. He didn't have to walk in Charlie's shoes to know how he was feeling.

'It must be handy living so close to Bromsgrove town centre?' Danny said, hoping to change the subject for a while, maybe clear some of the tension.

'Yeah,' Charlie said, his voice sounding far away. 'We bought it just after we got married, something to leave the kids.' His hand touched his bandage.

'How's your head?' Danny asked.

'Oh, just twinges a bit now. The kids call me Mr Bump after the Mr Men books we used to read them.'

It was obvious there was no way Danny could steer his thoughts away from family, so he decided to get to the point.

'Mind if we walk a bit? I'm starting to get chilly,' Danny said, wrenching himself up from the bench. Lack of sleep and worry were taking their toll now. God knew how Charlie must be feeling.

'Fine by me,' he said, and together they strolled down the high street, hands in pockets watching everything but seeing nothing.

A weak sun was breaking through the grey clouds and both men tilted their heads up, soaking in the rays, each hoping it would invigorate them with a blast of nature's finest.

Danny stopped at the end of the street where the stalls gave way to a chunk of town that had been left behind. Only a few shops remained; the rest of the row was boarded up, some with circus posters from events that had happened pre-pandemic.

'OK, here's the plan,' Danny said, the moment he was sure they couldn't be overheard.

There was no one else around apart from a homeless guy who was bundled up in what seemed to be a sleeping bag with a mouldy duvet over it. Only the very top of his head was visible, tufts of hair sticking out.

'We give Bernie till tomorrow to find who's responsible. Then, if we don't hear anything, we go to the police.'

'Won't he be mad if we change our mind?' Charlie asked.

'I'll call him first, say we've decided to go down the legal route. I'm sure he'll understand. He only wants to help.'

'So we are definitely not paying the blackmailers?'

Danny shook his head.

'And what if they make more threats, hurt the kids, break into the house again? What if they take it even further?' Charlie's voice was beginning to break.

Danny put a hand on his shoulder. 'Bernie's men are very good, ex-military. Nothing will happen. You're better protected by them than if the cops were informed. The police haven't the same manpower.'

'Why does Bernie want to help me so much, why does he care?'

'Have a listen to my podcast, listen to his story and you'll know why.'

Charlie was going to say something else when Danny's phone buzzed.

He grabbed it, and to his relief it was Bernie's name on the screen.

Boys are in place, all quiet at Charlie's house. B

Danny showed him the text and he could see Charlie shudder, in either relief or cold.

They turned around and retraced their steps.

'Thanks for helping me with all this,' Charlie said.

'It's fine. You came to me with a problem and I accepted you needed help. It's what I do these days—it helps me too.'

'Why?' Charlie stopped walking and looked straight into Danny's face. 'That's the part I can't get my head round. I've heard some of your podcasts about good people doing bad things, but what happened to you?'

Danny looked away for a second to mentally regroup. He'd been so close to telling Molly last night, and now here he was being asked the direct question again.

'It's not something I've shared much to people outside of the fellowship,' Danny said.

'You mean the AA groups?' Charlie asked.

'Yeah. Everything we talk about in those rooms is confidential, and it's only when I meet people who want to share publicly that I'll chat to them on my podcast.'

'You don't talk about what happened to you. You say "the incident" and that's all?'

They'd reached a small café, the smells of frying bacon squeezing through the doors.

'Shall we grab a drink? I can't go through this standing up,' Danny asked.

Charlie led the way inside.

The chorus of 'You Were Made for Me' was bleeding from a small radio behind the counter, where a woman with rosy cheeks seemed to be doing a dozen things at the same time.

She wore a floral apron and had a pen behind her ear. She could have been an extra from Emmerdale.

'What can I get you boys?' she said.

Danny couldn't remember the last time he'd been referred to as a boy, but Charlie turned on the charm straight away.

'Hi Denise,' he said.

'Charlie!' she gushed, looking up at them for the first time. 'How are you?' Then her voice went more of a whisper. 'How's Karen?'

Charlie smiled a confident grin. 'She's doing fine, thanks for asking. Now, could we have a couple of your finest coffees?'

Danny watched this transformation of the Charlie who'd been sat on a bench worrying, to the confident people-pleaser. He thought this was what people got when Charlie was pushing them around in wheelchairs and on gurneys at the hospital.

It was a defence mechanism.

'And your head?' she asked, pointing to the bandage.

'I keep walking into things, a senior moment,' he laughed, then shrugged his shoulders.

Denise laughed like it was the funniest thing she'd heard all week (another people-pleaser). 'You sit yourselves down and I'll bring them over.' She tapped Charlie's hand affectionately.

'Is the garden open at the back?'

'It's freezing out there, you'll catch your death.'

'It's OK, we're hardy boys,' Charlie winked, and led Danny through a door by the toilets that opened onto a patio area looking out at the back of a launderette.

They could hear the hum of washing machines and the aroma of soap powder coming from the fire escape door, which was wedged open.

They brushed snow off the metal chairs and sat down.

Within a couple of minutes Denise was back with two steaming cups.

'I've put the heater on,' she pointed to the orange lamp towering above them, already beginning to produce heat. 'Should be nice and toasty in a bit.'

She placed the cups in front of them. 'Oh, talking of toast, do you boys want anything to eat, on the house?'

'That's really kind, Denise, but we'll be fine with just coffee.'

She smiled at Charlie. 'Just pop back in if you change your mind. Nice to meet you, Charlie's friend.' Not waiting for a formal introduction, she disappeared back into the café.

The metal door gave a loud thunk behind her.

'She seems to have taken quite a shine to you,' Danny said.

'Yeah, her husband is forever at the hospital for treatment. He always asks for me to take him to the treatment rooms.'

Danny nodded. His gut instinct was right.

He watched Charlie take a sip of his coffee and saw kindness in his eyes—the way he'd spoken to Denise, the obvious affection she had for him.

This was a kind man, and any regrets about taking up this case were vanishing into the cold air, each one melting by the heat of the overhead lamp.

'So, we have privacy. How about you tell me what this incident was? You know all about me by now—what about doing some of that sharing?'

Danny took a sip of his coffee. It was surprisingly good, a cut above the bland bean concoctions you got at some places.

'OK, but I warn you, this may sour our friendship.'

'I doubt it,' Charlie said.

Danny sighed, sat back and cast his mind to that night almost a decade earlier.

Chapter 47

Danny didn't want to go but Kirsty had been badgering him for the past month.

All her work colleagues were as boring as the furniture they sold, and the idea of spending an evening stood around talking about corner units and sofa sizes was not his idea of fun.

It was one of those 'bring a partner' events where if you didn't show up with your other half in tow you were either a singleton or had an unsupportive spouse.

Danny liked to think he was supportive but these events were too much, even for his benevolent nature.

Plus he'd got a terrible day lined up at the office.

Three meetings back to back with clients who wouldn't know a good advertising campaign if Nike had turned up and presented.

Plus he was due an appraisal with his line manager later that afternoon and the prospects were not good.

Danny had promised to be home by six, they'd get ready together and take a cab to the event.

It was a black-tie dinner at the Whitehouse Hotel that he'd begrudgingly hired a monkey suit for.

The day had not gone well.

As predicted, the clients were not impressed with any of his presentations, just nodding in the right places while twitching to get out of the meeting room for another vape and a chance to catch up with their vapid social media posts.

His appraisal had been dispiriting to say the least. His line manager spent the entire half-hour talking to him about his timekeeping and how it wasn't the done thing to drag everyone to the pub at lunchtimes these days.

'This isn't the eighties now,' his boss had said, brogues up on the desk while he looked at Danny like he was addressing a naughty infant.

How he'd managed to hold his tongue and just nod at the onslaught he didn't know, but by the time he came out of the appraisal, with his tie hung loose and sweat oozing out of every pore underneath his jacket, he had a raging thirst and an excuse to get rid of it.

He escaped the office at 3pm, sneaking out of the back door so no one would notice him leaving.

He'd even left his coat on the back of the chair so anyone trying to find him would think he was still in a meeting.

The first pint didn't touch the sides, in fact he had no recollection of drinking it. The frustration, fear and anger were eating at him and he needed to numb the pain.

Three pints later he changed pubs. This was one of his regular haunts where he knew a scattering of local bar flies who were handy if you wanted to pass the time on peanuts and politics.

He was offered another drink and was about to accept when he noticed the time.

It was five o'clock, he was over the limit to drive home so he'd have to get a cab. Time for another drink while he waited.

The taxi never showed up, or rather he never heard the hooting from outside. Suddenly it was six and he should have been home.

His mobile had rung a few times but he'd let it go to voicemail.

He didn't want to hear Kirsty nagging.

Instead, he downed the last pint and dashed out of the door, nearly knocking over a group of girls who were just coming through.

'Watch it, pisshead,' one of them yelled as he sprinted towards the taxi rank.

He got a taxi fairly easily, drunk luck, and as it set off he let his head fall back against the seat and worked on his speech by striking up a conversation with the driver.

If he slurred his words when he got home Kirsty would lose it. He couldn't be drunk.

Just a couple after work, I've had the worst day, babe.

He practised what he'd say to her in his mind while conducting an interrogation of the taxi driver's family history and shift patterns.

It was six forty-five by the time the driver pulled up outside his house.

Danny spilt change all over the floor of the cab as he tried to count out the right money. He must have left an extra few quid in the footwell.

'Call that a tip,' Danny laughed as he fell out of the car, then realised he was shouting. Time to calm it down.

He put his house key in the lock but missed a few goes and by the time he managed to make contact the door opened, almost taking him with it.

He steadied himself and got a glimpse of something both beautiful and terrifying at the same time.

Kirsty looked amazing.

She had her dark hair pulled back into a bun, revealing sparkling earrings.

Her bare neck was accentuated by a gold chain he had bought her as a 'sorry for forgetting your birthday' present.

She was wearing a blue dress that tumbled to the floor. She must have been wearing heels because she was the same height as Danny.

The only thing that spoiled this image was the snarl she was wearing. Her deep red lipsticked mouth twisted in rage and her eyes filled with pent-up anger.

'Where the hell have you been? Or need I ask?'

She looked him up and down and shook her head.

'I've called you a million times but you were too busy getting pissed to even return my calls.'

'No, I can explain,' Danny began but got no further.

'I don't want to hear it, I've got a lift coming. You can stay here and drink yourself into a coma for all I care.'

'I'll go and get my suit on, I can be ready in ten minutes, we won't be that late,' Danny slurred, and not waiting for a response brushed past her and made for the stairs.

He took them two at a time but kept a steady hand on the banister.

By the time he'd got to the bedroom and flung the wardrobe open in search of the suit, he heard a car pull up outside the house.

He pulled back the curtain and saw a black BMW with its passenger door open and the driver leaning across.

The interior light gave the face away. It was Roger Carlsson, an impossibly handsome Swedish guy who was the company accountant and by all accounts was the buzz boy for all the girls at the store.

Danny had met him a couple of times when he'd picked up Kirsty from work. He noticed how she always acted differently around him.

What the hell was she doing accepting a lift from him? She was supposed to be engaged.

He pulled on his suit, ferreted under the bed for his best shoes and thanked the gods of menswear that the tie was a clip-on.

He could hardly lace his shoes without getting dizzy, let alone navigate a dickie bow.

Leaping down the stairs he missed the last two steps, causing his ankle to twist.

Kirsty had gone, leaving just the traces of her perfume behind.

His heart was racing now, he needed to calm down before he set off again.

There was a bottle of Peroni left in the fridge. He flipped the cap and drank it down in two journeys.

He had to even out the alcohol and this fresh buzz seemed to clear the nausea he'd felt from all the rushing. He felt less dizzy now and his ankle was only a twinge, so no harm done.

He had an obligatory extra-strong mint from his coat pocket where he also found the card of the taxi driver he'd just used.

An hour later he was hobbling from the cab to the entrance of the Whitehouse Hotel.

He walked into the reception and saw a party going on in the bar. He sauntered over, trying to look casual, but he didn't recognise anyone.

He knew some of Kirsty's workmates but there wasn't a single face to say hello to.

Ordering a whisky from the bar he surveyed the room.

Everyone seemed to be in animated groups.

Danny leant over and asked the barman if this was the office party.

The guy pointed a bar towel in the direction of the function room and he realised his mistake.

Peeping through the door there were one or two people he vaguely knew, but no sign of Kirsty or Roger, the Swedish hunk.

Something caused him to look up at the grand staircase and sure enough there they were.

Standing close together at the top of the stairs. He was whispering something in her ear and she was laughing.

Her earrings glinted as she tossed her head back and it was in that exact moment she locked eyes with Danny.

Something in them looked so guilty.

What had she been doing up there with this guy? Did he have a room booked? Had they been together in the hour that had passed?

Without another thought Danny took the steps and raced to the summit.

Roger turned round following Kirsty's eyeline and the next thing that happened went, in Danny's recollection, very slowly.

He grabbed Roger's arm and spun him around, ready to ask him what the hell he thought he was doing with his fiancée.

But the grab turned into a tug and within a matter of seconds Roger lost his balance and tumbled down the stairs.

Danny watched the events he'd caused unfold in slow motion, frozen in silent horror.

It was the screams from the bar below that snapped Danny out of his traumatic trance, as guests witnessed the man lying at the foot of the grand staircase.

It wasn't just the crumpled body lying still on the polished marble floor that caused the uproar, it was the pool of blood that was starting to spiral from under his skull.

Chapter 48

Monday 18th December, 4:03pm

Charlie's mouth had been open so long he could feel his fillings start to ache.

'My God, Danny, I can't believe that was you?' he said.

'It wasn't me, that's the point,' Danny said, sitting back, exhausted from reliving that terrible night again, 'it was my addiction. Don't get me wrong, I took full responsibility, still do, there isn't a day goes by I don't think about it.'

Charlie could understand why he was reticent to share it very often.

'What happened to the Swedish guy?'

'Roger,' Danny said, 'his name's Roger.'

Charlie shuffled uneasily in his seat, fearful of Danny's next reply.

'What happened to him?'

'Severe head injuries. He was in hospital for a few weeks, but thankfully, he recovered. He still walks with a limp and by all accounts has some memory loss issues.'

'And your girlfriend… Kirsty, was it?'

'She left me, wouldn't even visit me in prison.'

Charlie almost spat out his coffee. 'Prison? I didn't know you'd done time?'

'Yeah, throwing a man down a flight of stairs and almost killing him will do that,' Danny said. He'd gone for humour, trying to diffuse the tension that had brewed between them, but it had fallen flat.

'How long?'

'Five years, but I was out on parole in two for good behaviour and my work with other recovering addicts at the prison.'

'Did Roger ever forgive you?'

Danny looked at nothing in particular before he answered. 'I sent him a letter from prison and I tried to make amends when I was working through my 12-step programme, but he never responded. I can't blame him really.'

There were a million more questions Charlie wanted to ask, but it just didn't seem right anymore. Danny looked wrung out like an old wash rag.

They were silent for a while until Danny finally spoke.

'That's where I first met Bernie, we shared a cell.'

He was going to ask what Bernie was in prison for but thought better of it. It wasn't Danny's place to talk about other people's pasts, not unless they volunteered their stories on his podcast.

'Is he in recovery as well?' Charlie asked, then regretted it too. He was being way too intrusive now and suddenly felt bad pushing things just to satisfy his own curiosity.

'No, Bernie's been working his way through PTSD, he saw some terrible things when he was in the forces, lost some good friends.'

'Why haven't I read about you in the papers?' Charlie asked, wondering if this question was a step too far.

Danny looked at him and gave a faint smile, seeming to understand the curiosity. It probably wasn't the first time he'd been asked by those select few who'd heard the story.

'I changed my surname when I got out. I was Daniel Wadsworth, now I'm Danny Wade. It keeps those Google searches at bay.'

Charlie nodded, too stunned to say anything else.

Danny was tracing a line of spilt sugar along the wooden table when the friendly waitress Denise reappeared, the music from the café drifting a Beatles classic into the garden.

'Anything else for you boys?' she asked, scooping up both cups with an expert hand and cradling them into her ample arm.

'No thanks, Denise, but thanks for the coffee,' Charlie said with his brightest smile.

'Yeah, thanks,' Danny said, 'just what we needed.'

'Come back anytime, both of you,' she gushed, before disappearing back to the kitchen.

As they made their way through the café Charlie wondered if they would meet here again in the future.

He hoped that his relationship with Danny would last way beyond the hopeful resolution of his problems, and every time they came here they would sit in that same seat in the café garden whatever the weather, and he'd remember that this was the place he'd found out the real story of what happened to Danny Wade.

Karen was busying herself in the kitchen by the time Danny and Charlie returned.

It always gladdened Charlie's heart to see his wife doing domestic chores, it was like the old Karen was back, even if it was just for fleeting moments.

He'd learned after her first round of chemo that he should never tell her to take it easy or, heaven forbid, offer to do something that she considered her domain. He'd only done it once or twice but the tirade he got back put him firmly in his place. 'I'm not in my death bed yet,' she'd say, waving a dishcloth at him.

'You boys want some coffee?' she asked.

'No, we've just had one at Denise's café, she sends her best.'

Karen popped her head round the kitchen door. The earlier nap had done her good, there was even a slight colour to her cheeks.

'She's a nosy old bugger, I bet she gave you the third degree,' she smiled, 'I reckon she's got the hots for my hubby, what do you reckon, Danny?'

'You might be right there,' Danny winked, and sat down on the sofa.

'Where are the kids?' Charlie asked, taking off his jacket and throwing it over the side of a chair.

'Dylan's in his room playing on the PlayStation with one of his mates and Maisie is sulking on her bed.'

'Why is she sulking?'

'Because I told her she couldn't meet up with her mates or go to school for a few days.'

'Ah,' Charlie sighed, 'she wants to see that boyfriend of hers.'

'Yeah, well he's too old for her and anyway…' Karen stopped in mid-flow, spotting the jacket. 'Oi, hang that coat up,' she barked, pointing at the offending article.

When Charlie disappeared Danny took the chance to chat to Karen in the kitchen for a second on her own.

'Good call on keeping the kids at home, I'm sure we'll have this sorted very soon.'

She smiled at him and suddenly the energy seemed to bleed from her. She grabbed the kitchen unit and Danny gently held her arm.

'You OK?' he asked, leading her back to the chair.

'Yes, just a bit woozy,' she said. 'I try to concentrate on the day and then remember what's happened.'

Charlie was back in the room and knelt by her side. 'It's OK, love, Danny's friend is going to sort out things for us, no more big guys turning up at the door, eh?'

'Funny you should say that,' she said, wiping her brow with a tissue she'd pulled from her apron pocket, 'there were two large fellas at the door earlier.'

'Oh my God, why didn't you call? Are you OK?' Charlie was up off his knees and pulling out his phone.

'That's it, Danny, I'm calling the police.'

To both of their surprise Karen laughed, it was a small titter. 'No, the boys said they were working for a guy called Bernie and told me they were guarding the house. Very nice lads, they both had suits on.'

Danny and Charlie exchanged glances, then Charlie put his phone away.

'You see,' Charlie said, sitting back down again, 'Bernie's got it all under control.'

Danny smiled but felt uneasy. He hoped that he hadn't over-promised on Bernie, but what else was there left to do?

Chapter 49

'Why do pub hours go by so fast,' Molly slurred, as she glanced up at the huge clock that hung with majesty over the centre of the bar.

They had been in O'Neill's all afternoon and Molly's promise to herself of staying on Budweiser had been broken an hour ago when Gemma returned with a tray of shots.

They'd made their way through three exotic flavours each, making an incoherent toast, tipping back the tiny glasses and slamming them down hard on the table.

Now Molly was nursing a white wine spritzer and breaking the second of her promises by talking about Danny.

'Thing is Gem I really like him, he seemed like such a good guy.'

'You say he seemed like a good guy, he's not dead you know, there's still hope, maybe?'

'He's got a nice voice too,' Molly continued her monologue, ignoring Gemma. It was hard to hear anything anyway as 'Dirty Old Town' was bleeding out of the speakers and people were singing along even though they didn't know the words. 'He's good looking, in a geeky way, and tall-ish, tall enough, he likes…'

'Bloody hell Molly,' Gemma shouted loud enough to be heard this time, 'are you thinking of setting up his Tinder profile or what?'

'Oh God, I'm sorry, I'm getting drunk, not thinking straight.'

Gemma reached over the sticky table and grasped her best friend's hand.

'It's OK, I'm getting pissed too, let's say bollocks to the boys and go dancing.'

'I'll drink to that,' Molly said, grabbing her drink and missing the straw three times before making contact and sucking down the contents till she hit ice. 'Let's go.'

Dua Lipa was pounding from the speakers and Molly was lost in the music.

Gemma danced opposite her, swaying to the beat. Just at that moment life was good.

They hadn't bothered going to the bar when they'd arrived, just ran straight to the dance floor, the music pulling at them like a melodic magnet.

Some guys tried to barge between them, contorting their bodies in ridiculous ways that would have caused them to be hauled away for special treatment in the light of day.

They just ignored each interruption by dance-walking to a clear space of the floor until their admirers got the message. It was no more boys tonight.

After half an hour dehydration was setting in.

Molly went to find somewhere to sit while Gemma fought the bar queue to get a couple of lagers in plastic glasses and, being the good girl she was, two bottles of water.

Molly couldn't find a seat but there was a place to perch on the second floor by a ledge that overlooked the dance floor.

Gemma found her, placing the drinks by their feet while watching the carnival of characters below.

The strobe lights made it impossible to see each person individually, the whole floor looked like a blurry jigsaw puzzle of light and movement.

Dua Lipa had moved on to a pulsating David Guetta tune and there was a roar from the crowd when they recognised the hook.

'I love this tune,' Molly screamed.

'You go,' Gemma insisted, 'I'll sit this one out, I'm knackered.'

'Lightweight,' Molly laughed, as she stepped out of her shoes and skipped barefoot down the steps back onto the dance floor.

Whoever the DJ was knew his crowd well, one song blending into the next and every tune seemed to hit the mood perfectly.

Molly found herself spinning round when she bumped into a crowd of guys who had been leering from the side of the floor.

They looked like a poor boy band tribute in black hoodies, black jeans and whiter-than-white Reeboks.

They let out a huge cheer as she toppled at their feet.

Molly lay there for a few seconds, all she could see was the collision of lights swooping down at her in all directions.

She felt a rough hand grab her by the elbow and lift her from the floor.

'You owe me a kiss, babe,' the rescuer said, as she fell into his chest.

She could smell too much aftershave and the boyish musk of sweat and desperation.

'I don't think so,' Molly said, sobriety snapping into her.

'Oh come on, he saved your life,' another boy said.

They were circling her now like a pack of wolves hot on the scent.

The incident hadn't been witnessed by the rest of the dance floor, it had happened too quickly and the sound of Rita Ora bouncing round the room had them all back to the party.

'Kiss, kiss, kiss,' the boys chanted, and Molly went to push past but strong hands were grabbing her, pinning her to the spot.

The boy leant towards her. She could feel his peachy stubble brush her cheek as he went in for the snog.

And then he was gone, falling to the floor.

Someone had hit him from behind and before the rest of the gang could respond two bouncers came bounding over like excited bulldogs.

'You alright love?' one asked, while the other was chatting to the guy who'd hit her attacker who was still lying on the floor. Now even Rita Ora couldn't stop a crowd gathering round the event.

She nodded and was about to tell him what happened when she caught a glimpse of the man talking to the other bouncer.

She recognised the guy who'd hit the creep.

He turned his head and gave her a smile.

It was Stewart.

The stuffy office was situated just behind the VIP area on the third floor.

Molly, Gemma and Stewart were sat in mismatched chairs while the duty manager took some statements.

'Are you sure you don't want to press charges? It's fine if you do we can call the police?'

The manager had a soft voice but her demeanour was all business. She wasn't someone to be messed with.

She reminded Molly of her Year Ten maths teacher, who could silence the entire class with a raise of her eyebrow.

'No it's fine, I just want to go home,' Molly said. She was feeling sick, the alcohol leaving her body was making her dizzy and the hot cramped office didn't help.

'If you're sure?' the manager said, 'creeps like that need reporting, they won't get back in here that's for sure.'

'Thank you, I'll make sure she gets home OK,' Stewart had elected himself spokesperson for the event. Gemma seemed to be letting him take control. He was always good at dominating every situation, but then she remembered that he had just saved her from a frightening situation.

The manager gave Stewart a slight nod. 'That's good, sometimes people wait outside and finish what they started on the street, so it might be a good idea to get a taxi home.'

'She'll be alright with me, she only lives around the corner,' Stewart said, rolling back his shoulders as if preparing himself for action.

Gemma agreed and Molly was just desperate to get back outside and breathe some air, she was getting worried she'd throw up right there on the worn carpet.

The manager stood up and walked to a battered filing cabinet at the far end of the room.

She pulled out a squeaky drawer and ferreted around until she found what she was looking for. 'There you go, free entry for four whenever you like and a few drinks tokens, on us,' she said, handing them to Stewart.

This annoyed Molly as she was the one who'd been harassed and also Stewart was supposed to be out of her life. Now she'd as good as given them a pass for a night out together.

She said nothing apart from a 'thanks' before getting up unsteadily from the rickety chair and making her way to the door.

Stewart made a move for her elbow but she whipped her arm away.

He held up his hands in surrender.

She left the room with Gemma holding her steady and at the same time keeping herself upright.

'Thanks again,' Stewart said to the manager.

'No worries, give her some time, the shock of something like this can hit later on. Is someone at home for her?'

'I'll make sure she's alright,' he repeated, and gave a wink.

The manager gave a small smile back and lowered her voice. 'Good job on the lad who grabbed her by the way, I reckon you broke his nose.'

Stewart smiled.

'Not that I condone violence but if you're ever looking for a job we may have some positions free here. We'll have to work on your resolution skills though.'

'I'll keep it in mind,' he said, before catching up with the girls who were being let out of the rear fire exit.

By the time they'd reached Molly's house she'd thrown up three times. Once in a bin by the Grammar School, a second time in the doorway of a derelict betting shop and the last heave was just as they were approaching the turning for her road. Luckily there was hardly anything left to bring up in the garden of a semi-detached on the corner.

It took a while to get Molly's keys from her bag and once inside they got her upstairs and onto the bed.

She fell asleep instantly.

Gemma breathed a sigh as they crept back downstairs.

'Jesus that was quite a night,' she said, not moving from the doorway. It didn't feel right to go into the lounge without Molly's permission.

'I feel bad for her,' Stewart said, looking up the stairs. The faint sounds of Molly's snoring could be heard from the bedroom.

'You shouldn't, she'll be fine, and you did a good thing tonight,' Gemma said, and in spite of herself she smiled at him. For the first time she saw something in Stewart she hadn't seen in quite a long time.

He looked lost and yet concerned. Like the man she remembered when Molly had first introduced him.

In the dim light coming from upstairs and the alcohol buzz that was still lingering in her system she could see the guy that Molly had fallen for.

'Thanks for being a good friend to Molly,' Stewart whispered, moving a step closer. 'I'm going to leave her alone now and give her the space to find someone special, someone better than me.' His voice was low, with just a trace of regret.

'That's a nice thing to say,' Gemma said, looking up at him.

He was a good foot taller than her and there was no denying he looked good.

'I can be a nice person,' he said softly.

Then in a fleeting second he let his head fall closer to hers. Gently his fingers touched the back of her head, pushing ever so lightly till their lips met.

Chapter 50

Tuesday 19th December, 6:10am

Mr C. believed in what he termed 'strict simplicity'. This meant that every operation he ran had four options.

Option 1: Transaction

Option 2: Threat

Option 3: Extreme Threat

Option 4: Termination

In the last encrypted call he'd had with Andy and the two heavies, he'd been very clear what he wanted next. To show true intent, Option 3 would start with kidnapping one of Charlie's kids.

It was clear that Charlie and his podcaster friend had enlisted some kind of security round the Burrows house, as men in suits were obviously surveilling. Either that or they were very keen Jehovah's Witnesses.

B and G had got lucky while the protection were taking a break.

Their initial plan was to break back into the house.

They couldn't believe their good fortune when they saw the daughter opening her bedroom window and shimmying down the drainpipe.

They'd arrived just after six on the other side of the street and were about to start a vigil of the house, waiting for an opportunity.

They watched in awe as the girl's slender frame twisted round and round. She had obviously done this before, rebelling after being told she couldn't go out.

It was a bad decision on her part.

The men looked around to make sure they wouldn't be spotted and, with an agility belying their weight, ran towards the house.

One of them caught her round the waist before she even touched the ground, while the other smothered her face with a rag doused in chloroform.

She gave a muffled squeal and kicked out a few times, but it only took a few seconds for the drug to take effect.

The van was already parked close by and, in a matter of moments, the rear doors were yanked open and she was tossed like a rag doll onto the ratty mattress in the back.

One hour later Maisie blinked open her eyes and saw the blurry outline of two men taking photos of her on their phones.

Neither man knew mercy. Whatever empathy ran through the average human, there wasn't the faintest trace in B or G. It was why Mr C. used them so often.

They had been brought up on a diet of violence and survival, they knew who was in charge and what they had to do.

Age, sex, disability, race, religion or creed was of no consequence to them. The people they dealt with were all treated in the same way.

Charlie hardly slept, so once it got past seven he gave up the struggle.

He had to manoeuvre his hand from underneath Karen's sleeping body but woke her just as he'd thought he'd managed to untangle himself.

'Sorry, I didn't want to wake you,' he whispered.

'It's OK, I was only half asleep myself,' she replied, levering herself upwards and blinking her eyes into life.

The evening had finished in an argument with Maisie about her not going to school for a while. They didn't want to scare her too much about the situation and she thought she was being grounded unfairly, obviously desperately missing the boyfriend after more than twenty-four hours apart.

She expressed her feelings in no uncertain terms before stomping up the stairs and closing her door in a frame-splitting slam.

'I'll put the kettle on,' Charlie offered, opening the door onto the landing.

He could hear the gentle snoring of Dylan, still asleep and dreaming of Fortnite characters no doubt.

He didn't want to think about what Maisie's dreams were like, so just put his head against the door she'd slammed last night to listen for any signs of life. She invariably left her TV on but he heard nothing.

He knew better than to rouse the sleeping lioness, so crept past her door and down the stairs.

Padding into the kitchen, he flicked on the kettle then pulled the living room curtains to one side.

It was still dark outside but it seemed a little lighter with a covering of snow reflecting in the sodium street lights. The world would be waking up soon; this was the calm before the storm in more ways than one.

He'd call Danny in an hour or so, give him chance to recover after yesterday, and then they could find out if Bernie had revealed his plan.

He was adamant that if he hadn't, then today was the deadline for contacting the police.

While he was tossing and turning during the night, he'd gone over what he'd say to the authorities again and again. It was never the same thing twice.

He'd dreamt that he'd been arrested and was awaiting trial in a jail cell, the forged ring next to him on the wooden bench he'd been chained to.

As the kettle clicked he was just about to go into the kitchen when he noticed that the garden gate was wide open.

He'd shut it last night in his security frenzy before they'd gone to bed.

Opening the front door, he shivered in just his pyjamas and dressing gown, his slippers creaking against the hard compacted snow.

He walked up the covered path to the gate and closed it again, this time making sure the latch was firmly down.

A crow caught his ear and he looked up towards the noise.

That's when he saw that Maisie's bedroom window was wide open.

He almost took a tumble as he twisted round, bolted through the front door and took the steps in one breath before flinging open Maisie's door.

The bedroom was its usual chaos. Clothes all over the floor, drawers hanging open, hair straighteners and charging cables twisted together from a wall socket.

Charlie stood taking in the scene, trying to catch his breath.

There was no sign of Maisie.

He was just about to rush downstairs when his pocket vibrated.

The message liquefied his insides.

We want twenty thousand pounds delivered at 6pm tonight and the stakes are very high this time.

Underneath was a photo of Maisie and the postcode of a property in Redditch.

Chapter 51

Tuesday 19th December, 7:04am

Danny hadn't slept, even though he'd been running on nothing but fear and adrenaline for over twenty-four hours.

He felt helpless for Charlie at that moment, but the one thing he could do was finish the podcast.

He pressed play and sat back.

(Danny) Hi, I'm Danny Wade and you've been listening to Richard's story.

Another example of 'Good Gone Bad'.

I'm delighted to say that I now have the man we've been calling Richard with me, and alongside him is someone we'll call Steve — Steve the Santa.

So maybe, Richard, you could finish off the story. What happened after you had attacked Santa Steve and you were dragged away by the police?

(Richard) (Embarrassed laughter and shuffling) I was thrown into a cell and later charged with GBH.

(Danny) But the charges were dropped?

(Richard) Yeah, Steve said it was a misunderstanding and he'd rather not take it any further.

(Danny) Why did you do that, Steve?

(Steve) (Clearing his throat and more shuffling) Well, I... Or should I say 'we' had a bit of history, and I'm not really proud of it.

(Danny) Would you mind sharing for our listeners what that history is?

(Steve) A couple of years before the school Santa thing, I was a regular at the pub Richard used to go to.

We weren't drinking buddies or anything, but I used to see him a lot. I had a regular stool at the end of the bar.

I used to sell stuff, whatever came to hand. (More clearing of throat) Then one day there was a load of baby equipment that came into my possession.

(Danny) Your possession?

(Richard) I hope Steve won't mind me saying, but he was always handy for one or two bits that were cheaper than the shops in those days. It was before Amazon and stuff.

(Danny) I see. So what happened that upset Richard so much?

(Steve) I sold him one of those bottle washers, you know the type that cleans all the baby bottles in a plastic tub?

(Richard) We'd just had our daughter, so I bought one from him.

(Steve) I really didn't know that would happen. I only knew what the supplier told me when I picked them up. Safety standards were always followed — original boxes, manufacturing certificates, all that.

(Danny) Hang on, we're getting ahead of ourselves here. What happened with the bottle washer?

(Richard) I brought it home and my wife was delighted. I told her I got it from Mothercare on special, and she seemed satisfied.

(Steve) I didn't know there was anything wrong with it.

(Richard) It had a blue light when it was washing, it looked like my daughter's night light.

One night my wife was holding the baby up close to it, watching her eyes widen at the blue light and her reflection.

Then she put out her tiny hand and touched the side…

(Silence)

(Richard) (Voice cracking slightly) There was some kind of shock and my wife and our baby were jolted so much they were both blown across the room.

My wife smashed her shoulder against the wall and the baby's head fell heavily on the floor.

(Silence)

(Danny) Were they OK?

(Richard) My wife had a dislocated shoulder and the baby was kept in hospital overnight for observation. Luckily there was no damage, but it could have been so much worse.

(Danny) Where were you when all this was happening?

(Richard) (Voice close to tears) In the pub. I told my wife I'd been working late. When I got home and saw the ambulance outside my house, I'd never felt worse in my life.

All those emergency staff dashing round while I lingered in the hallway, smelling of booze.

(Danny) And then you tried to find Steve.

(Richard) Yeah, but he'd vanished into thin air. I asked around but nobody seemed to know where he was or even what his name was.

(Steve) I used to go from pub to pub selling whatever was on the market, but when I got wind of the dodgy bottle washers I kept low for a while. There had been a few more incidents with them, and some safety worries on the baby carriers I'd been selling.

(Danny) So the next time you saw him was when he was playing Santa at your daughter's school?

(Richard) Yeah, and I was furious. The idea that the guy who could have been responsible for my baby's death would be playing Father Christmas and giving her a gift — it made me sick.

(Steve) I don't blame you. It wasn't the only time I'd sold something dodgy. I never flogged drugs, but I would deal in knives from time to time. To me it was just business. I wasn't using the knife, it was just a transaction.

Then one day my brother's kid got stabbed at a party and suddenly everything clicked into place. It was like I suddenly realised what effect I was having on people by just selling this crap.

(Danny) So what did you do about it?

(Steve) Started trying to be a better person. Volunteering for stuff. Tin rattling, helping out at food banks and playing Santa.

(Danny) Is there anything you'd like to say to Richard?

(Steve) Just that I'm sorry it ever happened. If I could take it back, I would.

(Danny) Richard, what would you like to say to Steve?

(Richard) Thank you for not pressing charges. That makes up for what happened in the past.

(Danny) You guys up for a hug?

(Sound of chairs scraping back and pats on backs. Something is said but is muffled during the embrace.)

Danny hit pause, drew the microphone close and cleared his throat for the closing line.

'Another story of good people doing bad things, but I'm sure you'll agree that there's always hope for redemption, even if forgiveness seems impossible.

I'm Danny Wade and you've been listening to Good Gone Bad. I'll be back in January for our next story.'

He pulled his headphones off, letting them fall round his neck, and let out a guttural sigh.

As he began to save and share it, he wondered if Charlie Burrows' story would have such a neat ending.

A phone call minutes later would smash that hope.

Chapter 52

Tuesday 19th December, 8:35am

Gemma woke up and didn't recognise the pillow she had her head on. It was way more scratchy than the one she was used to and the duvet was poor quality too, it felt like sandpaper against her bare skin.

Her bare skin!? She sat up too quickly and blinked her eyes open a couple of times but the nausea hit her every time. She groaned and turned over.

The thin curtains were bleeding in morning sunshine as she began to recollect. Drinking all afternoon in O'Neill's, the trip to the night club, Molly getting grabbed on the dance floor and Stewart coming to the rescue.

The memory of him made he eyes snap open and she sat up again. It all came back now, the kiss at the bottom of Molly's stairs, the taxi back to his house that ended in this very bed.

She suddenly had the urge to vomit but had no idea where the bathroom was and wasn't sure if she'd make it on time. She saw a wastebasket by the window and crawled out of bed to throw up into it.

Kneeling on the carpet with her head over the basket she'd never felt worse in her life. She didn't normally feel this bad when she'd been drinking.

She had a foggy memory of them being together in back of the cab. Stewart pulling out a hip flask and offering her a slug. She'd taken more than one, her nerves and guilt were all over the place. Then they'd had more when she arrived at his house, she recalled drinking something from a teacup because he didn't have any glasses.

It was all a blur, but one thing was for certain, she'd betrayed her best friend. How could she have slept with Stewart?

She wondered where he was now and said a silent thank you he wasn't still in bed with her. Then a memory from last night swam into her mind. She remembered her mumbling to him about how she was going to be sick as he was pulling at her clothes, there was certainly no sex involved after that, which was a massive consolation.

He'd obviously overdone whatever alcohol and drug concoction he'd fed her. The last thing she remembered was Stewart snoring beside her on top of the duvet.

When she felt she could stand, she made a quick inspection of the room. Her clothes were on the floor and her phone was by the bed, she checked it but the battery was dead.

Pulling on her dress, glad that at least she'd had the decency to sleep in her underwear, she left the bedroom and stood on the landing. The floor kept rising up to meet her and she knew she only had a limited amount of time before she'd need to throw up again.

She crept down the bare wooden stairs, walking on tiptoe hoping to avoid splinters. The downstairs was a mess and it smelt bad. A mixture of weed and cat pee. There was no furniture as such, just dirty cushions on the floor. There weren't even curtains on the windows, only a filthy bedsheet hanging over the frame.

The chaos and the smell turned her stomach and she rushed back upstairs in search of the toilet. As she lay on the dirty tiles looking up at the rancid green shower curtain she wondered how the hell she hadn't noticed all this last night.

Then in patches of memory she pieced events together, stumbling through the door, Stewart rushing to the kitchen and grabbing the cups and booze before almost dragging her upstairs.

What was she thinking and more importantly what would she say to Molly?

Sitting back on the bed she noticed a piece of paper on the bedside table. It was folded over with her name on the front.

Yo Gemma
Amazing time last night but had to go to work
Sleep as long as you like and I'll be back later.
There's no food but make yourself at home.
Stew xx

She held back another urge to throw up. The audacity of the guy. To assume she would wait for him in this shit pit he called home while she nursed a hangover that he'd deliberately made worse.

She felt terrible and stupid. How could she have let him take advantage like this? How many times had Molly said what a control freak he was, how he always had to have his own way and in spite of all that, Gemma had fallen into the same trap like a lemming off a cliff.

She still had no idea what time it was so started rummaging round for a clock or a watch. She opened his bedside drawer and found a phone charger (not her kind) a dozen foil condom packets (wishful thinking) and a pile of polaroid pictures.

Sheer curiosity made her pull them out and what she saw took her breath away. At first she thought they were old photos from when Molly and Stewart were together but then she noticed they'd been taken with a zoom lens from a distance.

It was Molly in the shop serving a guy wearing a baseball cap with reindeer antlers sticking up. She remembered Molly saying about how she met Danny and what he was wearing.

The next photo was Molly and Danny together at a bar, which must have been taken on that first date. Then there were some photos of a man she didn't recognise. He was all wrapped up and was pushing a kid on a sledge.

The final two were pictures of a ring, it looked expensive, an engagement ring of some kind. The final one was a photo of what looked like a warehouse.

There was nothing special about it, all the windows were boarded up and if anything it looked like it was ready for demolition.

She was about to put them back when she thought about looking on the reverse of the photos for any information. There was nothing on any of them apart from the one of the warehouse. It had a series of letters and numbers she didn't recognise.

There was a banging coming from downstairs and then muffled voices. She slammed the drawer closed, put the photos in her bag and slipped on her shoes after finding them under the bed. Tossing her phone in her bag, she double checked she hadn't left anything else behind.

Creeping back down the stairs trying to make as little noise as possible she headed for the front door which was at the foot of the staircase.

'Where do you think you're going?' a husky voice asked. It didn't sound like Stewart.

She turned round to see a guy wearing a filthy vest and swigging from a giant can of off-brand energy drink leaning against the door frame. He had a cigarette dangling from his fingers and the ash was so long, flakes were dropping onto the threadbare carpet.

'I'm Noah,' he smiled, the way only stoners can, broad and senseless. His head was bobbing to a Jay Z track playing from a phone speaker.

'Hi,' Gemma said.

'You wanna stay and par-tay?' he spoke like a white man wanting desperately to be black. The irony was he couldn't have been paler, his arms were thin and reedy and he smelt as bad as the rest of the house.

'No I'm in a hurry but thanks.' Gemma turned the door knob but it was locked from the inside.

'What's your hurry girl?' he said dangling a house key from his nicotine stained fingers, 'why don't you stay and chill with us for a while?'

The 'us' turned out to be a second stoner who appeared from behind him.

'She's one pretty lady,' the new boy said. As he got closer she could tell by the ravages of acne on his gaunt face he couldn't be any more than nineteen.

'I'm waiting for my dad to pick me up,' Gemma said. reaching into her bag. 'He's a policeman,' she pulled out the photo of them together when she'd met him for lunch at work one afternoon. He was in full uniform and although it had been taken a few years ago there was no doubt it was her.

The stoner held up his hands in surrender, 'woah girl no need to fuss,' he said, squeezing by her and unlocking the door, 'you can wait for ya daddy outside.'

With that she ran through the door and down to pavement as fast as she could, with little idea where she was or how she'd get home. Whoever those guys were who shared Stewart's vile house, they were not about to be added to her Christmas card list.

She wondered around for a while, her high heels clomping past rows of identical houses. One or two odd looks were flung in her direction with an occasional wolf whistle as she experienced the ultimate walk of shame.

After fifteen minutes of aimlessly searching she found a phone box, the miracle was it still worked. She rang the only number she knew off by heart.

'Hi dad it's me,' she said.

Forty five minutes later she was sat in the passenger seat of her dad's car.

'You look terrible Gemma,' he said, and she couldn't argue. In fact she'd never felt more ashamed in her life.

'I dread to think what your mother would say, thank God she was at your auntie Maureen's when you rang. How did you end up in some random estate in Redditch?'

'Don't tell her where I was please dad,' she looked over at him hoping he would acknowledge the little girl lost expression she'd perfected since the age of five.

'What do you want me to tell her?'

'Just say I was staying with a friend and forgot to charge my phone, don't tell her what I….'

'What you look like?' Gemma nodded.

Then he began his speech on being careful when going out on her own and how he filed reports and had seen photos that would have kept her indoors for the rest of her life.

By the time he dropped her home they'd agreed he'd say nothing more about it.

'Oh before I forget,' Gemma said, reaching into her bag, 'what do you make of these letters and numbers?'

She passed him the photo of the warehouse she'd taken from Stewart's bedside drawer. He studied it for a few seconds before turning it over.

'Well it's some kind of disused warehouse and the numbers on the back are a postcode and the 18:00 is a time obviously,' he said.

'Thank you dad,' she leant over snatched it back and gave him a peck on the cheek.

'Wait Gemma what's going on with you?' he yelled out of the door as she made her way to the entry gate of her apartment block.

'Nothing I can't fix,' she yelled back, before blowing him another kiss and disappearing through the gate.

Chapter 53

Tuesday 19th December, 8:41am

'That's it, I'm calling the police.' Karen had the phone in her hand ready to dial.

Danny had driven back to Charlie's house as soon as he'd got the tearful call. Now he had Charlie's phone clutched tight in his hands and his eyes locked on the photo of Maisie's terrified face. This wasn't like the other pictures taken from a distance; this was up close, and it was obvious whoever took it was scaring her.

'OK, but let's work out what we're going to say first?' Danny said, handing the phone back to Charlie's outstretched hands. They were shaking uncontrollably.

'There isn't time,' Karen yelled.

'Time for what?' Dylan had appeared from his room. His curly hair was sprouting in all directions and he was still red from sleep.

There was silence, none of them wanting to be the first to explain to this twelve-year-old child that his big sister had been kidnapped.

'Dylan love,' his mother rushed to him and was about to explain when there was a loud banging on the door.

This was it, Danny thought. They'd finally come for the money, and as they didn't have it, there had to be violence involved.

'Go upstairs, all of you, and lock the bathroom door,' Danny said. He needed to take control of this. All that would happen next was down to his advice. The least he could do was keep this family safe.

'No way,' Charlie said, squaring up to Danny. 'I'm not leaving you on your own with these thugs.'

Another bang on the door. They were running out of time.

'Karen and Dylan, get upstairs and hide,' Danny barked.

Dylan started to cry.

Karen said nothing more, just grabbed his hand and hurried up the stairs.

Once Danny was sure they were safely in the bathroom with the bolt in place, he went to turn the lock on the front door. Charlie was right behind him, holding what seemed to be a heavy-looking vase.

'It's the only weapon I could find,' he whispered.

Danny flung the door open and got ready for a fight he knew he had no chance of winning.

Relief flooded him in a warm wave. It was Bernie, smiling at him. Three other men stood behind him.

'Can we come in, mate? It's kind of urgent,' he said.

Bernie took up most of the room even though he was sitting on a small chair by the window. His men were stood outside keeping guard while Dylan had been pacified and was back in his room playing with friends online.

'What have you said to your son?' Bernie asked, as Karen handed him a cup of coffee. The mug looked like it came from a child's tea set in his giant hands.

'I've just said that we need to be careful as there are some bad guys about and he has to stay home till they've been caught.'

'That'll do for now,' Bernie said, blowing the rim of his cup and taking a small sip. 'The less he knows the better. Hopefully when this is all sorted you can explain to him in your own time.'

'Talking of time, what about Maisie? I want to call the police right now,' Karen said.

'We know where she is and what we have to do,' Bernie replied without looking up from his cup.

'Is she at this postcode?' Charlie was on his feet, thumbing through the messages on his phone to get to the last one from the blackmailers. 'If she's there, we can go now.'

Danny put a calming hand on Charlie's arm but he pulled away. 'Come on, mate, stop pissing around. This is my daughter we're talking about here, it's not a game.'

'We need to go and get her,' Karen was pleading now, close to tears. 'I want my little girl back.'

Bernie looked at each in turn before speaking.

'Danny here will testify to you that I'm a man of my word and I will get your daughter back safe. Remember, we are dealing with people who want money, and they won't resort to violence until every avenue has been explored.'

'How do you know?' Charlie shouted.

'Let me just say one of my employees is familiar with their work and he has assessed the situation.'

There was silence now, nothing but Bernie's voice dominating the room.

'According to him, they just want the money and they will be out of your life.'

'But we don't have any money,' Charlie insisted, resisting Danny's invitations to sit back down with him on the sofa. 'They want twenty grand in cash at six o'clock tonight.'

'And you are going to give it to them,' Bernie said before getting to his feet and leaving the room.

A few silent seconds went past, just the bubbling of the fish tank in the corner. Nobody could think of anything to say.

When Bernie walked back into the room he had one of his men with him, who was carrying a black rucksack. He unzipped it, letting the contents fall on the carpet.

All eyes were on the pile of banknotes on the floor, dozens of rolls wrapped with rubber bands.

'Twenty thousand pounds cash,' Bernie announced to the astonished room.

Charlie thought about asking where it had come from but couldn't think of the right way to say it.

Karen was suddenly feeling faint, falling back into her chair, barely able to take her eyes off the cash.

It was Danny who asked the most pertinent question.

'OK Bernie, what happens next?'

Danny and Charlie were strapped into the back of Bernie's 4x4 when two messages arrived on Charlie's phone.

The first was a postcode and a picture of a dilapidated building with a reminder of 6pm. The second was a message saying '20,000 pounds in exchange for…' and then another picture of his daughter. This time she had tape over her mouth, just like what happened to Karen.

Charlie couldn't stop staring at his daughter's frightened eyes.

He was just thankful it had arrived after they had left the house. If Karen had seen the photo, it would have tipped her over the edge.

All her concentration now had to be keeping Dylan pacified while the two other men working for Bernie patrolled the neighbourhood.

'So you know where this place in the photo is?' Charlie asked, once they'd got on the motorway.

'It's like we predicted,' Bernie said, looking at Charlie through his rear-view mirror. 'This is what they call an option 3, where they hold hostages. Try not to overthink things too much. Once we get to the location we'll do a recce and then decide the best course of action.'

Charlie was about to ask something else but Danny put a hand on his arm and leaned over, whispering in his ear.

'Don't ask any more. I think the guy in the front seat used to work for the gang we're dealing with.'

'But…?' Charlie began to insist.

Danny put his finger to his lips and Charlie got the message.

After half an hour they were turning into what appeared to be a remote industrial estate. Not much trade around, just a couple of HGVs idly parked, their drivers either nestled in the sleeper section of the cab or checked into a cheap bed and breakfast.

The car skidded a little under the ice as they turned into an area that hadn't been used for a long time, the older units giving way to more modern facilities further down the road.

Charlie recognised the warehouse from the photo and was about to call out, but it was obvious both men knew what it was.

They drove straight past and then took the exit back onto the main road before pulling up into a pub car park.

Bernie switched off the ignition and turned round to face Danny and Charlie. 'I want you to make yourself scarce for a while now.' There was no humour in his eyes; the jovial big man was suddenly all business.

'No way,' Charlie said, snapping off his seatbelt and leaning closer to Bernie. 'My child could be in that building. Do you think I'm just going to hang around and wait?'

Danny was about to say something apologetic to Bernie, who after all was doing them the most enormous favour at great danger to himself. But before he could, Bernie gave Charlie his big smile again.

'Look, I understand. I'm a dad too. But believe me, if you do what I say, we'll have your girl back safe before the night's through.'

Charlie heaved a sigh. It was clear he wanted to say more as he looked at Danny and then at the back of the head of the guy in the passenger seat, who was just studying his phone.

'I just hope you're right,' Charlie said, before getting out of the car.

'Go and get yourself a drink or something to eat,' Bernie said, gesturing towards the pub. 'We'll come and collect you in a couple of hours.'

Charlie hoped the 'we' would be more than just Bernie and the silent passenger in the front seat.

As the 4x4 swept away, Charlie and Danny stood side by side in the car park, trying to piece together what on earth was going to happen next.

Chapter 54

Tuesday 19th December, 9:03am

The faces were getting nearer now.

They'd started far away, too distant to see, now they were crowding round her but the closer they got the more their features blurred.

It didn't help that the lights were coming in all directions. First green, then blue followed by a strobing bright white.

Now they were almost on top of her.

She had no way of breaking through the circle, it may as well have been made of concrete rather than a mass of human flesh.

There were howling noises, wolf like, then the snarling started. Soon they were almost at touching distance, she could see expanded lips slavering and hissing through rotting gums.

One of the group leapt forward to pounce and Molly screamed herself awake.

Her dress was soaked in sweat and she had managed to throw every pillow off the bed during the nighttime scuffle.

Her phone was ringing which had saved her from being consumed by the monsters.

It was coming from her bag which had been kicked to the bottom of the bed.

She plucked it out to see her work number.

'Shit,' she said out loud, but it was restricted in a throat that felt like it had been minced with razor blades.

'Molly is that you?' Graham's unmistakable voice. He was back to using the authoritarian setting, the tone he kept for special occasions.

'Hi Graham,' She said, her reply coherent but still fuzzy from the dream.

'Are you going to grace us with your presence?'

She looked at her phone and groaned, she should have been in at least half an hour ago. She could imagine him checking his watch, waiting until the no turning back time of 9 had passed, before getting himself worked up enough to call.

'Oh sorry I'm not feeling well, I had a terrible night and must have slept through the alarm.' The fact her voice sounded like someone had chewed it up and spat it out again helped to deliver the line with confidence.

'Is this to do with what happened in the store?' he asked, his officiousness dropping away like fur from a molting tabby cat.

She had a sudden memory of her putting the ring she'd taken on the date back in the display, had he spotted her doing that all along?

'What do you mean?' she tried.

'When you had the errr', he fumbled for the right word for a while and there was no way Molly was about to help him. She was hardly going to tie the knot in her own noose, 'the upset when you ran to the bathroom?'

The relief almost caused her to laugh, 'no,' she sniffed for effect, 'it's just a bug of some kind.'

'Well next time let me know before the store opens if you don't mind,' she could tell from his change in tone that he wanted to put the phone down but knew that his beloved management protocol wouldn't allow it, 'get well soon,' he said quickly, before disconnecting.

She fell back on the bed and was about to drift off again when the phone buzzed a second time.

It was Gemma's face on the screen.

Not quite sure she should answer as she had no recollection of coming home and what she might have said or done.

She let it go to voicemail but when it rang again she gave up and answered.

Before she could say anything Gemma spoke first, 'my God Molly thank God you picked up. I've found out something you really need to know, can you meet me in town?'

The cathedral bells were ringing as Gemma strode past.

There were a scattering of tourists leaving the main entrance, one or two stopping to chat in the gardens outside.

The snow had turned slushy but there was still plenty of photo opportunities for those new to the area or the occasional sightseer.

She passed Bygones an antique shop that always fascinated her. It had things in the window you wouldn't expect, she'd bought an old police whistle for her dad from there. She'd had to make an appointment to visit the shop first but what she got came gift wrapped and the look on her dad's face when he opened it was worth every penny she'd spent.

Thinking of her dad made her sad.

The concern on his face when he'd picked her up from the phone box, the state she was in and she must have smelt terrible.

She'd make it up to him by going on one of their dad-daughter days where they visited museums together.

He used to take her when she was little and the habit had stuck. She had been used to running round vast halls filled with glass display cases while her dad peered at odd paintings and bits of machinery.

For now she had to concentrate on Molly, how much should she tell her about what happened with Stewart last night?

The memory brought back the nausea she thought she'd vanquished in the long shower she'd taken back at the flat.

Nothing serious had happened, she reminded herself. They had a kiss and she'd foolishly gone back to his house and fallen asleep on the bed.

It was also fair to say there was more than booze in whatever cocktail he'd poured down her neck from his flask in the cab and in those disgusting teacups back in his squalid dump.

She still felt dirty though. The kind of filth a shower could not sponge away.

The important question was would Molly see that as a betrayal?

Whatever she thought there were more important things she had to disclose.

Poppins was buzzing.

The cafe had been here all their lives. From going with their parents and eating off the kids menu to now meeting as adults, they always felt more at home here than anywhere else.

The only thing that had changed in their lifetime was the decor and the ban on smoking.

When the law first came in back in 2007 it seemed odd not to have a waft of cigarette smoke along with your egg and chips.

Molly hadn't arrived yet so Gemma waited in the queue to get a table.

The smell of fried food would have turned her stomach a couple of hours ago but right now it seemed the best hangover cure in the world.

The only free table was at the back by the fire exit among a stack of high chairs. Behind her and the sound of gentle chatter and cutlery clinking all around.

This was her safe space, squeezed in with the rest of Worcester.

There were one or two faces she recognised, but not to talk to.

An old woman was scrutinising a copy of the Malvern Gazette using a magnifier over the print as if cracking a secret code while her tea went cold on the table.

A family she knew who lived somewhere down her mum and dad's street were by the window. The dad tucking into a mixed grill while the kids were playing with chicken nuggets and scribbling something on a play sheet with crayons.

She remembered doing just that with Molly when they were kids.

The door opened and there she was, windswept and looking like she'd done several turns in a fast spin washing machine.

It was obvious even from a distance she had woken up in a worse state than Gemma had, hardly surprising when she remembered her and Stewart laying her down on the bed, taking off her shoes and hearing her snore.

Stewart! What the hell was she going to say?

'You look as bad as I do,' Gemma laughed as Molly squeezed into the seat opposite.

'I doubt it,' she replied in a sigh, placing her elbows on the table and rubbing her eyes.

Gemma wondered if she should have waited, but then reassured herself that what she had to say to Molly couldn't wait.

'What happened last night?' Molly asked once they'd ordered.

'You remember the guys on the dance floor?' Gemma asked as gently as she could, by the look of Molly the merest jolt would have her gummed up like the cap of the tomato ketchup bottle in front of them.

Molly nodded, 'yeah I remember everything, reporting the attack to the boss in the club and then you guys walking me home, I just can't remember getting home at all.'

Gemma explained putting her to bed and them leaving her asleep.

What she said next would be the big moment. Either she would understand or not.

'I went back to Stewart's,' she said eventually, keeping her voice as soft and neutral as her ragged nerves would allow.

'What?' Molly shouted, loud enough for a couple of diners to turn round.

Gemma leaned in closer, 'it was nothing Mol, we were both drunk and…'

'Did you sleep with him?' Molly asked, thankfully quieter this time.

'God no,' Gemma scrunched up her face as if it were the most repugnant suggestion she could have made.

'I think the lady protest too much,' Molly said, pulling out her scratchy Shakespearian knowledge.

'No we didn't have sex,' Gemma reiterated.

More heads were turning now. The waitress paused from writing something in her notepad.

'But you did sleep together?'

'Sleep yes but not…' Gemma didn't finish before Molly grabbed her coat and stormed out of the door with the whole cafe watching her go.

Everyone's eyes returned to Gemma who just sat with her head in her hands.

A young waitress came over and leant towards her, 'do you want me to cancel her order?' she asked.

Molly had sprinted halfway down Foregate street by the time Gemma caught up with her.

'Molly please stop,' she said, grabbing her sleeve, but Molly pulled away.

'Get away from me you traitor. You're supposed to be my best friend and you sleep with the man who's been abusing me and stalking me all these weeks. What's the matter with you?'

'I didn't sleep with him,' Gemma protested again, hating how pathetic she sounded.

'You woke up in his bed?'

'Yes.'

'Well you slept with him then,' Molly pulled away again but Gemma wasn't letting her get away.

'Look at these,' Gemma was standing in her way now thrusting the photos she'd found in Stewart's bedside drawer into her hands.

Molly stopped and looked at them. Her face impassive at first and then shocked as she got to the photos taken on a zoom lens of her in the shop and then again at the bar with Danny.

The final one of the ring blew her mind. Danny asked to have it checked out, now here it was on a polaroid.

'Where did you get these?' Molly asked.

Gemma explained as carefully as she could about the discovery, 'I think Stewart's up to something bad.'

'I couldn't care less about Stewart,' Molly said, thrusting the photos back at Gemma, 'I don't care what he does, what either of you do.'

'But what about Danny?' Gemma said, just as Molly's was about to leave again.

'What about him?'

'Well he's in the pictures too and there's that guy on the sledge with his kids, maybe they're all in danger?'

'It's just a bunch of photos taken by a messed up stalker, it's got nothing to do with us,' Molly insisted although the frown lines appearing on her brow indicated otherwise.

'I think we should go to the address on the back of that photo,' Gemma said, flipping over the one taken at the warehouse, 'I showed my dad the picture and he spotted the postcode and a time,' she pointed at the numbers and letters.

'Why should we get involved?' Molly said, she was looking at Gemma full in the face now, hands on hips.

'I'll tell you why, if Stewart is up to something we can go to the police, get him out of your life once and for all. If Danny is involved we can work out what this is all about, maybe that's why he was acting so strange the other night. And if that family in the photos are in trouble we might be able to help them.'

'How are we going to get there?' Molly asked, beginning to thaw at the suggestion.

'We'll go in Sunny,' Gemma replied proudly.

Sunny was her battered VW Beetle, so called for its plastic sunflower perched on the dash.

'It could go very badly,' Molly said.

'My driving's not that bad,' Gemma replied.

Molly tried hard not to smile as they turned round and headed back towards Gemma's flat to pick up the car.

Molly hadn't forgiven her by any stretch, but the mention of Danny and the sight of that ring was way too much of a coincidence.

Something wasn't right and she had to get to the bottom of it.

Chapter 55

Tuesday 19th December, 5:01pm

Mr. C. had made it clear to everyone what their role was.

Andy would be keeping watch with his gun at the ready. Nobody expected him to use it, but it was there just in case.

B and G were the muscle and were also 'packing' as Mr. C. liked to refer to it. His love of all things mob or gangster came out in his terminology. His mind was a loop of Martin Scorsese scenes.

The new guy who'd just arrived to join them at the warehouse was not in the same league but another one of Mr. C.'s puppies, although he was well into his twenties, maybe even close to thirty.

They'd all been a puppy at one time. New recruits were always thrown in at the deep end early on to see how they performed under pressure. This formative apprenticeship wasn't work experience at the garden centre.

If they crumbled there was usually a pay off with a selection of threats to stop squealing. If they did well, a progression to more money and esteem within the firm could increase rapidly.

The puppy had been told to leave the photos at home in a safe place and commit everything to memory.

He'd taken the bus muttering the postcode of the warehouse under his breath in a mantra as he watched the scenery zip by.

It was only a ten minute walk from the bus stop to the location and as he walked through the concealed entrance into the darkness he squinted to adjust his vision. Even though he had an idea of what to expect, the scene before him made his stomach lurch.

A young girl was sitting in the centre of the room strapped to a chair, she was illuminated by a crude spotlight and even from a distance looked woozy as she fixed him with a pitying stare, her head lolling from side to side.

He had to look away.

Unlike Andy, B and G, who he'd only met on one other occasion, this was new to him. He reminded himself of what Mr. C. had told him in their brief meeting when he was first recruited. He could handle anything if he didn't overthink and stuck to his instructions.

He got up and waited by the door looking at his watch.

One hour before the money would be dropped. But what if they decided not to show?

Mr. C. had already notified them that the ring that was dropped into the litter bin at Pitchcroft racecourse was the forgery, so now they had no ring and no cash.

If Charlie didn't turn up with the 20 grand tonight it would go to option 4, termination. The puppy wasn't sure if that meant literal killing or just abandoning the job. He really hoped it was the latter. He could handle most things but murder was not on his bucket list.

He couldn't stop himself glancing across at the young girl again. God help her and the family if it got that far.

He reminded himself that he had little to do, just release the girl when the money was received, simple really.

There was another worry about the cash drop this time. There were guns involved.

Not that he had one, he was way too new in the organisation to be allowed a weapon yet, but he knew that Andy up in the rafters and both B and G were carrying something.

Each of the team were positioned somewhere different in the warehouse, out of sight but ready for action if needed.

B and G were stood hidden by the darkness on either side of the room, letting the shadows swallow them.

Andy had hobbled back outside to take in a last gasp of fresh air, his leg hurting more than ever. His rest at the Travelodge following the fruitless pick up at Pitchcroft seemed like years ago. Then after watching B and G grab the kid, follow on the bike looking for anyone tailing them and bringing her here, meant there wasn't much left in his tank.

It wasn't the first time he'd used a gun which was why Mr. C. favoured him on these missions, but he'd never fired a bullet to hit anything more animated than a practice target.

He made his steady way up the creaking stairs to the second floor, careful to navigate past the missing ones.

Laying flat on the floor he picked up the rifle and squinted down the scope of the telescopic sight fixed to the barrel. Through the broken floorboards he focussed on the girl tied to the chair below, he had a perfect magnified target.

Fifteen minutes before the cash exchange the puppy, wearing a grey tracksuit and balaclava, was approached by B and G who gave him a knife.

The serrated edge gleamed from the overhead lights, a beam illuminating the girl who was getting more restless as the chloroform began to wear off.

He looked awkward as he stood by her side, swaying to and fro with nerves.

The girl made an involuntary jolt and feeling her fist hit his back the puppy jumped and pierced himself in the leg with the knife.

B and G grabbed him before he used the knife on the girl. They needed her alive and well for the exchange.

Blood was already oozing through his pants so B, with military precision, pulled off the puppy's balaclava and tied it tight round the wound. He gave the puppy's trembling hand his knife back while he whimpered like a distressed spaniel.

B and G disappeared back in the shadows ready to pounce at the next incident.

Their instructions were to keep focussed on the money and the girl, while Andy in the rafters would shout instructions to Charlie from above.

All the puppy had to do was cut the bonds on the girl's wrists the moment the cash arrived.

It wasn't the first time a plan like this had been put into force.

B and G had been operational on five other occasions while Andy was on his third.

There was never any comeback, they always got the money.

With 10 minutes to go each man was in place.

Apart from the occasional moan from the bleeding puppy, muffled protests from the girl strapped to the chair and howl of the wind bleeding through the crude iron walls everything else went silent in anticipation.

Chapter 56

Tuesday 19th December, 5:05pm

Gemma's car was functional but noisy; it was also the coldest vehicle Molly had ever been in.

'Sorry,' Gemma said, catching Molly blowing on her hands, 'the heater's knackered and it would cost more than the car's worth to have it fixed.'

They were back on speaking terms now, although Molly was still reeling from the revelation that her best friend had spent the night with her deranged ex. The fact she'd found those photos at his house gave them something more important to concentrate on for the time being. Whatever issues they had to iron out they would have to park them until this mystery was finally solved.

'Turn left onto the M5 going south,' the satnav instructed. Molly had put the postcode from the back of the photo into her phone and, according to the screen, they were only fifteen minutes away.

'Why would Stewart have pictures of you and Danny?' Gemma asked, keeping her eyes on the road and her hands at ten and two. She was a good driver taught by her father, who, apart from working for the police, was also an advanced driving instructor. Molly reckoned they both had the Highway Code running through them like a stick of rock.

'That's easy,' Molly said. 'He's always been jealous and possessive. Maybe he wanted to try to prove that we were doing something wrong, or maybe just to torment himself. He was always weird like that.'

Gemma wanted to agree but thought it would be hypocritical, as she'd spent several hours sleeping on his bed. 'We know from the photos there's something going to happen at that warehouse, or whatever it is, but what about the photos of you and Danny? And who are that family sledging?'

Molly shook her head, deep in thought.

'It's the ring I don't understand,' Gemma persisted. 'Why have a picture of an engagement ring?'

'I think it may link to Danny in some way,' Molly said.

It was a rare instance where Gemma took her eye off the road, staring at Molly. 'What do you mean?'

For the next ten minutes Molly explained what had happened at the shop and how Danny wanted her to bring the ring along on the date so he could show it to his jewellery expert friend on the phone.

'Oh, this all sounds very dodgy to me,' Gemma said.

'That's not all. There was always something odd about the ring. It'd been reserved by a guy who never showed up and then, when I looked at it close up, it seemed wrong somehow, lacking sparkle...' Molly gasped as a couple of pieces of the jigsaw puzzle fell into place. 'Where are those photos, Gem?'

'On the back seat in my bag,' she answered.

Molly unclipped her seatbelt and reached back, fumbling blindly for the bag. She took out the photos and flipped through them, stopping when she got to the one with the dad and his son in the snow. She stared hard before speaking. 'That's him,' Molly said, her finger stabbing at the picture with a hint of triumph in her voice. 'That's the guy who reserved the ring.'

By the time the satnav announced their arrival they had thrown out so many conclusions that all ended in contradictions, they were both exhausted but secretly exhilarated by what was happening.

'Well, this is the place,' Molly said, holding up the photo of the warehouse. 'What now?'

'I guess we wait?' Gemma said. 'But I don't think we should park here. It's too exposed. Let's drive round to where that off-licence was and walk back round. We can hide behind those.'

Gemma pointed to a scattering of large yellow crates. They looked too small to be shipping containers but certainly big enough to hide behind.

They pulled up on a single yellow line and sat for a moment.

Molly was having a final flick through the photos.

'I'm going to get us something to drink from the shop,' Gemma said, undoing her seatbelt. 'Red Bull OK?'

'Yeah, but get me the sugar-free one if they have it?'

'You amaze me sometimes,' Gemma said.

'Why?'

'Well, here we are waiting for something to happen that could be criminal, involving people we know, and you're still worrying about your calorie intake.'

Molly giggled in spite of the situation.

Gemma got out of the car, leaving Molly focused on the photos scattered on her lap: the ring, Danny, and the bloke who'd reserved it in the shop what seemed like months ago.

This was all too much to be a coincidence.

Chapter 57

Tuesday 19th December, 5:12pm

The pub proclaimed to be 'family friendly' from a large banner draped over the entrance.

It had a long bar, sticky carpet and a small children's play area built into a crude extension that clung like a concrete carbuncle onto the rear of the building.

It smelt of fried food and bleach.

There was a mixture of hard drinkers leaning over tall tables while tiny children crawled around under the feet of disinterested parents preferring to stare at phones or the muted TV playing eighties music videos.

Charlie and Danny were sat by a window overlooking the car park, two Diet Cokes going flat on the table in front of them.

One of them would turn and check for Bernie every couple of minutes.

'I can't believe we are sitting here while my daughter is being held hostage in that building,' Charlie stage-whispered.

Danny had been staring at the TV where Madonna was singing on a gondola wearing a rah-rah skirt and lacy gloves. He found it hard to believe that it had been filmed almost forty years ago. He wouldn't have been born when that video was made. He was wondering where he would be in another forty years, if he were still alive.

'Did you hear me?' Charlie asked.

Danny turned to face him. 'Yeah… sorry, I was just thinking about the future. What do you think you'll be doing forty years from now?'

It was a distraction technique, but Charlie seemed to genuinely consider the question. 'Hopefully retired, the kids'll

be settled down with their own families and me and Karen…'
He stopped and his eyes became glassy.

Danny cursed himself at the clumsy question.

Luckily, a tap on the window broke up the uncomfortable silence.

It was Bernie, gesturing at them to come out.

Eight men stood just behind Bernie as they met in the car park.

Charlie pondered where he could have summoned so many people in such a short space of time, but he knew there wasn't the luxury of a third degree right now. It was a comfort to know Bernie was in charge.

'Right, here's what's going to happen,' Bernie said.

They'd all gathered at the pub entrance. The 4x4 was parked on the road with its hazards on; the silent companion who'd ridden shotgun on the way was still in the front seat.

'Charlie, you go in with the bag and when you've put it on the floor I want you to say "It's all there".'

'It's all there,' Charlie repeated.

'Good,' Bernie boomed. 'Make it loud, then take a step back from the cash, at least a yard.'

Charlie stayed silent.

'Danny, I want you to go in with him but stay by the door as you enter.'

Danny knew better than to ask why. The eight guys standing in the background and the fella in the 4x4 weren't just coming along for a trip into Redditch.

Bernie turned round and thanked the guys, who all disappeared into the darkness. He beckoned Charlie and Danny to follow him to the car.

He opened the back door hatch and pulled out the rucksack, tossing it to Charlie.

'Stay close to him, Danny, right up to the door, and remember to stick to the instructions I've given you.'

Both men nodded but stayed silent.

'You remember where the place is, just back down there and take a left past the off-licence. We can't give you a lift, they'll be watching you approach.'

'How will they think we got out here?' Danny asked.

'Probably think you got a cab to drop you off further down the road, but it doesn't matter,' Bernie said, his voice growling slightly, his no-nonsense tone back. 'Just don't overthink this, guys.'

They saw Bernie get back in the car as they began their short hike to the warehouse.

Charlie resisted the urge to run. The sooner he was holding his daughter the better. It was only the weight of the bag carrying the cash, and the nagging feeling that he'd do something to jeopardise her safety if he went in too quickly, that stopped him sprinting ahead of Danny.

They both walked in silence with only the sound of traffic hissing in the sleet.

'I'm scared,' Charlie admitted, as they turned towards the outline of the warehouse. 'What if I get this wrong? What if she's hurt or already d—'

'Stop it,' Danny yelled so loud Charlie stopped in his tracks. 'You can't think like that. We just have to follow Bernie's rules, everything will work out.'

Charlie said nothing, just trudged his steady way.

Danny was pleased he didn't look back. His face would have given away any sense of reassurance he'd just given.

Danny Wade had never been more terrified and uncertain in his entire life.

Chapter 58

Tuesday 19th December, 5:45pm

'OK, so we're just gonna stick around to see what happens at six o'clock?' Molly clarified. She still had the photos in her hand, trying to piece something together that seemed pretty flimsy.

'Yeah, that's about it,' Gemma said, before scrunching her Red Bull can and throwing it into the back of the car to join the collection of crisp packets and car park stubs that had accumulated over the years.

They bundled themselves up in big coats and left the car parked by the off-licence, hitting the lock on her keypad a few times just to be sure. It would be a nightmare if they had to make a quick getaway only to find the trusty VW had been nicked.

They turned the corner and navigated towards the warehouse and the yellow crates Gemma had spotted earlier.

Reaching the first one, they hunkered down together and got a good look at the dilapidated building in front of them.

There was definitely something going on inside because there was a sliver of light bleeding through a crack in one of the doors.

They were crouched down low but both had a decent view.

'Get your phone ready, just in case,' Gemma whispered.

'In case of what?' Molly whispered back, louder than she'd intended.

'In case something illegal happens and we need to take a picture as evidence for the police,' Gemma said sternly. 'And keep your voice down.'

Molly held back the urge to laugh. Gemma was certainly her father's daughter.

They could hear faint voices coming from inside, but nothing that could be discerned from that distance.

'Should we get a bit closer?' Molly asked, moving from one foot to the other. She wasn't sure she could stay crouched for much longer anyway.

'Yeah, you see over there?' Gemma pointed towards the entrance where a delivery noticeboard was still standing. It was certainly large enough to hide behind.

'Ready?' Gemma whispered, and then counted, 'three, two, one.'

They ran together, holding hands as they went, which was a good call as they both almost slipped on the slush, skidding together round the back of the sign before hunkering back down again, breathing heavily. Even though the situation was a little scary they both had to hold back the urge to laugh.

What were they doing?

They had only just got comfortable again when they heard shouts coming from inside.

Something was happening, but there was no way they could get any closer, even if they wanted to.

Footsteps were approaching and two men were just visible in the moonlight.

One had a rucksack on his back while the other was just behind him; he seemed to be on the lookout constantly.

The rucksack man whispered something to the other before disappearing inside while the partner waited at the door.

The beam of a security light fell on his face as he scoured the area, and that's when Molly felt her stomach flip. A mixture of surprise, disappointment and then sheer curiosity pounded through her. What the hell was Danny doing here? She just had to get closer.

Gemma saw Molly's face and followed her line of vision. She recognised Danny's face instantly from the photos. 'Oh my God,' she said, and then slapped her hand over her mouth. Had she spoken too loudly?

Danny looked directly at them and was almost ready to walk towards the delivery sign when there was a commotion behind him and he ran back to the door again.

A few moments passed when they heard him yell, 'It's all there.'

A matter of seconds later they heard the sound of engines approaching, then three 4x4s skidded to a halt within feet of where the girls were hidden.

An army of men, all dressed from head to toe in black, emerged from the doors and rushed in, almost knocking Danny over in the process.

There was shouting and threats, but the most incredible sight happened just after they'd stormed the warehouse.

The girls gasped as someone came rushing out of the building, crying and limping as fast as his bleeding leg would take him.

'Stewart.' They both said at the same time.

Chapter 59

Tuesday 19th December, 5:55pm

Danny and Charlie approached the building.

It looked even more ominous in the moonlight, like a haunted mansion—industrial estate style.

Its steel façade glinted, revealing holes in the structure, while wood panelling that would have indicated doors or entryways was all boarded up, some so disused green algae had attached itself.

All but one.

They took a steady pace on broken paving slabs past rusting yellow crates to the front of the building where they saw pale light piercing through a crack.

As they got closer it became more apparent that this was the only way to enter the unit.

The blackmailers must have broken in at some stage and were using this as the perfect space for their nefarious deeds.

Charlie slowed his pace and tried to catch his breath, which must have been pounding well over 100 bpm and rising.

'Are you OK?' Danny whispered.

'Not really,' Charlie replied breathlessly.

Their footsteps sounded loud even though there was still a covering of slush.

As they got closer to the makeshift entrance they could see footprints in the snow. They zig-zagged around each other as if people had been coming and going. Danny had an image of an army waiting for them as they entered.

To his surprise there were only two people in the room as they walked through the entrance.

A young guy was holding a knife in one hand while his other pressed against his leg with what looked like a rag tied around it.

He was rocking from side to side and blocking their view of what was behind him.

Danny stuck to Bernie's orders and stayed by the door as Charlie walked forward. The youth with the knife moved to one side.

Charlie broke the first rule of not saying anything until he delivered the money the moment he caught the first glimpse of his daughter. She was tied to a chair, her mouth covered with tape, just like Karen had been.

'Maisie,' he shouted without hesitation, and ran towards her.

A muffled response came from her and she began wriggling.

'You bastards,' Charlie screamed again, but before he could get any closer the guy with the knife stood in front of her and gave Charlie a push backwards.

Before he could retaliate there was a voice coming from above his head, somewhere in the ceiling, concealed in the darkness.

'Put the bag down and open it. Do not try anything or there will be big trouble for you and your daughter.'

Charlie got up from where he'd been pushed and tossed down the rucksack.

Say the words, Danny willed Charlie from the door. It was obvious from the shock of seeing his daughter he'd completely forgotten the signal.

'Now open the bag and show us the money,' the voice from above thundered, godlike.

Charlie did as he was asked, bending down, unzipping the front and letting the bundled notes tumble onto the stone floor.

For God's sake, say the words, Danny willed Charlie.

It was obvious Charlie wasn't going to do it. His shock and confusion were too much.

Danny cupped his hands to either side of his mouth and bellowed, 'It's all there.'

It went silent for a few seconds and then came the thundering of boots on concrete accompanied by shouting. The words were indistinct but the intention was obvious.

The man in the rafters looked down at the chaos below as a swarm of bodies stormed into the room.

It was like watching a cheap action movie.

This part of previous operations had never gone wrong before and Andy had never been in a position where he was thirty feet in the air witnessing its total collapse.

All the other exchanges had been very clean. The money would appear and the swap made. This was not in any playbook they'd experienced before.

Where had all these guys come from?

At first he thought it was a police raid but there was no indication of that. It was too quick and violent: no warnings beforehand, no sirens or blues and twos. These guys were working on their own ticket—but the question was, who had paid for their services?

He could see Charlie pulling at his daughter's bonds, trying to rip them off with his bare hands, but they were only getting tighter as he yanked at the tape.

She was screaming loudly now as he managed to tear the strip from her mouth.

'Daddy,' she sobbed.

Meanwhile B and G leapt into the action, appearing from either side of the room, jumping onto the backs of the men who were approaching Charlie, offering to help.

Mr C's new recruit had thrown down the knife he was supposed to be using to untie her once the money had been accepted and was now fleeing for the door.

He looked tiny compared to the brawling beasts on the floor and slid between them like a flame through petrol before disappearing into the night.

No surprises there, Andy thought while tracing the action through the scope of his rifle. Maybe the boss would think twice before giving someone so green such a big job next time. Not that he'd be around for a future mission. Once this mess was over he'd be gone.

A gunshot ricocheted through the building and everyone froze—even the brawling mass on the floor, each one checking they weren't the ones who had been hit.

Andy traced the source of the shot and saw a man standing at the entrance. He could see a bald patch from this high angle and below it a protruding shotgun, and further down shiny shoes polished to within an inch of their lives. Only a military man shined his shoes like that, and the way he held the shotgun and managed to cover the entire room made it plain that he was not to be messed with. People who held guns like that had no fear of using them. Nobody in that room wanted to die tonight, not even B and G.

'You two, stand up and walk to the side of the room,' the man with the gun commanded. He was pointing at B and G individually as they held up their hands and walked backwards to where he was waving the gun. 'Take out your weapons and throw them to the floor, nice and steady.'

They glanced at one another and in silent agreement pulled out the weapons from their waistbands. They fell to the floor with a clatter.

It had all gone very quiet; even the child had stopped screaming, pure horror and incredulity taking over.

'Charlie, pick up the knife and cut your daughter free,' he said.

Charlie reached down and did what he was told. A few bank rolls had come loose in the scuffle and were fluttering around in the breeze.

No one looked at the money. It had now gone way past financial gain. This was survival.

Charlie sliced away at the bonds and they came free pretty quickly.

Maisie sobbed into his shoulder as he picked her up from the chair, clinging to him like a limpet.

'You go back to the car and wait there,' the big man said while stepping further into the warehouse.

Charlie didn't need asking twice. He ran with his daughter to the exit and disappeared.

'OK, fellas, scoop all the money up, would you, while I have a private word with these gentlemen?'

The guys who'd been fighting with B and G were dusting themselves down and began picking up all the loose notes from the floor like the most diligent cleaning team ever.

Andy continued his vigil from the rafters, finger on his trigger but riddled with uncertainty. He now had a choice: should he fire a warning shot, exposing his position but maybe getting these men to scatter? Or should he try to take out the big guy pointing his gun at B and G?

There was also a third option: to stay where he was, let the situation play out, and when everyone was gone he could leave and forget about everything.

Like all smart operators he had what he called his 'go bag' at home: a passport in a fake name and enough cash to get him settled somewhere new until the dust settled.

The third option was unrealistic. Mr C would find him wherever he went, and did he really want to spend the rest of his life jumping at every footstep on the stairs?

Taking a deep breath he lowered himself further down onto one of the rafters and focused tight on the target.

The big man was in an animated conversation with B and G, who were leant against the far wall with their arms crossed, heads down. Andy wondered if the man giving them the lecture had any idea what these men were capable of once they were cornered. He could sense them marking time until they pounced on him before he had a chance to get a single shot off.

Sweeping the scope to the right he could see all the men busy picking up notes; the job was almost finished.

Sweeping his scope towards the exit, the figure of another man bled into view from the shadows. Andy adjusted the focus to get the image as clear as he could, not believing what he was seeing.

The man was holding a phone in landscape mode. He was filming the whole thing.

Now the situation had taken another twist.

Andy's new priority was the man taking the video. This would identify the whole operation. How long had he been filming, and who had he managed to capture? For all he knew this guy had been following them round for days, in the same way they'd been surveilling Charlie and Danny. Talk about being shot by your own gun—or, in this case, phone camera.

But if he shot the camera guy, the man with the gun would shoot B or G and then maybe kill him once he'd tracked where the shot from Andy's gun came from.

He had to do something.

He took aim, said a silent prayer and fired.

Chapter 60

Tuesday 19th December, 6:05pm

The gunshot was enough to make the girls run.

Keeping low, they fled from behind the delivery sign and within a few seconds they'd caught up with Stewart.

It wasn't hard as he'd fallen to the floor, clutching his leg.

'What the hell are you two doing here?' he yelled, before stumbling back up on his feet.

'We could ask you the same question?' Molly said. In spite of everything she couldn't stop herself offering her arm while he steadied himself.

'There's no time to explain, we need to get out of here before the cops come.'

'Not till we see Danny,' Molly said. She was more scared than she'd been in her entire life but there was no way she was leaving without some kind of explanation.

'You don't want to worry about him, he's no good. Him and his mate tried to steal that ring from your shop,' Stewart was shouting now. That controlling, confident manner she was used to had been replaced by a quivering, jealous little boy.

'We don't know the full story,' Gemma interjected.

Stewart looked at her like she was something he had just scraped from the sole of his shoe. 'You need to butt out of this, Gemma, you hopped into bed with me the first chance you got.'

When Gemma was about ten years old her dad had shown her a few moves to tackle someone if she was ever attacked. They were simple but effective manoeuvres, but she took to them very quickly. So much so, she had progressed to self-defence classes soon afterwards and even completed a couple of levels in mixed martial arts by the time she'd passed her GCSEs.

The punch she threw at Stewart was precise and effective. It wouldn't cause any lasting injuries but it was enough to make him crumple to the floor like a bag of dirty washing. He lay there for a while, hopefully long enough to rearrange his thoughts and put his manners back in, Gemma reasoned, as she looked down on him.

They were far enough away from the warehouse to avoid getting involved in any crossfire but close enough to see what was happening.

That was when they saw Danny running from the scene.

Just behind him was another man with a girl on his back. They could hear her sobs from a good distance.

Danny slowed down as he caught sight of Molly and Gemma standing either side of a crumpled heap of a man lying on the floor. He stopped, looked at each individually, unable to form a sentence.

'Who are you?' Charlie said, setting his daughter down on the ground but keeping his arms around her. She was shivering violently and her sobs were getting softer but more frequent.

Danny gave a confused smile. 'This is Molly, you remember from the…'

'Jeweller girl?' Charlie finished.

Molly nodded and introduced Gemma, who didn't think it was pertinent to hold out a hand. This wasn't a wine and cheese evening.

Charlie looked at the writhing man on the ground. Stewart looked up; his nose was bleeding.

'You?' Charlie said, and was about to tackle him when Danny grabbed his arm.

'We haven't got time for this, we need to go, get out of here right now.'

'We've got a car round the corner,' Gemma said.

Danny thought about his next move. They had the girl back and Charlie needed to get to safety.

'Could you take Charlie and his daughter home?' Danny asked. 'I'm going to stay here and wait for…' He stopped himself before he named the man who was currently aiming a gun at the bad guys. 'I'm going to wait for my friend.'

'What about me?' Stewart asked from the floor.

'You can stay here and face the music as far as I'm concerned,' Gemma said.

There was another gunshot and all heads turned to the warehouse.

'Someone's going to call the cops for sure now,' Stewart said, once again wobbling upright. He'd spent a considerable amount of time with his face against the pavement in the last few minutes.

'Go, all of you,' Danny said, waving them away.

Molly looked at him for a moment.

This was the Danny she'd heard on the podcasts. The man of action, the confident problem-solver. She only had the smallest understanding of what was going on—the ring, his police interview and now whatever this was—but she found it hard to believe he wasn't doing anything but trying to help. A quickfire memory of him sat opposite her in the bar, his kind eyes listening to her story, taking everything in, never judging, just listening and being kind.

'I'm staying with Danny,' Molly pronounced.

Everyone turned in her direction.

'No you can't, Molly, it's too dangerous,' Danny insisted. His words were firm but there was also an underlying hope in them.

'Go on, guys, get safe,' Molly said.

'Are you sure?' Gemma asked, her face up close, trying to gauge what her best friend was thinking. Maybe she'd just lost her mind.

'Please get away now, I'll be fine.'

Gemma hugged her and then helped Charlie with the girl, who'd stopped sobbing and was just staring into the distance, zombie-like, the shock now kicking in.

Another gunshot caused the group to run for Gemma's car while Danny put his arm around Molly and guided her to the street.

They stopped on the corner where he found shelter under the awning of what would have been a cinema, then a bingo hall and now a stopping point for couples to kiss, druggies to shoot up or drunks to urinate.

'Wait here,' Danny said. 'I'll be back soon with my friend and you can come back with us.'

'What about him?' She was pointing at Stewart, who was lumbering towards them, wiping blood from his face and limping from the knife wound in his leg.

'Leave him to me.' With that she saw Danny run towards him and whisper something in his ear. Stewart nodded while he spoke. He glanced at Molly once or twice but she looked away, pretending to read the police notice about no loitering that had been pinned to the very post she was leaning on.

The men parted.

Stewart walked towards her but didn't stop to say anything, he just gave her that smile. Even after everything that had happened to him tonight—and she had no idea what had gone on in the warehouse or what he was doing there—he was still the same Stewart. The smile he left her with was one that said, you may have won this battle but the war would always be his for the taking. She shivered, wondering if she would ever be truly free of that terrible man. Then she turned her gaze to Danny, who was striding back towards the warehouse. He wasn't rushing, just taking short yet confident steps, the way you might if you were going to a dental appointment.

Another gunshot was fired but Danny didn't flinch as he took more steps towards hell.

As she watched him go to the entrance she wondered if this would be the last time she would see Danny Wade alive.

Chapter 61

It was hard to get an accurate shot with a throbbing knee on one creaky rafter and an elbow wedged between two others.

Andy had the guy's phone in the crosshairs of his sight.

If he missed the phone he would blow his head clean off. Out by an inch, he'd take a hand at least. The chances of the man coming out of this well were pretty slim.

Mr C had always said that guns were a final solution. Threats, fists, knives and then guns—that was the order. Usually they only got as far as fists with the threat of knives, although they always came tooled up with everything just in case.

This would change everything the moment he pulled the trigger.

He took one last sweep of the room with the scope. It was the big guy's fault for bringing a gun into play; he was the reason this had escalated as quickly as it had.

Back to the guy filming, he realised he had no choice. He felt a trickle of sweat running down his forehead and he blinked hard as the salt hit his eye.

He put the gun down for a second and rubbed gently at his eyelid while wiping his brow with the back of his sleeve.

A thought suddenly crossed Andy's mind. Even if he did shoot the phone, wouldn't whatever he'd filmed have gone to some kind of cloud storage somewhere anyway?

The clean-up of the money had happened; there wasn't a single note left on the floor. No one was getting paid for this operation, that much was certain now.

Andy knew he would have to take out the guy who was filming as he would be the only link to him. If he'd been followed by this guy and his camera, he might have footage of him picking up the package at Worcester racecourse or perhaps filmed him coming here today. It would be easy to link him to whatever outcome there was for this catastrophe.

There was no way he would carry the can for this mess.

He resumed his position and took aim.

The shot was loud, the way only a double-barrelled shotgun being fired in a warehouse with a corrugated iron roof would sound.

It was a small explosion.

At first he thought he had squeezed too early and the shot had come from his own gun, but the barrel was still cold between his tight fist and the man with the phone was still standing, although rocking slightly from the noise.

An acrid smell of cordite rose in the air as once again he turned his scope to B and G, who'd obviously gone for the big man who'd fired the gun.

By the plaster falling from the ceiling it was obvious that he'd fired a warning shot into the air.

All he saw now was a swarm of bodies beneath him. Men in black reappearing after hearing the shot and now scrumming together on the ground.

Then another gun had come into play. It must have been one of the pistols B and G had thrown to the floor.

Another shot and then more shouting.

Both B and G were down. G was writhing round in a pool of blood oozing from a wound in his side, while B climbed on top of him and started to shout. Andy had hardly heard either of them speak before, let alone show any emotion.

Taking the cue, the big man fled the scene, followed by his faithful soldiers, and finally the man with the phone also disappeared outside, leaving just B and G.

It was too late now, Andy had missed his chance, but at least he was still alive.

He looked down at his colleagues who from this height looked like small children making up after a row.

He didn't feel any pity for these men; he had seen them do some brutal stuff in the past so in many ways it was payback time. This was the first time they'd been defeated and it was beyond their comprehension. Andy's only thought now was getting away unnoticed.

Pulling apart the rifle took him less than ten seconds. He was well practised in the set-up even though he'd never used it. Today was the closest he'd got. It fitted snugly in a case which he put under his arm before creeping back down the stairs.

B was nudging G, who was still lying on the floor. Andy trod lightly to get past them, each step seeming like a mile.

He'd just got close enough to the exit to feel the breeze blowing through the makeshift doorway when B spun round. 'Help us,' he said.

Andy wasn't sure how he could, and he was pretty sure that B didn't either. They could hardly call an ambulance in the middle of a felony and the last time he checked he wasn't a doctor.

'What can I do?' Andy yelled helplessly.

'Call Mr C, tell him to send someone quick, maybe he can get a doctor or something?'

'I can't,' Andy said, moving another step closer to the door. 'I'm sorry but I've got to get out of here.'

'You're not going anywhere, chicken shit.'

Andy took a step back at the sight of the gun which had found its way towards B in the scuffle. 'Call the boss now.' He waved the gun and then cocked the trigger.

Andy held up one hand and with the other went to pull out a phone from his pocket.

Assuming Andy was going for his own pistol, B fired, throwing Andy three feet back against the wall, taking a couple of wooden pallets with him.

Andy lay dead on the floor, the bullet hole square on his forehead killing him instantly. The phone dropped out of his hand beside him as a river of blood began to pool around it.

The sound of sirens came as G died in the arms of B.

The last of the gang was all alone, taking one last look around, thinking of an option to escape.

There was only one way this could end now the police were approaching.

He took the pistol he'd just killed Andy with and put it under his chin. It still felt hot against his skin. B wasn't a religious man, but tonight he said a silent prayer that whatever awaited him in the next life would be better than he deserved.

His finger rested on the trigger and a breath later he pulled it hard.

Chapter 62

Tuesday 19th December, 6:19pm

Bernie sat in the driving seat and fastened his seatbelt. Next to him was a man with a phone who was showing him the footage he'd taken of the events that had just unfolded. For all the world it could have been old friends looking at the highlights of a holiday reel. Everything seemed so matter of fact.

In the back seat Molly sat next to Danny. They were both silent, lost in shock.

When Bernie had come out of the warehouse Danny was just about to go back in; they'd almost collided with each other. Both men and the camera guy had run towards Molly, who was stood under the disused cinema entrance watching spellbound.

Danny had grabbed her hand, pulling her along as they followed Bernie back to his car.

The other men had all pulled their 4x4s away, leaving only Bernie's vehicle.

They started back towards the motorway when Bernie dialled 999 on hands-free.

The answer came through the car speakers, asking which emergency service they required.

'Police and ambulance,' Bernie said, and then gave the address before hanging up. 'Untraceable on this phone,' he told the back seat.

Molly didn't know where to start. Luckily Danny had made up his mind to fill her in on the details. 'I'm sorry you had to get involved in all this,' he said. 'I was just trying to help an old friend and things got out of hand.'

Molly was so confused. She wanted to be angry but the way he said "out of hand" seemed such an understatement that she laughed. Whether it was genuine humour or just the release of all that nervous energy was anyone's guess.

'What's so funny?' Danny asked, but started to laugh himself, then Bernie joined in from the driver's seat, his booming guffaw bouncing off the roof. Only the man studying the phone kept quiet. He probably thought they were all losing their minds, and in a way he would be right.

Once the laughter had died down Bernie began to talk to his silent passenger about the film he'd taken. He spoke in hushed tones, so Danny took this as a cue to tell all to Molly. This would be his last chance to lay everything out for her, and what better place than strapped into the back seat of a car? She could hardly storm out in disgust—well, not until they'd got back into Worcester anyway.

He started at the beginning with Charlie swapping the ring, then making contact with him after all those years. Everything came out over the next half an hour. He didn't omit a single thing—there was really no point at this stage.

'So the only reason you wanted to go on a date with me was to swap the ring back?' Molly said once he'd finished the story.

Danny shook his head. 'No… well yes, but…' He couldn't explain that it had been for both reasons.

She turned away from him, looking out of the window, even though there was nothing to see but her own reflection.

'I just wanted to help him and knew I'd have to return the ring. He stood too big a chance of being recognised.'

Molly looked back at him. 'But you didn't manage to do it?'

'No, but I really wanted to ask you out and I also really needed to swap the ring back and finish all this mess.'

Molly went quiet, trying to take it all in. 'What did you say to Stewart just now?' she asked, never taking her eyes off him. She was fairly certain he wasn't a liar, but there was no harm in paying attention to the whites of his eyes.

'I told him we knew why he was there and who he worked for. His best choice was to go as far away as he could.'

They took the turning for Worcester North and navigated a roundabout before Bernie pulled into a small patch of land at the bottom of a winding muddy track. 'Let's stretch our legs and have a chat,' he said, silencing the engine.

Everyone got out apart from the passenger with the phone. His sole function seemed to be taking video and avoiding others.

Molly and Danny followed Bernie as he strode along a small path.

Above them was a steep hill that keen motorbike scramblers used as a track, slaloming their machines through the mud. It was a little slushy underfoot, but the trees grew thicker as they walked until they reached an area that was perfect for privacy.

'I used to come here with my little brother when he got the biking bug,' Bernie explained. 'I wanted to have a word with you both alone before I drop you back in the city,' he said.

Molly noticed a small bruise developing around his eye, and his jacket had a slight tear on the shoulder.

'Things got ugly in there,' he said, as if reading Molly's mind, 'but it's over now. You won't hear any more from those guys. And the other fella…' It was obvious he was referring to Stewart. 'He should be miles away if he's any sense.'

'But what about the money, the threats—won't they want some kind of revenge?' Danny asked. He felt Molly shudder with cold and fear, realising he'd put his arm around her without thinking about it.

'That's not how they work. And remember, I'm the one with video evidence now. If anything happens to any of you, I can release it to the authorities—or even worse, the Daily Mail.' There was a smile in Bernie's voice, but neither Danny nor Molly could see the humour.

There had been guns, knives, kidnapping and home invasions.

'How are we supposed to trust people like that?' Molly asked, looking up at Bernie while moving closer into Danny's embrace.

'You can't,' he said. 'But you can trust me.'

'I owe you,' Danny said, as they began back down the path to the car.

'Just call us even,' Bernie said, opening the door for them.

Molly slid in, followed by Danny, and they sped off back into the city.

She let her head fall on Danny's shoulder while the gentle rocking of the car took over her senses for a while.

She liked the feel of his hands squeezing her tight and, although there was still so much of this she didn't understand, she was fairly certain there was some kind of future for her and Danny Wade—although she hoped the coming months would be a little less eventful.

Chapter 63

Mr C slammed down the receiver so hard one of the metal holders broke, the piece flying off into the deep carpet. The phone was a classic imitation of a 1970s direct dial which he'd had specially made, and it would cost him a fortune to have repaired—but at that precise moment he couldn't have cared less. Someone could have come through the doors and smashed every one of his highly collectable Ming vases and he would have barely turned a hair.

Tonight had been a bad night. He had lost three of his most valuable men—they were all dead. The only person who was not accounted for was the puppy, the lanky streak of piss he'd given the easy job to. All he'd had to do was let the girl go when they arrived with the cash. He'd only chosen this Stewart guy because he seemed keen and had connections with the girl at the jeweller's. It was rare to find someone that close to an ongoing operation. He wouldn't get far. The only way people left his organisation was with the cash requested, or with a damn good reason for coming back empty-handed. There was going to be some payback, and it wouldn't be pleasant.

The hospital porter, his wife and kids, that interfering podcaster—the lot of them were going to get their just desserts. All he had to do was assemble a new crew. There were always enough lads ripe for recruitment.

Mr C only let a select few use his direct mobile line. His phone was very much an evil necessity in his mind, but sometimes he had to be updated while on the move.

He didn't recognise the number now appearing on his screen and was reticent to accept. He'd heard of attachments with viruses embedded. This one was too tempting not to be downloaded.

It must have come from his inner circle, someone he trusted—no one else would know how to contact him. And he never got phishing emails or calls on this phone.

Download complete, he hit the arrow.

The video played instantly and he watched the screen with mounting horror and anger as his latest operation played out before his eyes.

The kid strapped to the chair. The dad arriving and shouting. B and G lumbering in and out of shot. A blurry mess of men he had no connection with. There was even a sweeping shot of Andy up in the rafters. It had been skilfully edited, and every face was quite clear. If this ever got out, it would come back to him and his organisation.

He watched it all the way through with rising fury, and just as he was about to play it a second time another message pinged.

LEAVE US ALONE AND THIS GOES NO FURTHER

He threw down the phone and scrunched it under the heel of his shiny brogue.

Chapter 64

Thursday 21st December, 6:30am

The headlines on the Worcester News website, BBC Hereford & Worcester radio and Midlands Today TV had been buzzing with the stories coming out of a disused warehouse in Redditch.

Danny turned up the radio in his cab as the news jingle started.

Fresh reports are coming in this morning of the shooting incident that happened in Redditch on Tuesday night.

We now believe that the killing of three men who have yet to be named was gang related.

A police spokesperson at the scene has told the BBC that no further information would be forthcoming until after Christmas as forensic teams and the major crime squad had to continue a full investigation which could take some time due to the complexity of the case.

The BBC understands that this may be linked to several other incidents across the Midlands where ransoms, kidnapping and threats of violence have been reported.

Danny turned it off the moment the news turned to predictions for a white Christmas. Incredible to think the press could move from something as serious as three men being killed in a shoot-out to a fluffy piece about the weather in one step. It gave him hope that the story would disappear eventually and Charlie's family would be left alone. Bernie's threats may well have done the trick; only time would tell.

He had a busy day ahead. The van was full of parcels—last-minute gifts to deliver for those who'd left it too late to get a note for Santa. He'd got a present for Molly, nothing too lavish—he was afraid of overstepping the mark. Their relationship had hardly started in a conventional way.

They'd agreed to a Christmas Eve date and he'd booked a table at an Italian restaurant on Friar Street. He had no plans to leave her for any other business this time. In a way, it was his second chance at wooing Molly Gardener, and he wasn't going to blow it.

Driving towards Bromsgrove he wished he had time to stop at Charlie's house, but he reckoned it was good they had time to get back to normal without him bringing back bad memories. Maisie was still in shock according to Charlie, but she took comfort in knowing that the house was still being watched by Bernie's men.

Thinking of Bernie, Danny wondered how he could ever thank him. What would they have done without his help? If the police had been involved Danny would have been questioned hard—much worse than his experience after being picked up at the racecourse on his first date night with Molly.

The next few weeks were going to be tense, but if they all kept their nerve everything would work out fine.

Pulling onto his drive at half past five he was thankful the traffic had been pretty light, but he was totally shattered. His head was buzzing with the events of the past few days, reliving all that had happened on a crazy loop while he went about his business delivering parcels and smiling when people wished him a happy Christmas.

Bernie had advised him to stay busy and try not to think about things too much. It was easier said than done when he almost went through the roof of his cab every time his phone buzzed. He still couldn't believe this was the end of it—there had to be some kind of repercussions. His 'one day at a time' mantra was currently 'one hour at a time', with the adage of 'no news is good news' for good measure.

About to unlock the front door with the tantalising prospect of a shower and an early night ahead, he felt a hand on his back.

He spun round, dropping his keys.

It was Bernie, his big face glowing from the security light above the door. 'Sorry mate, did I scare you?'

Danny let out a breath. 'You could say that,' he said, and then felt something nudging his leg. Tinkerbell was on a lead and looking for attention, yelping and slavering her long tongue on the back of Danny's hand.

'Just taking Tink for a walk,' Bernie said, 'and thought I'd drop by to see how you're doing—and wish you luck on your date with Molly.'

'That's good of you, Bernie, but how did you know?'

It was a stupid question. Bernie just winked before adding, 'It's on Christmas Eve, isn't it?'

Danny didn't have time to respond.

'Hope so—I've left a nice bottle of plonk reserved for you when you get there.'

'Thanks,' Danny said, amazed at the calm demeanour of a man who'd been in a shoot-out only two days ago. The only sign that anything untoward had happened was the bruise on the side of his face, colouring like a bad tattoo.

Bernie just smiled and held out a package wrapped in Christmas paper. 'Oh, and I also have a little gift for you,' he said, handing over a box.

'Oh no, I can't accept this,' Danny said, taking it anyway. 'It's me that should be giving you a gift after everything.'

The big man held up his hand. 'It's not over yet,' he said sternly, 'but give it a little while, and once the dust settles you and Charlie can breathe easy again.'

'OK—thanks again, Bernie.'

Bernie gave his broad smile and walked away, the dog running obediently behind.

Danny slammed the front door behind him and strode into the living room. Flipping on a lamp, he began unwrapping the box.

He couldn't stop laughing as he tore the paper away and pulled the present out. It was a toilet plunger with a message attached on a piece of string.

Don't get stuck again. Bernie

Epilogue

Hi, this is Danny Wade and welcome to a new season of Good Gone Bad.

This is the podcast where we meet extraordinary people who make one bad choice that leads them down a road they never thought they'd take.

This time we hear from someone who we'll refer to as Benny. That's not his real name—for reasons that will become obvious—but his story is completely true. Only names and locations have been changed to protect the innocent.

It all started when Benny had a plan to swap an expensive engagement ring for a forgery.

Gemma and Molly were laid together on Molly's bed.

It was a rare Saturday off for both of them, and they'd just downloaded Danny's latest episode.

'You're right—he has got a lovely voice,' Gemma said, pausing the audio.

'Yeah, but there's much more to him than that,' Molly giggled.

'So it would seem,' Gemma replied, grabbing Molly's hand and staring at the ring. 'Strange how you met him because of a ring and he ends up putting one on your finger.'

Molly pulled her hand back. 'It's only an eternity ring, we're not rushing to get engaged or anything,' she insisted, with little conviction.

'Whatever you say,' Gemma laughed, pulling her best friend into a hug. 'I expect with your promotion at the jeweller's you'll get somewhere to live together?' she teased.

'Maybe,' Molly replied dreamily. 'I still can't believe Graham recommended me to take over when he left.'

'Goes to show you never can tell. Graham was a good guy after all,' Gemma said.

'I never thought he was bad, just…' But Molly couldn't come up with a word. Graham was too unique to be labelled, and if truth be told she missed him a little bit. Since she'd taken over as manager, she'd appreciated his frustrations as she tackled a new recruit who didn't seem capable of stringing a sentence together, let alone serve customers.

Molly rearranged her pillows and sat back again as Gemma resumed the podcast. She thought about Stewart for a second and wondered what had become of him. Since that night in Redditch he'd fallen off the face of the earth, but she still jumped every time she got a message. It was extraordinary to think he'd got recruited into a criminal gang like that, but looking back it was hardly surprising. According to Danny, he'd got involved when he moved out of Molly's and started looking for work in Birmingham. She'd met many of Stewart's dodgy mates in the past, and it was only her insistence that they never spent time with them that kept him on the straight and narrow while they were dating.

Just as she was wondering if she was a bad judge of character, she heard Danny's voice again reminding his listeners that even good people do bad things.

Gemma paused the podcast again at the moment Charlie Burrow's voice started speaking. Even though it had been altered considerably she would never forget him and his daughter as she drove them back home from Redditch that night.

'Have you heard anything from Charlie's family at all?' she asked Molly, who seemed lost in thought herself, staring at the ceiling.

'Yeah, actually—his wife…'

'Karen?'

'Yeah, Karen. She's in remission from the cancer.'

'Oh, that's great. And how about the daughter… Maisie?'

Molly shook her head. 'Don't know. Danny said something about her going to counselling, but I'm not sure what she can say—even in confidence.'

'I hope they'll be OK. They're such a lovely family.' Gemma recalled the moment she'd helped Charlie and Maisie back through the door, and Karen had jumped out of her chair, enfolding the girl in her arms as she started to cry for the first time after being locked in a cocoon of horrified silence all the way back in the car. 'And you and Danny?'

Molly just smiled but stayed silent. Their Christmas Eve date had been the first of many, and one night on the same sofa where he'd tried the first time, he finally got around to telling her all about his bad thing. At first she was stunned into silence, not sure how to take it. She had been waiting so long to find out what he'd done that her imagination had built it up into something much bigger, and yet the fact he'd served prison time—and that Bernie had been his cellmate—was the big kicker.

They'd talked the whole night and into the next day, until the words dried up and physical emotion took over. By the time the sunshine was bleeding through the curtains they were fast asleep, holding onto each other like the planet was about to lose its gravity.

Now, six months later, lying with Gemma listening to his podcast, she said a silent prayer that Danny's bad thing was all he'd ever have—because secretly, she had some very good things planned for both of them.

THE END